THE THREE HEADS OF DR. CUBA

Dr. Cuba II

By Christopher Paris

ISBN 979-8-9993812-1-7

Chapter 1: The Fourth Floor

The whore believed she had learned how to live in a man's world. Men ruled the economy. They ran the governments, steered elections, led the corporate boardrooms, dominated the labor unions. When women were needed, they were used as breeding stock, political pawns, or — worst of all — advertising.

The whore was convinced she had turned the tables and reversed the power dynamics. Now it was *she* who was in control, using men's universal weakness to her advantage, dangling before them the one thing they could not resist. She was taking their power away from them, one dollar at a time.

That belief did her little good when the needle stabbed her skin. She fell, blinded and in agony, grasping for the assailant behind her.

Within forty seconds, the whore was dead, and her philosophy gone with her.

Inspector Heiner Thumann set the box he was carrying down, breathing heavily. There were four flights of stairs to his new office in Paris, and many more boxes waiting in the truck downstairs—but the others would have to haul those; he was finished with physical exertion for the day.

Thumann, whom many in Scotland Yard called the "German Brain," had received a promotion, of sorts, for his role in bringing the Invisible Devil to justice. It was not the promotion Thumann had expected — he'd been "shipped out" of Scotland Yard, loaned to the nascent International Criminal Police Organization. His superiors at Scotland Yard insisted the move was because they had the greatest respect and gratitude for Thumann's work. And, because they had such great trust in Thumann's abilities, he was now tasked with representing the United Kingdom during the ICPO's post-war rebuilding.

Thumann was not convinced. He knew that his "reallocation" — as some bureaucrat called it — was at least partly due to his German heritage. The war may have ended, but suspicion against Germans remained, and there were still many that never believed Thumann's tale of having fled Berlin to escape the Third Reich after decades of working as a dedicated German police inspector. The side glances and whispering that shadowed Thumann suggested some felt he was a Nazi spy and the rumor was that a high-ranking Yard official grumbled, "Let the French have him for a while."

There was also the nasty fact that the previous International Criminal Police Commission, as it was called at the time, had been under Nazi control since 1938. They had even relocated to Wannsee in 1941, the same region where, just a year later, Hitler's men met to formalize their "final solution to the Jewish question." With the surrender of Germany, Belgium took control of the ICPC, restructuring it as the "ICPO," and announced the new provisional headquarters would be set up on Rue Bonaparte in Paris. This was the de-Nazification of what was already being called, by telegraph operators, "Interpol."

Despite all this cynical gossip and rumormongering, Thumann's old friend, and superior at Interpol, Section Director Dr. Brühl, was happy to have him.

But it had been a struggle to get approval for his assistant's transfer too. Scotland Yard had remained suspicious of the young Chilean girl with far too many names, Ximena Alejandra Torres Orellana. Many at the Yard resented Thumann for pushing them to grant her a role other than fetching coffee for the "real" detectives. The atmosphere at the new ICPO, however, was more welcoming of fresh ideas and, most of all, people who could speak more languages than the King's English. Thumann had quickly noticed that the Paris building bustled with people speaking English, French, German, Portuguese, Hindi, Japanese, and — yes —

Spanish.

Thumann's request to transfer Ximena to ICPO had originally been rejected; it was Scotland Yard's plan to terminate the position Ximena held entirely. At the last moment, someone had stepped in and convinced the brass to allow Thumann to take Ximena with him. The Dr. Cuba crime wave earlier that year proved that having someone familiar with the "Español" of Latin America was as useful as the traditional "Castellano" of Spain.

Ximena was granted the not-quite-official title of "Co-Inspector," which she quickly adopted regardless of whether anyone had been serious in giving it to her. In truth, the ICPO cared little for official titles like "inspector" or "detective inspector" and simply wanted crimes solved. Titles were something its bureaucratic leaders argued over. In the end, Thumann was an inspector and Ximena his co-inspector. That was that.

The work of Interpol was, on paper, simply to coordinate criminal investigations between member nations' police agencies. Brühl had pushed for a more hands-on function and created what was quickly dubbed the "Fourth Floor." This was an unofficial cadre of hand-picked international detectives tasked with investigating crimes that fell beyond the scope of any single nation's police force. Once again, the Dr. Cuba crime wave the year before had forced many organizations to rethink their approach, and Brühl restructured Interpol with the vast scope of Dr. Cuba's operations in mind. Thus, the "Three-Country Rule" had been born.

The Three-Country Rule was an informal guideline set by the new Interpol for when a remit for Fourth Floor investigation could be requested. Interpol did not get involved in criminal cases limited to one or two countries, but when things expanded to three or more, Interpol began paying attention.

The Fourth Floor department was, quite literally, positioned on the fourth floor of Interpol's provisional headquarters in Paris. The joke amongst Interpol office-skulkers was that the bosses were stationed in the basement, where it was more secure; the disposable agents were put on the top floor of the building, where they were more likely to be firebombed. Thumann knew this was not a joke, but a real security measure. Replacing Brühl would have been difficult, but there were many other Thumanns floating around the world if they needed a replacement. As a result, Brühl was secured underground while Thumann was put in an office anyone could toss a hand grenade into.

Thumann was warned, however, that the credit and glory in solving Fourth Floor cases would likely remain buried within the basement of the new Rue Bonaparte building. Once a Fourth Floor case was closed, it would likely be handed off to a nation's police force for the credit, since explaining Interpol's cross-border finagling might get too sticky for any one nation's courts. Thumann was just fine with that arrangement—he was never one for flashy promotions or ticker-tape parades in his name. If he earned enough to stuff his pipe with latakia and then swig it down with a £2 bottle of Scotch, he was satisfied.

And so, whereas in London Thumann had to put up with whispers and glances when he and Ximena walked the halls, here in Paris they were treated as valuable assets. No ticker-tape parade was necessary.

There was, however, the problem of alfajores. The Peruvian blancmange cookie had become Thumann's obsession, and now — nine months after closing the Dr. Cuba case — he had long since run out of the damned things. Sans alfajores, the damned French macarons would have to do. But they were certainly a lesser-tier replacement.

Settling in his chair, Thumann finally caught his breath. He had lost none of his considerable weight since that business in South Dakota, and now he let his full weight sink in his new, comfortable leather chair. The office was small, but had two desks — one for him, and the other for Ximena — with ample cabinets for files and paperwork and evidence and bottles of Scotch. The desk was new, the chair was new, and the cabinets were new. An interior window looked out to the busy hallway outside, and another window overlooked the buzzing Paris boulevard below. The door to his office had a small, third window, with his name hand-painted on it. He felt like a private eye from one of those Bogart films.

Thumann reached into his new desk and pulled out a macaron, shoving it into his mouth. Thumann grunted; he had already resigned himself that a macaron was not a an alfajor, but a lesser-tier replacement.

"Not quite an alfajor," a woman's voice said from the door. It was, of course, Ximena who had become so familiar with her mentor that she was now reading his thoughts. The pretty twenty-six-year old Chilean wore stylish, albeit reasonably priced, clothing that not only suited her, but simply made it easier to move in: high-waisted wool slacks and a light blouse, plus a woolen overcoat to battle the occasional cold breeze. Gone were the traditional, maid-like dresses and uncomfortable black shoes the Catholics in Arica had raised her to wear. Ximena's style was now more practical, with an added bit of French flair.

Thumann, for his part, wore the same wool suit and strained-button vest he always had, with his giant, clomping shoes and messy, always-askew necktie. He wore this in the dead of winter and the blaze of summer, more religiously than those Chilean Catholics. He still had the same battered fedora he wore when he first met Ximena in Santiago, and the same XXL shirts. He smelled better, however, not wanting to be known as the "smelly bear" forever by his protégé. Thumann had taken up regular soap and water, even if his French contemporaries still debated the practice.

Ximena hung her overcoat on the rack next to the door, then settled into her chair, concealing her pride behind a practiced, neutral expression. But inside, she was thrilled to have come with Thumann to Paris and to Interpol. Her life had changed entirely after meeting this big, stomping, bushy-bearded detective.

"Is there no way to buy alfajores in France?" Thumann

asked, perhaps not at resigned after all.

"I haven't found any, but I can have my friend send me her mother's recipe. I hear they're that difficult to make." Ximena used to brush alfajor powdered sugar off of Thumann's vest, but he still made enough of a mess with the crumbly macarons to require at least a little clean-up. It was her way of signaling to him that she cared for him like a father, while maintaining their professional relationship.

For his part, Thumann was thrilled to think he might get homemade alfajores but decided to remain aloof. "Nonsense, we can survive on these French things for now. No need to make a mess in your kitchen. Besides," he said, already regretting he had turned down Ximena's offer, "you'll have too much to do here. There won't be much time for baking."

Thumann stood and walked to where he had hung his coat. He pulled out a small envelope from the pocket and handed it to Ximena. With a curious look, she took it. "What's this?"

"Something from the basement for you. Open it," Thumann said.

Ximena slowly opened the envelope and pulled out the single, folded sheet of paper inside. A note, written in English, on official ICPO letterhead.

"I don't understand," she said after reading it.

"It's a commendation, dear miss," Thumann said, using his preferred means of address for Ximena. He did this out of respect, yes, but also to hide the fact that he still could not wrap his mouth around the pronunciation of her name—*Hee-MAIN-uh.*

"They're praising your work on the 'M' case last month. This will ensure many more such cases come your way."

Ximena smiled, but it was forced. Thumann noticed.

"Go ahead, dear miss. Tell me what you see."

"It is what I don't see ..." she said, trailing off.

Thumann nodded knowingly. "You don't see your name on

that letter. But the commendation is understood as being yours all the same."

Looking up at him with a raised eyebrow, Ximena said, "The letter only mentions you. How is this a commendation for me?"

Thumann sat again but leaned forward. "You know how it is. We're in better shape here in Paris, yes, but it's still the same old boys' club. They weren't going to issue a commendation in your name, so they issued it in mine, but referenced your work. Don't worry, though, the right people know who's really being praised in that letter. The rest is irrelevant."

Ximena smiled again, but it was still forced. She knew she was still not a real person to the "powers that be," no matter their change in location.

"Never mind that for now," Thumann said, realizing the compliment was not going over the way he thought it would. "Let's read the wires."

Ximena put the letter away and pulled some papers out of her bag. "I've been through last night's," she said. She flipped through a few sheets. "Two blackmails reported, but they appear unrelated. One in Madrid, another in Estonia. Both were high ranking political officials, but no other similarities."

"Mmph," Thumann grunted, taking out his pipe and tobacco pouch. He knew Ximena loved going over the wire reports and was glad he was able to shift the mood.

"Some reports of gold missing from St. Petersburg, but it is so difficult to get details from Russia."

"Yes, but worth watching," Thumann said, thinking of Dr. Cuba as he stuffed his pipe with his favorite Burley and Latakia blend. He'd seen Dr. Cuba die himself, his corpse turned into a golden idol after being dropped into a stream of vaporized gold by some red-fingered creature who claimed to be Dr Cuba's "Father-Brother." After Dr. Cuba's streak of gold heists, Thumann considered anything related to gold worth watching. Just in case.

"And I believe our 'Golem' serial killer has struck."

Thumann perked up. "Still in Stuttgart, dear miss?" he asked.

"Yes," Ximena said. "Witnesses at a movie theater say a giant wrapped in burlap killed two Nazis who were hiding their identities. The cinema was smashed up in the process."

The nickname "Golem" was given to the killer by the news reporters, a nod to the ancient Hasidic tale of the Golem. In that tale, a huge monster made of clay, wrapped in burlap, launched attacks to defend his Jewish people. The nickname stuck. Some of the reports claimed that former Nazi officers or soldiers, in hiding after the war, were killed in the attacks. This led the locals to believe this new "Golem" was exacting revenge for the Jewish people. Because of that, it was becoming harder and harder to distinguish facts from myth on the reports. Witnesses were becoming unreliable in their desire to believe fiction.

"That's how many now?" Thumann asked.

Ximena checked her notes. "Hmm ... well, it's not easy to track. In Stuttgart, we have at least ten. But before that, some from Czechoslovakia and Austria." Ximena looked up. "We've satisfied the Three-Country Rule."

"Are all the victims former Nazis?" Thumann asked.

"No, but a lot are. There have also been murders of prostitutes, beggars, rich men, and yes, some Nazis. All levels of society. I'm not sure there's a pattern," Ximena said. It was difficult to tell yet which murders were the actual serial killer's, and which were not. Every crime in Germany and its surrounding neighbor countries were attributed to a mystical giant "Golem" lately.

Thumann lit his pipe, sending rich smoke through the room. Ximena inhaled a bit of the scent; she enjoyed it when Thumann lit his more expensive tobacco, as he had now.

"Map!" he said loudly as he stood. To any observer, it might have looked as if Thumann were demanding Ximena retrieve him a map. Yet she remained seated. He was not asking for anything of

Ximena, he was just announcing his next move.

Thumann went to a wall detailed with thin strips of wood; each strip was fitted with a small copper handle. Thumann pulled one such handle, and a huge map of Germany and its neighbors, framed and at least five feet high, slid out and then rotated on hinges to cover the wall. The map was new, highly detailed, and fully colored. More ICPO investment for their new Fourth Floor inspectors.

Thumann allowed himself to sink for just a moment into his memories of his home country. He wondered with frustration why it was always Germany causing problems.

Ximena stood and walked to the map. Scanning it — she was still not familiar with European countries — she finally found Prague. "The earliest reports came from here, in Czechoslovakia, then ..." She traced her finger downward. "Later here, in Austria."

"Literally a Golem from Prague," Thumann grunted rudely, as if he had degraded his own mouth by uttering the ridiculous words. "Then he moved south."

"Right. Next, we received reports along the German-Austrian border here, in Julbach."

"And then he moved west," Thumann said.

"Then steady reports moving westward into Germany, until the movements stop in Stuttgart," Ximena continued. "He has not moved any further west. Have we received our remit yet?"

"No, nothing," Thumann answered, scowling. He did not want to go to Germany and dredge up all those memories and had found a reason to dismiss the entire matter.

"Without the remit, there's not much we can do," Ximena admitted. She put her hands on her hips and stared at the huge map, as if trying to make sense of it.

Secretly, Thumann was relieved. With no remit there would be to trip to Germany. "Coffee!" Thumann announced; again, it was not a request, it was an intention. He stood with a bolt of surprising agility, threw on his coat, grabbed Ximena's from the rack, and thrust it at her. She smiled. She knew this meant a trip downstairs and across the Rue Bonaparte to the café across the street.

"You will make me fat," she said, taking her coat from Thumann's meat-slab hands. *"No quiero ser una gordita."* She occasionally tossed a Spanish phrase at Thumann to keep his attention.

"You couldn't be fat if you ate all the cows in France," Thumann said, stomping out of the office. "But we can discuss your strange ability to remain thin over slabs of bacon and those flaky pastry things they serve down there."

Jeffrey Crandall was tall, slim, and bore the face of a rich scion: thin nose, long chin, wispy mustache. The suit he wore was elegantly tailored, and the gold-buttoned waistcoat, delicate leather gloves, and shoes of the latest fashion all screamed of an obscene wealth. He walked across the tarmac towards two men standing next to a shiny, polished aluminum aeroplane. The plane sported wings covered in bland white fabric, each supported by two thin struts; the tail end sat on a single tail wheel, angling the plane's nose upward, its propellor still. It was powered off.

Crandall reached the two men and shook their hands. They seemed to be eyeing him with some level of judgment. He did not have the appearance of an aviator, and he knew it.

"This is the new Cessna 140, Mr. Crandall. It comes fitted with the latest luxury seats, rear windows, full electrics, and our latest flap system. Have you flown a Cessna before, sir?" The question was meant to ensure Crandall knew what he was doing.

"I don't fly, sir," Crandall said, sniffing. He ran a gloved hand over the wing strut nearest to him, as if to look for dirt.

"You don't fly? How, then ..." the man asked, brows raised.

"I have someone for that. A pilot on salary."

The two salesmen visibly relaxed. This made sense; Crandall

was shopping for planes to be ferried around in, not to fly himself. This immediately prompted a greater deal of respect from the men.

"Of course, sir," one said. "Well, the 140 is the best aeroplane a private businessman such as yourself can own. The Piper Cubs cannot come close the advances in quality and design you see here, with our 140." Crandall knew that was not necessarily true, but he was in a hurry and needed to buy a plane today. Right now, in fact.

But he would not telegraph his urgency. "The color?" he asked, sniffing at the bare, polished metal and bland wings.

"We recommend the fuselage remain unpainted, but can add livery striping, some tail details, and of course dye the wings. All to your specifications."

"Can that be done later?" Crandall asked.

"Later?" one of the salesmen asked.

"If I were to purchase this now, might I have my man break the aircraft in, so to speak, first and decide on a livery later?"

"Of course, sir! Would you like to arrange a demonstration flight with your pilot, perhaps later this week?"

"I'll buy it," Crandall said. "Let's finalize the contract of sale now, and I can have my man come by later to fly it to my property."

The salesmen both raised their eyebrows in happy surprise. "Today? Right now?"

"Right now, yes. I assume you don't mind being given money on Thursday morning?"

"Of course not!" one of the men said. "Let's head to the office and finalize that contract."

And, so, within the hour, the salesmen had their cash and Crandall had his airplane. With the signed purchase agreement in his pocket, Crandall strode across the tarmac, back to his waiting car. Slipping behind the wheel, he shut the door and removed his gloves, then started the engine.

He had not removed his gloves previously, lest the salesmen

notice the bright red forefinger on his left hand.

Chapter 2: The Island of Vipers

"There is more to this than meets the eye," Brühl said, pointing his finger at a stack of papers related to the Stuttgart murders. "I am frankly surprised you haven't noticed this, Heiner."

Thumann remained stoic. He found himself sitting in front of his superior's desk and was beginning to feel as if he was being dressed down in front of his assistant, Ximena. Her eyes remained politely fixed towards the floor. "Miss Torres has been watching for patterns, Erik," Thumann said sternly. He wanted to calm Brühl down a bit while giving Ximena some credit, but now it sounded as if he was blaming her. Just in case, he added, "But we haven't received our Three-Country Rule remit."

Brühl snorted, leaning back in his new leather chair. "You never *requested* a remit, Heiner. They don't just appear out of thin air. You have to file a requisition."

Thumann shifted in his seat; he had tried to do so without notice, but the damned chair creaked noisily, drawing attention. "You can file them, too, Erik," he said. Had it been anyone else saying this to Brühl, they would probably have been fired on the spot. He and Brühl had enough history that Thumann could – on occasion, at least – be rude.

Brühl stood. "I did file the requisition. And that's why you have your remit now. The Three-Country Rule was met weeks ago, if not before that. This isn't another Jack the Ripper scandal, Heiner. There's more to it." He turned to Ximena, and her eyes darted up to meet his. "Miss Torres, what connections did you see?"

Thumann watched her face sadden ever so slightly. Sensing she did not want to make him look any worse, Thumann whispered, "Go ahead, dear miss. This is part of the job."

"There have been similar killings here in Paris," she said delicately.

"There have been killings in Paris since there was a Paris," Thumann snorted.

"Reports of bodies drained of blood," Ximena added.

"Yes, yes, yes," Thumann said dismissively. "Attributed to a group called 'Les Vampires.' Nothing has ever come of that, and the Vampires are just a group of street thugs."

Ximena nodded, "Yes, Inspector, you are right. But the similarities between the scattered reports from Paris and now these from Germany, well, they could be connected."

Brühl interjected now. "To be completely honest, Heiner, no one thinks that we have a group of organized serial killers."

"I would hope not, as even the newspapers couldn't dream up a story that fantastic," Thumann said. He anxiously fiddled with his coat lapel.

"We think there may be two possibilities," Brühl said. "One, this is the work of two or three entirely different killers, wholly unrelated to each other and simply capitalizing on post-war chaos. Or two, an organized crime ring using murder as a form of terror to either strike fear into the streets or to create a distraction for other crimes we might not have spotted yet."

Thumann snorted once more, attempting not at all to mask his ridicule. "This is getting more nonsensical by the minute. Erik, you want us to believe that someone is committing killings to cover up crimes no one ever knows happened?"

Brühl moved closer to Thumann, raising himself to an equal height and fixing his face into a severe glare. Thumann recognized this look: it was Brühl silently reminding everyone in the room that he was the boss, not Thumann. "On more than one occasion, Heiner," he said, his eyes unblinking, "you have reminded me that I hesitated when you came to me with a story about an insane master criminal who could alter his facial appearance and was stealing gold to awaken ancient gods buried in the earth. I daresay the remit is based on a story far less fantastical than that."

Brühl was right. The Dr. Cuba plot had sounded insane, and yet it proved to be true. Thumann fell silent, yielding to both the grim look in Brühl's eyes and the logic of his argument.

Ximena spoke, a welcome break in the brief moment of tension. "My opinion, if it matters, is likely there is no such organization to this," she said.

Thumann turned. "You don't have to placate me," he said gruffly.

"I am not," she responded with surprising quickness. "Let's look at the facts. As we saw on the map, the murders appear to have started in Czechoslovakia and then moved west, into Germany. That does not suggest an organization but a lone man or a small group of killers. The victims in these killings were, as far as we can tell from the wire reports, mostly Nazis. But the killings of prostitutes and rich men were elsewhere in the country, yet at the same time."

"You think someone else is responsible for those?" Thumann asked, relaxing a bit.

"I do. They don't appear linked." She turned to Brühl. "With all respect, sir, I think this is not the work of an organized criminal gang, but…" She paused.

"But what?" Brühl asked.

She glanced at Thumann for a moment. "Not every remit needs to be for the crimes of an organization. The Fourth Floor exists to investigate all crimes that may not be within the reach or capability of any single national police force. If we do have a rash of murders, or even two such rashes, and if they span so many countries, then it is still within our responsibility to act. The police of Austria and Germany and Czechoslovakia and France cannot connect the facts the way we can."

The men remained quiet for a moment. She had just reminded them of their true mission.

Somberly, Ximena added, "I think we must go to Germany."

Professor Jakob ten Brinken slid the body of the dead prostitute through his rear doorway, being careful not to be seen by his few neighbors. The body was wrapped in canvas, and his laboratory — if you could call it that — was on the far end of the street, towards the rail yard and away from most of the rail workers' living quarters. The Professor intentionally rented this run-down, smoke-blackened building in the worst, run-down, smoke-blackened end of Mülheim so he could work with some level of seclusion. Because Mülheim was outside of Essen, Germany's major industrial and coal processing city, it did not suffer the intense scrutiny of Allied forces during the post-war rebuilding efforts. The building itself had housed a butcher shop on the ground floor many years ago, but was now just an empty shell. The second floor held a small room with a mattress on the floor in case the Professor should need to spend a night, and one larger room where he experimented on the bodies of his dead whores.

To be fair to the Professor, he was not really experimenting *on* the bodies of the whores, but *with* them. He was trying desperately to repeat his first experiment, which had borne fruit, but for nearly two years, a second success had eluded him. This was the sixth prostitute he was forced to kill in pursuit of scientific progress, and he was no closer than he had been twenty months ago.

Frustrated, he wondered what he had done right back then, and what he was doing wrong now.

The problem with this string of failures was not so much that he was running out of whores — the industrial towns of Germany had plenty of those — but that with each victim came an increased risk of being caught. A single dead whore raised few eyebrows. Six in two years, though? The press might soon be reviving the story of Jack the Ripper. He did not want that attention.

The Professor was brilliant, however, and had — so far — eluded the police's notice. This was because there were never any bodies left behind; a failed experiment left no body behind at all. The police were left only with prostitutes whispering about other prostitutes going missing. They could do little with that information.

Now, however, he was confident he would see renewed success. One of the missing factors in his last four failed attempts was the *wañuchiq saphi*, the "killer root" that proved to be the exact opposite of its name. The strange plant was not a killer at all, although it could be used as a poison in specific preparations; no, the plant was the giver of life, perhaps the very fountain of youth sought by Ponce de León himself. Professor Jakob had precious little of the root and had dismissed its inclusion in the first experiment as a flight of fantasy. Only in examining the differences between his five prior experiments did he identify *wañuchiq saphi* as being the single ingredient missing in the last four.

He would rectify this. Now, he worked to "transeminate" the body of his latest whore with what his notes referred to as "formulation 13," which not only included the semen of a hanged man but also the *wañuchiq saphi* infusion. If this formulation worked, the whore's corpse would soon begin to grow new life and eventually give birth to his second creation.

Thumann and Ximena were now on an aeroplane to Berlin; from there, they would head by military bus to Stuttgart. For her part, Ximena had become used to flying — somewhat — and was looking forward to visiting her mentor's home country. Thumann, on the other hand, was not looking forward to the trip at all.

It had been six years since he'd set foot in Germany. The moment he'd received a letter informing him that his wife, Hilda, was dead, killed in a "work camp incident"—he knew better than to believe that—he rejected his country entirely and fled by escaping through Belgium. That was January 1939. By late 1939, he was in the United Kingdom and working at Scotland Yard, trying desperately to heal his fury at his country and recall the best memories with his love, Hilda.

He'd married Hilda, his sweetheart, when he was only twenty-one. At age twenty-five, Thumann was conscripted into the

German army and fought his antiwar instincts as much as he fought the enemy from filthy, mud-soaked trenches. By 1918, he was freed of this forced service and left the army as a *feldwebel*, or sergeant. This helped him get a job as a simple beat cop in Berlin, and he settled with his beloved Hilda for what would be a peaceful life. By 1924, he had become a *kriminalkommissar*, or detective inspector, and ten years later, he rose to *kriminalrat*, or senior inspector. Things were looking good for Thumann and Hilda.

But Fate threw spite at the couple. The Nazis rose to power.

Hilda was Jewish. Only Thumann and a few others knew—or so they thought.

Their home, above a small bakery that specialized in various sweet pastries covered in powdered sugar, was razed to the ground. It turned out someone in the Nazi party did know. Hilda was dragged from their home and taken to a "camp" in Dachau, Thumann was beaten and left behind. His years of service in the first Great War were ignored, and his pleas to have Hilda released were tossed out.

He had no desire to return to Germany after what it did to his beloved wife. And, thus, the Scotch. The whiskey may have made Thumann walk crookedly and slur his words at important department meetings, but it kept him from murderous, vengeful rage. In all truth, Scotch was the only thing keeping Thumann from becoming one of the monsters he now hunted.

Now, Thumann — fifty-six, obese, and exhausted — felt rage, yes, but it was weighed down with a new emotion: surrender. Having gone through so much over so many years, Thumann was breaking down. He secretly yielded to the Fates who, he believed, wanted him to suffer. He would no longer rage over Hilda's death. He would no longer rage over the death of his previous assistant, Gentleman, brought by Thumann's own hand, forced by the manipulations of Dr. Cuba. Thumann would simply accept the fact that he was meant to die from grief.

And soon.

Unknown to anyone, Thumann — who refused to carry a gun and only used a set of brass knuckles molded with a Celtic knot design — kept a hidden pistol under his mattress in his small, moldy apartment. It had one bullet loaded.

The bullet would have to wait. As Thumann and Ximena stepped down from their plane, it was immediately apparent to the inspector that this was a very different Berlin from the one he had left. US and Soviet soldiers were everywhere. The skyline was destroyed. Everything seemed black: the cratered streets, the burned buildings, the filthy soldiers' uniforms, the sky, the faces. There was no music, no laughter, just officials and soldiers shouting in a variety of languages. Noise and black, as if Berlin had been turned into a monochrome image shot on silver film stock and played back during an earthquake.

Unlike most of their other trips abroad, Thumann and Ximena were not greeted by police officials in Berlin. Police officials had been replaced by British, American, and Soviet military police, and this was not the time to spend resources on greeting some criminal inspector from Interpol. The transitional government's inability to investigate the Golem may have been why the Germans reached out to Interpol in the first place, having failed to get either the Austrians or the Czechs to do their work for them.

With Heiner Thumann now assigned, they had gotten lucky.

Their official paperwork lubricated Thumann and Ximena through every checkpoint they encountered, although Russian Zone areas were decidedly more difficult; Russia had barely heard of Interpol. Fortunately, the Russians relied more on the appearance of official-looking stamps and fancy embossing than they did the purpose of the document ornamented with them. And the ICPO documents had many official stamps and embossing, even a watermark or two.

Thumann knew that Ximena noticed he was sullen and uncharacteristically silent during their military bus ride out of Berlin. Perhaps she knew he was thinking of Hilda and his old home, he pondered. Perhaps she knew he was debating visiting; perhaps she knew he was also afraid it might now be a blackened crater? If she was thinking these things, Thumann noted that she opted not to ask. They both knew that if Thumann wanted to talk, he could, and she'd listen.

The Homunculus landed the Cessna 140 on the small grass airstrip of Ilha da Queimada Grande, pleased with how his new purchase had performed. It took eight refueling stops to reach the Brazilian island, a number which would have been much higher had the Homunculus not fitted an additional fuel tank above the aeroplane's canopy. The tank looked ungainly, but the welded rack assembly kept it in place, and its oval shape presented less drag than one might think. While flight time was not necessarily a priority — he'd chosen Queimada specifically because of its inaccessibility — shaving off ten hours or so by simply slapping an extra tank on the roof had proved worthwhile. Queimada had no fuel on it, so this also ensured there would be enough fuel to make it back to the Brazilian mainland.

Queimada, also known as "Snake Island" since its inhabitants were nearly entirely golden lancehead pit vipers, was located some twenty-two miles off the coast of Brazil. The venomous snakes had become trapped on the island after the last Ice Age, leaving it uninhabitable by men. Just one bite would be fatal to. Man, and it was impossible to walk without encountering dozens of the vicious vipers. The Homunculus, of course, was not a man, and the bites of the golden lanceheads had no effect on him. It was moot anyway since, for some reason, the snakes allowed him to pass through their ranks without even attempting to strike him. Perhaps they viewed him as one of their own.

The landing strip had been meticulously carved out of the island's foliage along the western side of the hilly landscape; the Homunculus did this himself, having previously used a small ship to bring the necessary equipment to the island. The landing strip was unlit and not visible to most overhead air traffic, so Snake Island would likely remain uninhabited for another twenty years. That would be sufficient.

The island would be the Homunculus's new primary laboratory, replacing the Father-Father's original lab on Monito Island, floating between Hispaniola and Puerto Rico. The Father-Father, the Homunculus's progenitor, had used that lab to develop the original methods for creating the Homunculi from a mixture of extracted genetic fabric taken from his own tissue and other chemical strands and substrates that were available to him at the time.

But with increased shipping traffic through the Mona Passage, the Homunculus began to see signs of visitation by curious fishermen and tourists on Monito Island. While he remained confident his hidden base had not been compromised, the risk of exposure was increasing, and Monito was simply too small to be accessed by aeroplane. A new location had been needed.

Snake Island proved perfect. It was close enough to the Americas for the Homunculus to easily manage his exploits when needed, while being remote enough to ensure his secrecy. As he exited the Cessna, the Homunculus made his way to a dug-out path that led slightly downward and into the island's interior. Above were strung a set of camouflage nets, fitted with leaves and vines, to ensure the entry could not be easily spotted by anyone flying overhead. The path appeared to end abruptly as the stone of the mountain jutted upward. The Homunculus pushed his weight against a portion of the stone, revealing a large hinged door. A normal man would not have been able to move it, but for a soulless genetic abomination with abnormal strength, it proved a temporary obstacle.

Inside, the blasted-out section of mountain had been refitted with generators, lighting, and sufficient equipment for the Homunculus to continue his Father-Father's work.

There was a sleeping area, a library, and a set of vertical, iron-lung-like chambers that opened like copper-clad iron maidens, allowing the Homunculus—and others like him, should there be any—to be rejuvenated. Whereas Monito Island had only a small tank of the mixture needed for rejuvenation, the Homunculus's Snake Island lab had a tank with four times the capacity. And, whereas he previously relied on creating a blend comprised largely of blood and gasoline, his latest formula now utilized 99.99% pure gold in suspension. This, he found, helped him go for much more extended periods on the same amount of mixture.

The Homunculus's previous attempt at growing his own set of "Brother-Sons" only resulted in one viable batch in 1929, which had been transported accidentally to Peru. The Peru mass grew outside of laboratory controls entirely. Embedded with only partial memories of the Father-Father, this homunculus – the first surviving mass from the second generation of the creatures – became the criminal mastermind "Dr. Cuba."

Without the full set of progenitor directives and guidance, Dr. Cuba's mind twisted—he believed that he was destined for Godhood and believed he could awaken the "Sunken Gods"—King God Skyx and his cruel Queen Macapax—by injecting a vast quantity of pure gold into the earth. Dr. Cuba's worldwide gold heists drew too much attention, forcing the Homunculus to hunt down his Brother-Son and kill him, with a small bit of unexpected help from the intrepid German inspector, Heiner Thumann. With Dr. Cuba dead, the Homunculus returned to work in the shadows, along with his two mysterious Brother-Brothers, the Doktor and the Fantôme.

But the Homunculus learned some things from his Brother-Son during the conflict. First, how to manipulate his skull and bones to change the shape of his face, as he had done when posing as Jeffrey Crandall. This was something Dr. Cuba had done routinely, and yet the Homunculus had never even attempted it before. The bones of the homunculi were not at all soft but instead grew like tiny, shell-like plates, forming a strong lattice that nevertheless allowed for some manual manipulations when enough pressure was applied at the right points. Dr. Cuba found the process painful and became addicted to morphine as a result; the Homunculus felt no such pain and was now adept at altering his appearance to the extent his bones would allow it. He was grateful to his Brother-Son for the learned skill.

The morphine addiction likely contributed to Dr. Cuba's insanity. The entire "Sunken Gods" delusion was madness, as all delusions inherently are, but there was a benefit to be gained by the Homunculus from this, as well. The Homunculus experimented and learned that by injecting gold into himself, rather than the Earth, his soulless, inhuman abilities were improved. The irony: Dr. Cuba never needed hundreds of metric tons of pure gold to find gods buried in the Earth; he needed only a few milliliters to find the Sunken God hidden within himself.

And yet a third benefit came from Dr. Cuba's blunt, grotesque crime wave: that the Homunculus might use some of the terror created simply by the name "Dr. Cuba" to further his ends. Where he and his two Brother-Brothers had attempted to remain entirely hidden and had only gained their names "the Doktor" and "the Fantôme" from the press, perhaps there was a benefit to controlling the mystery, creating the mythology. If these Sunken Gods could create their own religion, before man even existed in a form that could worship them, perhaps the homunculi could do something similar.

And, so, he had decided there was terror to be had in using the name "Dr. Cuba," as well as respect it could demand from the criminal underground. The Homunculus realized there was a use for a religion around the so-called God of Crime.

As the Homunculus flipped the switches to turn on the lights in his new Snake Island facility and walked towards the copper iron maidens, he had one lingering concern. He started the mixture pumps, opened one of the iron maidens, stepped inside, and shut the door. Steel needles penetrated his torso as the chamber's door shut, beginning the rejuvenation process.

One lingering concern.

He *had* heard the voices of King God Skyx and grim Macapax, like distant, low-frequency foghorns, a rasping metallic sound, as if it came deep from the earth, repeating a two-word phrase, in perfect English:

KILL ME.

Chapter 3: The Big Gray Golem

Friedrich Becker walked home alone after a particularly grueling chess game with his old rival, Herr Weber. The two had been battling each other on the boards for at least ten years and were once part of a thriving chess club in Stuttgart. Now, after the war, Becker and Weber were the only two members left and so resumed weekly matches between themselves over coffee at a local bar. Ignoring the dirt and the cold, the two old men would sit outside and shout profanities at each other as each accused the other of cheating.

To the neighbors, hearing Becker and Weber argue meant the world was still rotating on its axis, the bombs had stopped, and life was returning to old Stuttgart. No one complained about the noise.

Now, another loss in his ledger, Becker muttered to himself angrily as he walked back to his house, some ten blocks away. "Cheater," he grumbled. "I should have thrown the board at that old bastard."

Becker turned down one bombed-out street, stepping carefully over fallen bricks and collapsed wooden walls. He did not need a twisted ankle to ruin his night any further.

Before he could think one more thought, a scarf tightened around his neck with such force it seemed it might sever his head entirely. Becker did not even have the time to realize that a twisted ankle would have been a far preferable outcome for the evening. Within seconds, his throat choked shut, and he turned blue. He could not gasp loud enough for anyone to hear him, so no one came to save the old man. Not long after that, he fell to the ground, quite dead.

The bus pulled over in Leipzig to refuel and allow the passengers to stretch their legs. Thumann grunted as he stood from his seat, made his way outside, and promptly lit his pipe. The air was cold.

Ximena stepped out behind him. She stood behind Thumann and then, politely, excused herself to an area of the petrol station away from the crowd of stretching, yawning passengers to grab a few minutes of isolation. She had already accustomed Thumann to accept her occasional escapes to privacy; he never questioned her about it. If he did not know what she was doing in those moments, he never asked.

In fact, Ximena was praying.

Standing away from the crowd of passengers, Ximena reached inside the neckline of her blouse and pulled out a wooden rosary. She may have updated her wardrobe since she moved to Europe, but her rosary was a constant accessory.

Silently mouthing the *Padre Nuestro*, she ran the beads through her fingers.

"Padre nuestro, que estás en el cielo," she whispered, nearly silently. *"Santificado sea tu nombre. Venga tu reino. Hágase tu voluntad en la tierra como en el cielo."*

She no longer needed to think about the words; they had become like a sound she would make to trigger a deeper thinking process. The words of the Lord's Prayer were a meditative trill, enabling a higher consciousness of sorts. And so, as she prayed, she thought, asking God to forgive her for being forced to fight on this path He had set her on, which seemed in opposition to many of His lessons. Ximena wanted to serve Him. She fought to stop bad people from doing bad things, but that meant that she, too, sometimes did bad things. This path she was on, though it felt right, confused her. She wanted guidance.

She spoke their names, calling her ghosts to her side once more.

Tears welled up but did not fall. She was already too old for that sort of thing. She prepared to ask for guidance, but was interrupted.

"Young miss!" Thumann called from the bus. "We are leaving."

With a long exhale, Ximena put her rosary back into her blouse, then turned and walked back to the bus.

The ghosts retreated.

Professor Jakob ten Brinken did not kill old Friedrich Becker in Stuttgart because he was far too busy killing prostitutes in the northern town of Mülheim. Besides, old men did not have what the Professor needed, and the Professor did not kill for sport. This was for science.

In his laboratory, the Professor waited. The whore's corpse was not yet showing signs of transemination. His notes from the only successful trial indicated that the process had taken nine hours.

The thought filled him with satisfaction. A woman could create a life in nine months, yet he could do it in nine hours.

He knew his experiments made him an abomination. But he had tried to be attractive. He had tried to succeed. He had tried to be popular. And in all these things, he always failed. He had grown overweight and balding and was forced to work in secret, on dead whores in abandoned butcher shops. He was always rejected, always shunned. An outcast with no hope of redemption.

There was no reason to keep trying the same things only to face the same result. No, he would take an entirely different road.

Jakob ten Brinken was not really a professor. He merely adopted the title and wore the appropriate clothes. He was surprised, at first, that the ruse worked so well on so many. This simple lie won him a modicum of respect at the druggists or the library, but he was still laughed at by men and rejected by women.

The Professor had studied as best he could at university, learning about the sciences and human anatomy in his attempt to become an attractive, successful, popular surgeon. But his grades were never good enough, his thinking was never original. Mocked and abused by his fellows in school, shunned and laughed at by women, the Professor decided to return the favor.

He had begun to dedicate his life to changing those around him. No ... more than that. *Creating* those around him. If he created his own society, that society would respect him. But to create a society, he would first have to create a person.

He would start by creating a woman. A woman who would love him and, if she did not, could be discarded and replaced with another of his making.

Nearly by accident, he discovered the notebook. In January of 1944, he learned that a bookshop somewhere in Berlin was selling a book on the creation of artificial life. An anonymous letter arrived by post, warning the Professor to act quickly; others would be pursuing the book, as well, and there were only a small handful of copies.

The Professor never thought to question the source of the letter, and instead rushed to Berlin, hoping the notebook might be genuine.

It was.

The notes spoke of genetic fabrics and chemical strands, of biological processes combined with metallic reactions. Acids and bases, suspensions and solutions. Blood and gasoline, pumps and hypodermics. He understood all of it as separate pieces, but how they all came together made no sense. He studied the notebook for months before attempting his first trial.

The Professor had already studied the profane science of how the mandrake, whose root took the form of a human body, had been used to attempt to create life. But the theories and stories of these experiments dated back to the ages of mysticism, kabbalism, and alchemy. The notebook provided a modern roadmap, relying not on the mandrake but something far more ancient and more complicated to obtain: *wañuchiq saphi* from the Andes.

The Professor had been able to obtain a small sample of the root—enough for just one trial—and only after tremendous effort;

no druggists in Europe kept a supply of an unknown root that required teams of men — and llamas — to find it.

Accepting the fact that he was unlikely to get more *wañuchiq* any time soon and thinking the root to have been largely irrelevant to the trial, he continued his additional trials without it.

But the evidence now appeared clear. The only trial to have successfully produced a child was the one that used *wañuchiq saphi.* With his first creation having survived birth but then gone mad, the Professor knew he would need more of the Andean killer root to ensure another success. He eventually managed to obtain a new sachet, enough for a few trials more.

Absent from the notebook was a description of the womb. Some scrawling in the margin suggested, perhaps, a machine was to be used ... an artificial womb. But if so, its construction was documented in some other notebook and was no doubt lost in time. No, the Professor knew he'd have to create his own womb for his trials and theorized that a *real* womb would be far better than any man-made machine. He gambled that since a machine was not alive, his wombs might not need to be either, but an organic birthing environment would clearly be superior for birthing an organic mass.

And killing whores was not particularly difficult work. In fact, Professor Jakob ten Brinken did not even mind it.

Now the Professor sat next to the whore's corpse, listening to the clock on the wall ticking quietly, advancing time. In the silent, dead womb, tissues were growing, cellular reactions bubbling.

And the Professor was sure that this time, she would live.

Before encountering Dr. Cuba, the Homunculus was quite pleased with the level of control his Brother-Brothers had exerted over the world, using crime to realize their ambitions. Much of their work was eventually carried out by the world's citizens themselves, rather than an army of surly—and potentially unreliable—street criminals. The Homunculus had controlled 250 men across several countries. The Doktor's network in Germany added another seventy key operatives, and the Fantôme skulked through France with a meager thirty. But Dr. Cuba's organization was thought to be at least two thousand men strong, across at least thirty-five countries.

The Homunculus could not deny that events might be pushed along at a faster pace if he were to command a greater number of men, as Dr. Cuba had. For this reason, as Dr. Cuba had dismantled much of his organization leading up to his doomed attempt to awaken the Sunken Gods, the Homunculus carefully recruited or took control of Dr. Cuba's detritus. Within two months of Dr. Cuba's death, the Homunculus had gained a thousand men, entire warehouses of equipment, and caches of weapons all over the globe.

But the Homunculus was not Dr. Cuba, though he fully intended on carrying on the name. He preferred to manipulate events without military hardware, if at all possible. A well-placed pack of TNT could accomplish as much as a full squad of armed men, and a whisper in the ear of a prostitute sometimes as much as ten such squads. Dr. Cuba had to die because his methods were too brash, too uncontrolled, too chaotic. But this did not mean there were no lessons to be learned, no opportunities for improvement to be exploited.

The Homunculus did not carry on the obsessive-compulsive practice of his Brother-Son's regular radio commands, issued at key hours of the day to trusted agent-recipients spread across the globe. Instead, he ordered operators to man their radios twenty-four hours a day and simply wait. If there was something essential to be transmitted, the Homunculus would do so. If not, the radio would remain silent. A dead radio was less of a risk than a chatty one.

Likewise, he ordered his men not to send transmissions unless absolutely necessary. Which made the incoming buzz of the radio at Snake Island all the more unusual. The radio had not made a noise for months.

The Homunculus sat down at his radio desk and placed the headphones over his head before toggling the transmitter switch.

"Collapse. Blue. Integrate." The code he used was entirely different than that of his Brother-Son. He spoke slowly, knowing his agents were still learning the new code. "Blue. Blue. Admonition. Garish."

The earphones crackled. "Tether. Random. Glow. Yellow. Glow."

The Homunculus paused and then switched to a different frequency and adjusted his radio to upper sideband. A stream of electronic gurgles poured from the headphones, not quite beeps but not unlike them, either. To the normal ear, there was no pattern to it. An astrophysicist might have mistaken this strange squeal as the remnant radio bursts of a neutron star, far in the heavens. But it was very much made by man, and the Homunculus was able to decode the signal, in real time, using nothing more than his brain.

As the signal squealed from the headphones, he wrote the message down quickly. Once it was complete, he returned his dial to the original frequency and set the radio's mode back to AM.

"Gray. Calumny. Treasure." This indicated the signal may be cut off, that the message had been received. The Homunculus shut the radio power off and watched as the vacuum tubes' glow faded back to darkness.

Once the room was again calm, he looked at his note. The message was troubling. A disaster, in fact.

DOKTOR, FANTÔME DEAD. UNKNOWN PLOT. BERLIN, PARIS OPERATIONS IN DISARRAY. FORMULA MAY BE COMPROMISED. NEED ORDERS.

The Homunculus could have sent someone to look into the matter and to ensure the German and French operations continued to function normally. But the truth was, he had no communication with his Brother-Brothers since their departure for Europe. They were left to their own designs *by* design, and communication between them was unnecessary. The Father-Father, the progenitor, had told each of them what to do before they left, without revealing each brother's orders to the others, and they then separated to carry out those orders. Those orders continued until now, more than fifty years after the progenitor's death.

The Homunculus had known the day would come when one of the Brother-Brothers would have to take the progenitor's place and update the orders or begin issuing new ones. So long as their work continued with success, as it had, that day had not yet arrived.

This message changed everything.

If true, two of the three Homunculi were dead. If both brothers had been killed at the same time, this pointed to an adversary, not an accident. Most likely a new adversary. An unknown adversary.

Making matters worse, the progenitor's notes on creating more Homunculi had somehow been released to normal men. Either one of these problems would be a dramatic setback; both at the same time were apocalyptic. If souled scientists learned the secrets of creating soulless men, the possible ramifications were unthinkable. The Homunculus's efforts would be for nothing, and the world's power structure would be thrown into complete madness.

And so, no: this could not be left to an agent. The Homunculus would have to travel to Europe personally.

But he would have one stop to make before flying to Germany. He had to visit a witch.

Deborah Abend was six years old and frail as a wet leaf of paper. She wore a dress that may have been, at one time, light yellow, but was now caked in mud. Her skin may have been, at one time, pink, but was now caked in mud, as well. Such were the conditions in Stuttgart West, a camp for displaced Jews being built up in the American Zone of Stuttgart. Perhaps someday the camp might be bright, clean, and refreshing. This was not that day.

Deborah was separated from her parents and scared. She had reached the point of fear where no tears formed, no trembling occurred, and no expression crossed her face. Lost and terrified, she entered a damp tunnel that was part of an old rail system. Now the tracks were destroyed, the landscape made into an alien world of mud and gray and damp.

Going into the tunnel was the worst decision Deborah could have made, but she had not really made it at all: she was simply moving forward, her dirty legs carrying her forward out of simple instinct, nothing more. Adults would have avoided the tunnel for fear of thieves or rapists using it as a hideout, but Deborah did not know of such things. She only knew to walk forward. Forward.

Even as she passed the entrance and was now encompassed in near-total darkness, she continued. The lit entryway behind her was growing smaller, the echo of her feet on grimy wet rock louder. She did not hear the deep rustle of fabric, nor the low creak of stones rubbing together behind her.

Deborah fell, tripped by a thick, exposed root protruding from the ground. She could never have seen it, not in this darkness. She fell and lay flat, face down, the shock fully embracing her now. She would be dead from the cold in half an hour.

The two men following behind her may not have cared. From their vantage point, closer to the entrance, they could still just barely make out Deborah's form and saw her fall. This would make their efforts easier. They no longer needed to worry about scaring Deborah into running; she was not going to be running anywhere now.

The men relaxed, no longer worried about making noise.

Laughing between themselves, they called after Deborah, shouting, "We're coming for you, little Jew!" Knowing their prey had nowhere to go, frightening her would make their fun all the more exciting.

When they finally stood over the fallen Deborah, one began to undo his belt. Their laughter and mocking were so loud that they, too, did not hear the rustle of fabric, the sound of stone rubbing stone, behind them.

The first man's head crunched like a coconut crushed by a pneumatic press. Blood and brains sprayed in all directions, with much of it covering his friend. His friend screamed, unable to clearly see what had just happened. Now he heard the rustle, the stone. Oh, *now* he heard it.

A roar thundered throughout the tunnel, a terrifying sound, as if someone were dragging an iron bar across a granite pit while screaming. The second man turned to run, towards the entry, towards the light, but before he could take even two steps, he felt something clamp onto his shoulder. Not a hand, but a vise. A stone vise. His shoulder collapsed under the pressure, bones turned to splinters, muscle tore apart, blood sprayed. His blood now.

The vise yanked him backwards, spinning him until he faced the thing that had him.

And *thing* was precisely what it was. A shadow of black and gray, eight feet tall, at least. Made of mud, clay, and stone; wrapped in burlap, the thick, coarse fabric held in place with endless ropes covering its arms, legs, and torso.

The thing gripped the man's shoulder even tighter and then pulled, tearing him apart to the sound of his screaming. Limbs and chunks were tossed in different directions until the man screamed no longer.

The tunnel now silent, the great giant thing turned to Deborah. It picked her up, with two enormous hands, and carried her towards a fire.

Deborah would be found, warm, fed and alive, just days

later. No one ever entered the tunnel in Stuttgart, so no one ever found the bodies of the two dead criminals.

Chapter 4: The Silver Girl

Lady Petra did not enter the room; she slid into it. Her movements were perfect in every way and enticing to every man. Lady Petra was one of about sixty wealthy Germans sliding across Schwetzingen Palace's immaculate marble floors as a small quartet played portions of the Winterreise.

Around the opulent hall, elegantly dressed men and women flirted over trays of imported champagne.

Heidelberg, the palace's seat, had been liberated early by US forces and thus enjoyed relatively less damage than nearly every other major city in Germany. Because of that, the would-be aristocracy of smoldering Germany gathered here to relive an era before bombs and camps and Nazis.

Upon closer inspection, many of the men and women at Schwetzingen were not as well-off as they wanted to appear, and their elegant suits and immaculate dresses were not so elegant or immaculate. These were older clothes, re-washed, re-dyed, and re-stitched to fix or hide damage from storage during the war. No one here was wearing anything particularly new or modern.

Except for Lady Petra. Her silver dress lay on her thin, perfect frame as if someone had poured liquid silver over her and then dusted her with diamonds. The dress dipped low on her chest, revealing enough to catch the eye but without causing scandal; the hem fell nearly to her ankles, but allowed a pair of white, crystal-dusted shoes to remain in view. Her blonde hair was pulled up tight and adorned with a few diamond pins. She was a walking shimmer of light and glint, with a small emerald pendant as a single point of color.

Her skin was pure white; cream, in fact. Her eyes were blue and shining, the whites of her eyes unblemished with even a dot of red. She had a perfect upturned nose, perfect lips, and perfect brows. Lady Petra would have been beautiful if she had walked into any ball at any of the richest social events anywhere in pre-war Europe.

But here, post-war, at Schwetzingen, she was a goddess. It was as if she had stepped down from the heavens themselves to join Man just for a short while, to remind them that gods existed.

Perhaps it was ironic that such a specimen of German perfection appeared only *after* her country was forced to abandon its pursuit of racial purity.

If Lady Petra shared the views of Germany's fallen leaders, it was entirely hidden. If she had contempt for the working class or loathed the Jews, this was obscured. She floated through the crowd as if such things were beyond her notice, entirely unimportant. Now, in this moment, only one thing mattered:

"Champagne, and lots of it," Lady Petra said softly to a wandering palace footman. "I quite intend on getting drunk."

The truth was that Lady Petra had no such intention, and she could not stand drinking champagne, nor any of the cheap German imitations that were passed around during these years, pretending to be it. Instead, her concern was blending in and, in this group, appearing to be both elegant and an alcoholic was expected.

A former banking official, no doubt now broke but still in possession of a tailored suit, approached Petra. His hair was fine enough, but the style of his mustache was ten years out of date, and he had the slight smell of bacon.

"I am Lord Bassermann," he said, extending a hand in greeting. "Of the ... Bassermanns," he added, as if it mattered. The German aristocracy had been scattered to the ends of the earth after the abdication of Kaiser Wilhelm in 1918. The people here were pretending, for sure, but so long as everyone was in on the pretense, it was all very acceptable.

Of course, Lady Petra was no "lady," either. She came from a different stock entirely.

Petra allowed her hand to be taken, but did not do so enthusiastically. "Very nice to meet you," she said out of politeness.

"And, your name, miss?" he asked.

"The Lady Petra. I won't lie to you and say I'm from some

family, since, as we all know, those families don't exist anymore. No, I'm the first of my family line. I won't say otherwise." Petra managed to tell the complete truth with an innocent smile that shone as brightly as her dress.

As she spoke, her gaze wandered until it landed on a tall man across the hall. Petra immediately took notice. The man was forty-ish, with dark hair with flecks of silver beginning to appear, but still very German. He was well-apportioned and smartly dressed in what seemed to be a new suit. Nothing re-stitched for him.

The waiter returned, bringing champagne, but now Lady Petra waved him off. She had found something else of interest.

"Excuse me," Lady Petra said to Bassermann. She took both his hands and looked him in the eye to fully engage him. "I do promise to come back, you've ... enchanted me." Her smile was the perfect balance of youthful innocence and wholesome flirtation. Lord Bassermann could do nothing but smile back and nod.

The Lady Petra then slid away, ever so gently, allowing Bassermann's hand to linger for a moment on her pinky. But this other man, this tall rake, begged her attention. She had to know who he was. Her legs, hidden behind the shimmer of her slinking dress, carried her to the other side of the hall. She put herself within his eyeline and, without ever looking directly at him, drew his attention immediately.

He came over, of course, because there was nothing else he could possibly do.

"Hello, miss," he said, offering a hand. "I've not seen you here before."

Petra pretended to be surprised by his approach. She glanced at his hovering hand, and then offered hers, but only after the perfectly timed delay. He took it and kissed her hand near its gentle white knuckles.

"I am Lady Petra. I won't lie to you and say I'm from some family, since, as we all know, those families don't exist anymore. No, I'm the first of my family line. I won't say otherwise." Fortunately, the baconly Basserman had not been close enough to hear her repeat herself to this new rake.

"I am Hans Müller. I did not come prepared with a fictional title, but you can call me Baron, I suppose. Or Duke?" His smile was clean, his hair neat, his skin well-maintained. Up close, she reevaluated his age as closer to thirty-five years.

Petra uttered a sound that existed somewhere between a giggle and a hiccup, as if she intended to laugh, caught herself, and cut it off abruptly, all in a single second. It was delightful, of course. Müller was already captivated. "Perhaps Baron, then?" she said. "It sounds powerful and with a bit of menace."

Müller raised an eyebrow at her. "You like a bit of menace?"

"The only people who don't like menace are cowards and the boring," she said, showing a bit of pearl teeth with her girlish smile. "I strive to be neither."

Müller did his best to pretend to be aloof. It was not working on Petra, of course, but she was impressed by his skill at it. He was a handsome man, likely used to the flirtations of any woman near him, but she could still see through much of his pretense. "Well, I shall try to be menacing, then," he said.

"Dance first?" she asked boldly. No matter how demure, how charming, how delicate Petra appeared, she wanted him to know that she also knew how to take control when she wanted to.

Müller nodded, taking her hand and whisking her away to the floor. The crowd quickly threw their eyes at the couple, as they were beyond a doubt the most handsome — and youngest — attendees at the event. The older people smiled, the vision of Petra and Müller dancing reminding them of happier times, decades ago; the middle-aged men smiled, but only to hide their jealousy.

The beautiful couple remained a couple for the rest of the evening, until the musicians packed up and it came time to leave. They had shared an enjoyable conversation, a pleasant dance, and now Müller clearly intended to finalize his evening with an appropriate conquest of Lady Petra's body.

That did not happen.

Inspector Thumann and Ximena arrived in Stuttgart after a quiet and pensive twelve-hour bus ride from Berlin. Thumann's mood had not improved since arriving in Berlin, although Ximena sensed some of his anxiety may have lifted now that they were out of Thumann's home city. At least the scenery was lovely, making their passage through the rural parts of Germany pleasant; in between the cities, there was less evidence of outright wartime damage.

"I know you're still unhappy with this assignment," Ximena said. She wanted to discuss the case, perhaps to change Thumann's mood, but she was also aware that the case was the thing affecting his mood. She felt guilty for having taken Brühl's side on the matter.

"I am," Thumann admitted. "It's a simple serial killer. We are being wasted here."

"But shouldn't we stop serial killers, too?" she asked. She realized she was repeating what she had said in Paris, and instantly regretted it. Ximena feared appearing unshakeable in her opinion.

"Hmmph." There was the grunt Ximena had expected. "I spent decades poking around murder scenes. First in Berlin, then for Scotland Yard. I suppose I thought I had matured sufficiently not to be sent out on every minor case."

"Dr. Cuba," Ximena said, leaving the words to sit in the air.

Thumann was silent for a moment and then exhaled. "Perceptive, as always, dear miss," he said. In this instance, Ximena was not sure if he meant it as a compliment or an annoyance.

Ximena nodded. "For you, the Dr. Cuba case was something bigger. I think I understand."

"We should be investigating crime. Crime in the broader sense, on a larger scale. Yes, the Dr. Cuba case probably spoiled me, if I have to admit it. In that case, I felt I had reached my calling, as they say. I was finally where I was meant to be."

Ximena knew this was true. She also knew he was unhappy to be in Berlin, to have the memories of his earlier life — a happier life, no doubt — intruding on him. That was where his real misery lay now. She tried to find a way to change the subject but found none.

"Golems," Thumann muttered, more to himself than to Ximena. "Ridiculous."

Ximena fell silent and elected to remain that way for the rest of the trip to Stuttgart.

The Homunculus arrived by fan boat. He had never piloted one before, but the principle was simple enough; he could have killed the foul-smelling captain and simply taken the boat, but he had no idea how to navigate in the maze of sawgrass. Eventually, the boat's noisy fan was cut off, and the dock came into view.

The Homunculus stepped onto the dock and stood straight like a statue, facing the black, rundown shack of Madame Blavatsky.

"I'll be back in an hour to getcha," the pilot said.

The Homunculus turned, staring the sun-baked, stinking man in the eye. He raised one hand — the one with the red finger — and pointed downward. It was as if he were telling a dog to "stay," and the pilot did just that. He stayed.

Turning towards the shack, the Homunculus began walking. Occult symbols decorated the dock and the front of the shack, a combination of legitimate curse-warders and phony tourist trappings. Off to one side was a garden growing cannabis and other questionable weeds. Crickets whined, and cicadas screamed. A dog slept on the porch, as if dead.

The door to the shack opened. "Do not approach, Thing," a woman's voice said.

Madame Blavatsky stood at the door, dressed in a shamble of cloth and beads that vaguely looked like a dress made by blind seamstresses during a hurricane. Layers upon layers of material hid her real shape, but it was large, very large. She was also nearly as tall as the ivory-skinned demon she saw in front of her. Her mass of hair was a nest of dreadlocks, beads and matted braids. She had a black eyepatch over one eye, embossed with the symbol of a red dragon. Her skin was cragged from the Florida sun and too many years of smoking cigars, pipes, and all manner of illegal substances. Despite her habits, her hands were steady, which was all that mattered for the moment, since she held a sawed-off shotgun aimed right at the Homunculus's heart.

The Homunculus remained motionless, except for his lips as he spoke. "You are Madame Blavatsky. I am Dr. Cuba." It was one of the first times the Homunculus had overtly used his Brother-Son's prior name.

"You are no more a doctor than I am pinup queen," Blavatsky said without an iota of fear in her being. "To be a doctor requires first that you be a human, and you are not that."

The Homunculus did not move, but his curiosity was triggered just a bit. "You see me, then? I mean, as I am."

"I see you, Thing. And I don't *want* to see you, so turn around and get back on your boat. Take your walking carcass to some other witch's hut." Blavatsky raised the gun slightly higher.

"I will leave, but only after I have an answer from you, Madame Blavatsky. I only need an answer, which means I will only ask a question. Then I will go."

Blavatsky remained silent. She was not about to ask this creature what its question was, but she was also curious as to why it shambled up her dock.

The Homunculus continued. "You are, they say, the great-granddaughter of the Russian theosophist Helena Blavatsky. Some say this is a ruse, to sell trinkets to curious tourists. But I know better."

"How so, Thing?"

"You helped Inspector Heiner Thumann defeat my brother."

"Did I?" Blavatsky asked. "You mean I helped rid the world of a soulless, damned beast, and I hadn't even realized it? I'm even better than I thought."

"I'd laugh, Madame, but we both know I have no sense of humor, and I would only be doing it as a pretense. Having no soul makes it hard to understand, much less appreciate, things like humor or music."

"What's your question, Thing? The faster you ask it, the quicker you get to leave here with your head still attached." Blavatsky was not bluffing.

"You advised Thumann on the Sunken Gods. These gods pre-dated humans. My question is this: how did you come to know these things?"

Blavatsky snorted. "I read a *book*, you dimwitted, skulking bugger. That is how one learns things."

The Homunculus now fell silent, pausing on the thought. Blavatsky's raised shotgun never wavered, never lowered.

"Give me this book," he said.

Blavatsky raised one eyebrow, the one without the eyepatch. "You said one question and you'd leave. I'm not a library. Now turn around."

What happened next could be called a blur, but a blur presumes someone was watching and could see it. No, this happened within the tiny second that Blavatsky's eye blinked. For that moment, as the lid shut and prepared to reopen, the Homunculus had moved. With her unpatched eye open again, she now saw he was gone.

But he was not.

Behind her, a hand now grasped her windpipe. Another hand forced her arm down, sending the shotgun rattling to the ground. It fired, a loud bang that shook the sawgrass outside for miles. The dog woke.

"Give me the book, I will leave, and you will live," the

Homunculus said, gripping Blavatsky's windpipe. "If you don't, I will just kill you and search your shack for it. I will leave with the book no matter what. You decide whether I do it over your corpse."

Stuttgart itself was as bad as Berlin; buildings were collapsed, hotels left half-standing, and rubble was everywhere. The Rathaus, or City Hall, still boasted a single clock tower, but the surrounding buildings were roofless and shattered. There were cleanup efforts underway, but it was still too soon to claim that Stuttgart was even more than a quarter of the way to being restored.

Thumann and Ximena headed towards a cinema, which, reports insisted, had been left untouched by Allied bombs. It was there that two men were murdered by the alleged "Golem." The ICPO wire said the cinema had been torn to shreds by the beast.

A short taxi ride took them from the bus depot to the cinema. It was very much intact and did not appear to have been the scene of any great drama other than whatever might have been projected on its weathered screen. A sign out front read, in German, "Stuttgart's Best Cinema is Open Once Again."

Thumann crunched his way over gravel and street debris into the cinema's lobby, where he was met by a young usher. Ximena followed behind; she spoke not a word of German, so had to rely on her instincts — and context — to tell her what was being said.

"Your manager?" Thumann asked.

"One moment, sir," the young usher said, scurrying off to find an adult. The inside of the theater smelled like mold and stale cigarettes; the carpeting was red—or would have been if it was not covered in dirty footprints and water damage stains.

"Sir?" an older man asked, emerging from an office.

"I am Inspector Thumann of the International Criminal Police Organization."

"The what?" the man asked with a frown.

"Some refer to us as 'Interpol,'" Thumann said. "We are here to ask questions about a murder."

The man nodded. Ximena only understood about fifty percent of the conversation.

"Oh, yes. Two men were killed, right here in the lobby." He pointed to a spot near the center of the room. "You can see the bloodstain."

In fact, you could not. At least not apart from the rest of the filth on the war-damaged carpet. Thumann nodded anyway. "Can you tell me what happened?" he asked in German.

"A street thug, dressed in an overcoat and hood, shot them dead. It was all over in about one minute. It shocked us, of course. We cancelled the matinee. The police took the bodies, and that was that. I can't tell you much more."

Thumann took out his pipe. "And this killer? What happened to him?"

"Gone as soon as the deed was done. Disappeared into the streets while the people here screamed and ran around like rats."

Thumann lit his pipe now, scowling. "We heard reports of a large man. A wrestler or circus performer, perhaps. Dressed in burlap."

The cinema manager shook his head, looking confused. "Sir?"

"How large was the killer?" Thumann asked, smoke spewing from his pipe.

"A normal man, thin. Difficult to say, but normal. Not a giant, that I am sure of. Dressed in burlap? No, a normal wool coat."

Thumann nodded. "Thank you, sir. I believe we have been misled and will leave you to your cleanup."

As Thumann turned, the man said, "Cleanup? We already cleaned."

Thumann did not argue. He and Ximena exited and stood underneath the tattered marquee sign.

"Inspector?" Ximena asked. "I didn't understand all of that, but it sounded like the killer was not a giant?"

Thumann took another puff from his pipe, liberating a large cloud of tobacco smoke into the Stuttgart air. "That's right, dear miss. It appears this was a normal criminal act, a robbery gone wrong, something of that sort."

Ximena scowled now.

Thumann noticed; she was likely beginning to regret her decision in Paris. He pointed the tip of his pipe towards a bakery across the street. "Let's get coffee," he said.

The two entered the bakery, and for Ximena, it was as if she had entered an entirely different world. Gone were the gray bricks and craters and piles of garbage. Inside the bakery, there had been no war, no bombs. There was only the sweet smell of fresh cakes and bubbling coffee. The display case held what must have been over forty million different types of desserts, or so it seemed to Ximena. Tarts, cookies, pastries, pies, cakes; every one of her senses was rewarded. She looked around and thought it strange that the bakery was nearly without any patrons.

Thumann sat at a table near the window.

"It's so empty," Ximena said, sitting across from him.

"It's the hour," Thumann answered. "Germans don't eat many sweets at this time. In another two hours or so, the place will be a madhouse."

"So many different types of ... of ... everything!" Ximena said, wide-eyed.

"I felt the same when I was in South America, in the bakeries there, dear miss. It only looks amazing because the items are different. But we will still not find your delicious alfajores here."

The waiter approached.

"Two coffees," Thumann said, "and whatever the young miss would like." Ximena pointed at a decadent slice of chocolate cake, and the waiter left to fill their order.

"Danka shane," Ximena attempted to say, then huffed. "My German is terrible," she grumbled.

"Again, now you know how I felt in Chile and Peru," Thumann said. Someone in the back put on a record of traditional German music; Ximena smiled. "They think you're a tourist," Thumann said. "That's for your benefit."

Ximena's momentary joy here, in this bakery, lifted Thumann's mood slightly. The waiter returned with two hot coffees, fresh and steaming, and a plate of what Ximena thought was the biggest slice of cake she had ever seen. "I can't eat all that!" she said.

"Yes, you can. I have faith in you," Thumann said, smiling under his thick, tangled beard.

"Inspector," Ximena said, suddenly a bit serious. "I don't…"

Thumann interrupted. He knew what she was about to say. "There are a lot of emotions running over us, between us, dear miss. We need to stop this nonsense."

Ximena froze for a moment, the cake hovering near her mouth.

Thumann continued. "We are professionals. Investigators. Inspectors. The facts must guide us. You are worried about me and my hesitance to come back to Germany. I am worried about your memories of Lima. Both of us are worried about each other, and I am afraid this is hindering our ability to do the work."

Ximena lowered the cake back down to her plate. Thumann snorted. Gently, he placed his hand over hers, raised it, and repositioned the cake near her mouth. "You see? You're so worried about me that you won't even eat cake. Even Catholics know there is a small room in Hell used to put women who won't eat cake because they are worried about old Germans."

She smiled and bit. "Dios mio," she said, rolling her eyes. "It's good."

Thumann reached down to her plate and broke off a piece of the cake for himself. "I don't want to go to Hell, either," he said, as he nibbled. The mood was lighter now.

"Facts," he said, cake falling onto his whiskers. "Go back and think. What did you say in Paris? What are the connections? Facts only."

Ximena sipped her coffee to clear her throat. "Killings of Nazis, a string of them, moving from Prague to Julbach and then to Stuttgart. These appear linked, based on the facts."

"Agreed," Thumann said. He resisted reaching for more cake.

"Then, random killings elsewhere in Germany, some near Stuttgart, some not. These are of prostitutes, beggars, even people of station."

"What's left of it," Thumann snorted.

"These don't seem related to the Nazi murders. The victims in those cases have no political affiliations, no sympathies, no real pattern. These are similar to what the wires had been reporting for years, sporadically, through France as well."

Thumann nodded. "But these recent German reports have something new. Witnesses recount property damage, smashed houses, toppled brick walls, and a giant man in burlap. Fantastic elements."

Ximena paused. "We missed something," she finally said.

"What's that?" Thumann asked, sipping his coffee now.

"We never tracked which of the reports included a Golem appearance. I would bet the Golem attacks are those coming from Prague, as you said."

"The Golem of Prague," Thumann repeated.

"These other killings are more ... I don't know what the word is. Traditional? Can you have traditional killings?" Ximena asked.

"I know what you mean. More textbook," Thumann said.

"Yes! Like out of the textbook," Ximena said, nodding. "Simple killings. The Golem attacks suggest a motive: revenge against the Nazis. These other killings might be sex crimes or just a serial killer, but they don't seem to be related to the war or politics. I think we may have *two* crime waves, not one."

Thumann thought for a moment. "The Golem attacks met the Three-Country Rule. What about these other murders?"

"Only Germany and, perhaps, France," Ximena admitted. "At least that I can see from these wire reports. And, frankly, the French reports are old. They may not be connected at all."

"Our Fourth Floor remit didn't specify. We can safely investigate them all and find out for ourselves if we are dealing with two problems or one larger one."

"Sir?" a voice said.

Thumann turned. It was the young usher. "Yes, boy?"

"I heard you speaking of the Golem," the boy said sheepishly.

"Hmmph," Thumann said, turning his attention back to his coffee. "What of it?"

"The Golem struck the other cinema. Not this one. The one on Schellingstraße."

Thumann paused to look at the young man. "Boy, make sure you know what you're talking about. We are not in the mood for being sent all around town chasing ghosts."

"Not a joke, sir. The roof was smashed, the walls caved in. It's only a ten-minute cab ride there, sir. You can see it. I swear by my mother," the boy insisted.

Thumann reached into his pocket and handed the boy a coin. "If you're wrong," Thumann said gruffly, "we will come back and swear *at* your mother."

The usher ran off, the coin gripped tightly in his hand.

"A lead?" she asked, chocolate smudged on her lip.

"A lead," Thumann acknowledged. "We can relax here a bit more, and then we are off to another cinema. Apparently, murders in cinemas are more popular now than the films themselves."

Chapter 5: The Red Herring

Franz Gogel was twenty-four and not going to get any older. As he walked back from the pub, his legs going in one direction while his drunken brain aimed his torso in another, he whistled a tune he had heard on the radio a few days before. He was not whistling particularly loudly, nor particularly well, so no one would have noticed him as he took the roughly straight route from the pub to his flat, with one short detour to piss in an alleyway.

He had finished pissing when he felt the air choke from him. Suddenly, someone was behind him, wrapping something tight around his neck and pulling with the strength of a team of workhorses. His eyes rolled into his head before he collapsed, but he did collapse, being entirely dead before his body even hit the ground.

Thumann and Ximena arrived at the cinema on Schellingstraße and found it just as the young usher had said: heavily damaged, with much of its roof collapsed. The theater looked like any other building that might have been smashed by the Allies. The damage certainly could not have been done by a single man.

The theater was closed for business due to the damage, but the massive hole in the front wall allowed the inspector and his protégé to walk inside anyway. They were met with a crew of older men, dressed in coveralls, who were clearly tasked with helping clean and restore the fallen cinema.

Again, Thumann and the others spoke in German, leaving Ximena only to guess what was being said.

"What do you want?" one of the workmen said rudely.

"I am Inspector Thumann from Interpol, and this is my co-inspector, Miss Torres. We have questions about this alleged murder."

"Do you have papers or something?" the worker asked.

Thumann grunted, annoyed that Germans could never seem to stop asking for papers, but produced his identification.

"This says International Criminal Police Organization," the worker said with an eyebrow raise.

Thumann figured this man must have been a bureaucrat before the war and was now reduced to cleaning rubble. "'Interpol' is our telegraph address, and people seem to know that more readily."

"I've never heard of either," the workman said.

Thumann was getting impatient and moved his giant, six-foot-four, refrigerator-sized body so it towered over the man. "We are here to investigate a murder. You should let us do that before there's another." He knew bureaucrats respected fear.

Thumann had calculated correctly; the man handed Thumann back his papers and moved aside. "Talk to Scheiner," the man said, hooking a thumb over his shoulder, towards a bookish-looking man near the box office booth.

Thumann walked past the man; Ximena was sure he clomped his feet a bit louder than usual, if only to emphasize his size to the poor worker.

"Are you Scheiner?" Thumann asked.

The bookish man looked up. "That's me. Scheiner."

"I'm Inspector Thumann, and this is Co-Inspector Torres. We are here investigating this alleged murder." Thumann held his papers up again, but the bookish man didn't look at them. "And," he waved his hand in the air towards the collapsed roof, "whatever caused all this."

"The Golem," the man said nervously.

"Yes, we hear this man calls himself that. Or the newspapers do, anyway. We want to know more about him."

"That's not its name, Inspector," the man said, looking down at his book of receipts, pretending to count something. "It's what it *is*."

Thumann looked at Ximena, rolling his eyes. Exhaling, he turned back to the man. "Let us start with this: who was murdered?"

"Two former Nazi officers. I don't know their ranks, but I was told by people who recognized them that they held somewhat high positions. Of course, they were in plain clothes."

"I'm sure," Thumann said. The German landscape was lousy with Nazis who had shed their uniforms to blend in with the people they had, just a few months earlier, sent to work camps.

Like Hilda.

"The beast broke through the front there," the man said, pointing to the hole in the front wall. "Broke through it as if it were made of paper. It found the men there, near the left entrance to the theater, and snapped them in half."

"What did this man look like?" Thumann said. "And how did he break the wall?"

"You don't understand, Inspector," Scheiner said with a shake of his head. "This is not a man. It is a golem. A living, walking golem. Two-and-a-half meters in height at least. Made of stone. Wrapped tight in burlap and ropes. It broke the wall with its fists. It roared like a blast furnace!"

Thumann was not in the mood. "Golems don't exist, man. That's a myth from the Talmud. This was a man, a large one for sure, but a man. Dressed up, I imagine."

"Not a man!" the bookish man insisted, growing angry. "It snapped those men in half! When it heard the police whistles, it smashed its way through the ceiling, and the rest of the roof collapsed. Do you think a man could do all this?"

Thumann raised an eyebrow. "I think an old bomb did all this."

"Fine, then go search for bombs," the man huffed angrily. "Leave us alone, then!" He walked into a back office and slammed the door.

Thumann sniffed, looked around a bit, and turned to

Ximena. He explained everything the bookish man had said, adding, "Obviously, this is all nonsense."

Ximena thought for a moment. "No one would have believed Dr. Cuba existed, but we saw him. And that strange creature who called himself his brother."

Thumann shook his head. "Strange men with odd habits and sick minds are one thing. Living statues tearing down brick walls is another. These people saw a murder, probably by a large man, and their post-war trauma conflated the stories. I know Germans. They love to speak of myths and Valkyries and angry Teutonic gods. Get them drunk, and they will insist the world is sitting on the back of a turtle instead of floating in space."

Thumann began walking out of the theater. Ximena was surprised at his sudden desire to leave.

"Inspector?" she asked.

"Let's go back ot the hotel. This is absolutely nonsensical. There must be some factual basis for all this. We are missing something. My Germany has gone mad, yes, but it cannot have lost all its sanity."

Petra sat in her apartment wearing a simple skirt and blouse; the silver dress hung in the closet. Yesterday's ball was over, she had made the long ride back from Schwetzingen Palace to Stuttgart and was now, once again, simply "Fraulein" Petra, not Lady Petra.

Petra's apartment was one of the nicest in Stuttgart, in a relatively safe zone that was heavily patrolled by handsome French soldiers. The building was a small three-story home converted into flats, with a shared bathroom on each floor. Petra was on the top floor, in what must have been an attic, as her room's ceilings hung at odd angles, with strangely angled windows jutting out here and there.

The view from those windows might have been nice when Stuttgart was in its prime; now it only offered a view of blackened streets and bomb-damaged neighborhoods in the distance. The building's owner, Frau Jannings, tried her best to lighten the environment, planting flowers near the front fence and in a garden along the side and hanging brightly colored curtains in the windows; Petra's were pink.

This had been one of the wealthier parts of the city before the bombings, and now the wealthy were slowly returning. It was still highly damaged, but compared to other parts of Stuttgart, there was a greater — and more organized — effort underway to make repairs. This offered Petra a more comfortable place to live, at least for the time she would stay here.

Which would not be much longer, she was certain. She hoped she might move on from the city within a week or two, as her efforts here were proving fruitful. But Stuttgart was not a place to live. She'd have to get out of Germany entirely, though she thought she might one day return after the Allies figured out what to do with it.

Wanting some fresh air, Petra went downstairs and stood outside her apartment, near the front gate and its yellow flowers, to gaze at the gray city before her. She wore a light sweater to keep the chilly air off of her.

Frau Jannings came out to greet her. "Fraulein Petra," she said kindly, "you should wear a heavier coat. You will get sick!"

"I'm fine, frau, but thank you so much for your worries. You always treat me like a daughter, and I'm grateful." Petra smiled her charming smile, a tiny glimpse of pearl teeth visible.

"You remind me of my late daughter, Fraulein Petra, but even if you didn't look like my late Anna, I would still nag you." Frau Jannings dabbed a handkerchief over Petra's cheek. "Look at you, you're still dripping wet from the bath. You are going to catch a cold, dear."

Petra smiled again. "I'm fine, just fine. I have a hearty constitution, don't worry."

"May I fetch you some hot tea, fraulein? Just a cup?" the

landwoman asked.

"No, no, thank you, Frau Jannings."

"You never drink my tea. Have you been to America? Did you switch to coffee? Should I make you some of that instead? I must have coffee somewhere in that kitchen of mine."

Petra smiled. "I have not been to America, Frau Jannings, no. Someday, I hope. But thank you for the offer. Again, I'm fine. I will have some soup later at that little bistro down the road. I love that little place."

Frau Jannings pouted. "I do hope you're not fibbing, fraulein, and will take care of yourself. You're too thin, you need to eat. Forget about attracting the boys, make sure you are healthy. That's what I say."

Petra issued her strange giggle-burp. Had any boys been in earshot, they would have melted in a mere moment. "I will try, Frau Jannings. I will eat a fat steak today and dedicate my fat belly to you afterward. How does that sound?"

Frau Jannings smiled broadly. "Very good, fraulein! Very good! Did you enjoy your ball at the palace? You looked so elegant in that silver dress, even if you were showing a bit too much skin."

"It was a nice party, yes, but it ended abruptly," Petra said sadly.

"Oh, dear. What happened?" Frau Jannings asked.

"Some German police arrived, with their French counterparts. They claimed someone at the ball was a suspect in those murders all over town. They dragged a few of the men out, kicking and screaming. It was all very loud and scandalous."

Frau Jannings gasped. "Oh, goodness! I'm sorry you did not have a good time, fraulein. You looked like a fairytale princess."

"Oh, I had a fine time. At least until the end. But it was fine. A very nice evening with champagne and dancing. I met a very nice man."

"Will you see him again?"

"Oh, no. That won't be possible," Petra said, looking off into the distance. "But I am going on another short trip, perhaps I will meet a different handsome man and have better luck."

"When will you come back?"

"In just a few days. A very short trip."

"Well, dear fraulein, that is exciting! I wish you well. I will leave you to your peace, then." Frau Jannings turned to walk back into the house, but turned around suddenly. "Oh, dear Petra, please be careful if you travel. I heard something on the news that the horrible criminal Dr. Cuba may be responsible for all these terrible things happening in Stuttgart. They say he's here, right now, in the city!"

Petra raised her eyebrows slightly, thinking how silly the name Dr. Cuba was. "I don't know who that is, Frau Jannings. I'm sorry."

"A devil! The 'Invisible Devil,' in fact, is what they call him on the radio. He brings crime and death everywhere he goes. They say he's the Golem! Or did he bring it with him? I don't know, the news reports are so confusing, and my radio always sputters, I can't hear everything. But please be careful," Frau Jannings pleaded.

Petra smiled. "I will, don't worry. I will go to the bistro, get big and fat, and come right back. No one will bother me."

Frau Jannings smiled one final time, and Petra watched as the woman disappeared back into her ground-floor flat.

Sitting in her hotel room, Ximena was worried about her giant, smelly bear. Inspector Thumann was sullen, quiet, and appeared ashen. He cheered up somewhat while they were in the bakery, but only for a moment. Once they returned to the streets of Stuttgart, his mood soured again. It was something she had not seen before, at least not with such persistence.

She knew what was bothering him. She did not know the details, but colleagues at Scotland Yard had gossiped that Thumann lost his wife in the war to the Nazis. Whether Thumann's Hilda was a Jew or simply someone caught up in the net of the Nazi war machine was not clear, but something most certainly happened.

And Ximena knew that Thumann loved his Hilda very, very much. He had precious little in his flat back in London and had brought even less with him when they moved to Paris. But he had one yellowed, weathered photo of Hilda that he kept flat, without any frame, on his dresser. Ximena swore she heard Thumann talking to that photo a few times while she waited outside for him on some mornings.

Ximena had tried to discuss Hilda with Thumann, but he simply would not allow it. He would make excuses for dropping the matter or change the subject entirely. One time, he ran to the bathroom, saying his bladder was going to explode. Eventually, Ximena stopped asking. If he wanted to talk about Hilda, he would in his own time, she was certain.

Ximena had still not fallen in love, even though in her hometown, she likely would be married by now. At her age, being single and without ever having kissed a boy, much less married one, Ximena would be considered a spinster or, worse, a whore. Ximena was neither; she was just a young woman who had been given some professional opportunities she intended to pursue. She really did not understand the fuss around love, and therefore decided it could wait.

But seeing Thumann's deep love for Hilda did make her wonder about such things. What would it be like to love someone so much that when they were gone, you felt that much pain? What if you could live your whole life with that person, avoid the pain, but feel that level of love and dedication every day, without interruption? These were interesting questions that Ximena allowed herself to ponder, though she knew she could not speak to Thumann about them. Perhaps eventually she'd make new female friends in Paris and have other girls to talk to about these thoughts.

Unlikely. Despite the more liberal atmosphere of the new

ICPO and the special freedoms they gave the Fourth Floor, Ximena was still struggling in Paris. The women in France were given a slightly higher level of respect and admiration for their work, but they were still not considered equal to men. She still had much to do to prove herself equal, if not better, than the men at Interpol.

Having settled that, she returned to her two current problems: the investigation before her and how she could somehow improve Thumann's mood, so the German Brain was once again functioning at his best. She realized that by doing the first, she might achieve the second.

Yes, Ximena would work hard, focus on the investigation, and help Thumann solve it. With the file on these German matters successfully closed, Thumann might have his confidence restored and be able to move on from the death of this former protégé, Gentleman, and whatever was haunting him about his dear Hilda.

She laid out the facts as she knew them. A series of incidents was reported where destruction of property and murder occurred, often with former Nazis being the main targets. These they called the "Golem attacks" and the path was well established: they began in Czechoslovakia, traveled down into Austria and then into Germany from the east. Would the Golem stop here, in Stuttgart? If so, why? If not, would he go further west after that, towards ... France? Switzerland? Spain?

Ximena made a fist, frustrated that she struggled to remember the strange European map and all its odd countries. All she remembered of it was that France looked like a boot and Scandinavia like male genitalia.

Ximena did not rule out that this "Golem" might be an organization and not a single individual, especially given the damage that was reported in these attacks. She recalled they had the same debate about Dr. Cuba in South America, and she did not want to rule out any possibilities. While the victims tended to be individuals or small groups, the damage to the surrounding area or buildings suggested weapons of some kind. Bazookas? This meant someone with access to military hardware, which again pointed to an organization.

Then there was what Ximena was theorizing was an unrelated *second* crime wave: a string of murders not accompanied by any property damage or particular drama, and not following any predictable pattern. These murders were mostly of men, but not exclusively. A rich man here, a poor washwoman there, also clustered in Stuttgart.

Separating them from the Golem attacks, were these just random murders occurring in the chaotic lawlessness of post-war Germany? A natural eruption of frustration and emotion given the horrors that the region must have seen during the bombings and street-to-street combat?

Ximena shook her head, sure she was missing something. She told herself to zoom out, like they did in the pictures. To take in more than she could currently see.

She opened her single piece of luggage and pulled out two maps: one was of Europe — she noticed it was Italy that was shaped like a boot — and the other of Germany. She unfolded the German map onto her bed and found Stuttgart.

Ximena pulled more papers from her luggage: her set of exhaustive summaries of the ICPO wires received over the past year for Germany. She crossed off any wires that had been reported to have occurred along the presumed "Golem" path from the east.

Then, Ximena started looking at dates. She began making more marks on her map, numbering each occurrence by date. Now, a new pattern emerged.

Ximena saw that a rash of murders exploded in Stuttgart at least six months before the Golem attacks. These then split off into a new branch, specific to the murders of prostitutes, which led to the north, near Essen. But the other murders continued in Stuttgart at the same time. Only the prostitute murders had branched northward.

Ximena put her papers and map down, as well as her pen.

She knew, in her bones, that she had found something. But it was something Thumann was not going to like.

Not two crime waves. *Three.*

The Homunculus arrived in Berlin, bringing no luggage with him. He was met by a driver named Belknap, who insisted the "k" be pronounced, following ancient tradition. Belknap had been a trusted associate of the Homunculus Brother-Brother, known only as "Herr Doktor" or "Doktor M" in Germany. Unlike Dr. Cuba, who had taken the name and title partly out of madness, this was a name used purely by the press, which then spread through the German criminal underground. The Doktor did not allow any of his associates to call him that, but he also did little to stop the press from spreading the name within society.

The Doktor had been responsible for a wave of crimes throughout Germany, Austria, Hungary, and even further on, but with much more subtlety and stealth than the garish crimes of Dr. Cuba. The Doktor worked within Germany to agitate political parties, foment anti-government sentiment, and foster a culture that sought to blame outside elements for Germany's ills. It was the Berlin-based homunculus that convinced the Nationalsozialistische Deutsche Arbeiterpartei to abandon its socialist leanings and adopt more right-wing, nationalist policies. The Doktor operated a lean but effective network of criminals who bribed and extorted key figures in power to undo the liberal trends after World War I and enflame anti-immigrant and anti-Jewish sentiment. Together with his two Brother-Brothers in the US and France, the Doktor helped bring about World War II.

All of this was part of the grand plan by their Father-Father, the progenitor, of course. The path to global autocracy was being paved by stones laid, in secret, by the Homunculi.

Now, Belknap was a trusted associate of the Doktor, and now, by default, he would be a trusted associate of the Homunculus, or have his head removed.

Belknap drove his new leader to one of the Doktor's headquarters, constructed beneath a large pre-Weimar mansion once owned by a count, on the outskirts of Berlin. A hidden drive led down a tunnel to a series of iron gates and steel doors to an underground parking garage. There, the Doktor maintained a small fleet of road vehicles to be used in various German operations.

Belknap exited the front of the car and then opened the rear door for his black-clad leader. The Homunculus stepped out into the garage and followed as Belknap led him towards a stairway, taking them a few levels deeper into the subterranean facility. It was not large, but it was well-equipped and, as all things the Doktor had managed, efficient.

Below, the Homunculus was greeted by another of the Doktor's key personnel, a physician named Singh. A Sikh, Dr. Singh wore a formal, white pagri turban and spoke with a genteel British accent.

"Sir," he said, bowing slightly before the Homunculus. "I will take you to the body."

"What happened?" the Homunculus asked. The homunculi could survive even serious injuries, but, as powerful as they were, they were not immortal.

As Dr. Singh led the Homunculus through a series of winding stone-lined hallways lit by modern ceiling-mounted bulbs, Belknap returned to wait in the car.

"He was poisoned," Dr. Singh said.

"That is not possible. You know he was not susceptible to poison," the Homunculus said.

"Nevertheless," Dr. Singh said as they entered a square room; it was a morgue.

The two approached a drawer in the wall, and Dr. Singh pulled it out. A metal slab slid out, a sheeted body lying on it. The Homunculus pulled back the sheet. The face of the Doktor was his own, identical in every way, except dead. The skin was still smooth and poreless, but its ivory color was even more like marble now: cold and lifeless.

The Homunculus checked the dead body's left hand. The ring finger was colored with a deep ruby red, identical to the coloring on the Homunculus's own forefinger. No tattoo or birthmark could produce this detail. This was the homunculus known as Herr Doktor.

"Do you know the nature of this alleged poison?" the Homunculus asked.

"It appears designed specifically to target your unique body chemistry." Dr. Singh clearly knew of the Doktor's unique nature, but also that the Homunculus before him was identical. "This means someone knows your nature and is exploiting it."

"How was the poison introduced? By dart? A weapon of some kind?"

"He drank it," Dr. Singh said.

"Imposs —" The Homunculus cut himself off. "How?"

"His sustaining formula was compromised. Someone added the poison to the mixture." The mixture, of course, was the gasoline-and-blood cocktail required to keep the homunculi alive. Few knew these creatures ingested it, fewer knew its exact formulation, and nearly no one should have known where a homunculus would keep his supply.

"Where did he keep his maiden?" the Homunculus asked.

Dr. Singh escorted the Homunculus outside the morgue, down another hall, and into a larger, round room. It resembled, to some degree, the Homunculus's room at Snake Island, with a set of copper-colored iron maidens standing along the perimeter. These were attached to various pumps and devices via tubes and electrical cables.

"Why didn't he feed here?" the Homunculus asked. "Why did he drink instead of using the maiden?"

"Herr Doktor was engaged in a complex operation,

involving the long-term ... shall we say 'wooing' of an opera star. She was crucial to ensuring the compliance of a senior government official. He was spending much of his time with her and could not return for sustenance."

"Someone knew of this plan and exploited it," the Homunculus said.

"Security of the organization here in Berlin is handled by Brentley. He insists the operation was not exposed."

"And yet my brother is dead. Someone knew he would be with this opera singer, knew of his body chemistry, and knew he'd need to drink instead of use the maiden."

"Herr Doktor trusted Brentley with his life multiple times over decades. It could not have been Brentley," Dr. Singh insisted.

The Homunculus knew this to be true. Brentley had been a point of communication between the Berlin operation and his own in the Americas.

The Homunculus stood stiffly. "My brother in France is also reported dead," he said.

"I am told that, too, was poison, sir," Dr. Singh answered solemnly.

"Then someone has penetrated our secrecy."

"Will you go to France?" Dr. Singh asked.

"There's no point. The evidence will be the same. The Doktor and the Fantôme are dead. I need to find out who is killing us, and why."

Chapter 6: The Haunted Bookshop

The Homunculus stood down the street from the bookshop, scanning the area. This was an older part of Berlin, less damaged than much of the city due to its relatively low risk of having anything of interest to the Allies. The shop itself fell within the American zone, thankfully, since the Homunculus had much experience blending into US society as one of their own. His forgers had proper papers for all the Allied checkpoints, but US control of this area made this trip much easier.

The shop itself was old and looked like a German shop from the 1800s, as imagined in a film by that animator the film world was making a fuss about, Walt Disney. The wood was old but featured ornate carvings over the doorway, and it boasted a small storefront window that held a small selection of the shop's latest bestsellers. Through the curtains of a side window, the Homunculus could see a single lamp lighting the interior.

This was a trap.

A note left in Berlin, found by the Doktor's men, indicated that the formula for the homunculi had been compromised. It claimed that a copy of the progenitor's notebook had been sold from this shop, exposing the Father-Father's most closely-held secrets. The idea seemed implausible on its face; only the Homunculus had the progenitor's notebooks, and he had certainly not made any copies. These had been safely stored on Monito Island for years and were now held securely in the new facility on Snake Island.

But, so far, everything the message from Berlin reported was true; the Doktor and the Fantôme were dead, the homunculi operations in Berlin and Paris were in disarray. If two-thirds of the information from the message was true, it was likely that the last third was, as well.

He was certain he'd been summoned here, not led by luck or chance. The Homunculus scanned the area again but saw no one out of place, nothing suspicious. A few pedestrians walked the evening street, lit by gas lamps, and some cats fought in an alleyway. Little else.

The Homunculus, still dressed in his black overcoat with black fedora, approached. Now outside the shop, he peered in. A single old woman sat behind the counter, sleeping, her eyeglasses perched on her nose. No one else was inside.

Stepping in, a bell rang above the doorway, waking the shopkeeper. She sniffed and coughed slightly. The Homunculus towered near the door, the top of his red-banded hat nearly touching the low-beamed ceiling.

"May I help you, sir?" the old woman asked.

"I am Dr. Cuba," the Homunculus said. "I believe you are expecting me."

The old lady stood, adjusted her glasses, and squinted. "I am afraid I don't know the name. You are a doctor? We didn't call for a doctor."

"Dr. Cuba," the Homunculus repeated. "From the Americas. I was summoned here."

"Here? To my bookshop? I can't believe that. We don't know anyone from America. And no one here is sick. We don't need a doctor."

The Homunculus remained in place, only moving his eyes from left to right to slowly scan the room. There was no evidence of anyone else, no apparent threats. No scent of bullets or weapon oil. Nothing.

"Very well, then," he said. "I want to know about a notebook you sold. It had medical procedures in it, with drawings and diagrams. It would have been very unique, easily distinguished from anything else you have here."

"Does this book have a name?" the old woman asked.

"No. Just a simple notebook. The original had a leather cover, but this would be a copy. I don't know what the copy's cover might look like."

The old woman shook her head. "It doesn't sound like something we would carry. Was it fiction?"

"A scientific notebook. Mostly written in English. Nothing in German."

The old woman shook her head. "I'm sure I didn't sell it."

The Homunculus was growing impatient. He'd have to tear the shop apart, which was not something he wanted to do, knowing he was likely standing in the middle of a trap.

"My husband," the old woman said suddenly.

"Your husband?" the Homunculus asked.

"He must have sold it. I may have been outside or in town, doing the shopping. But we keep records, I can check."

Perhaps this shop — and this old woman — might survive yet. "Please look," the Homunculus asked.

The old woman retrieved a tattered old ledger from a shelf under the counter. It was thick and yellowed, but apparently the old couple still used it; the entries must have dated back decades.

"Do you know when this book was sold?" she asked.

"I can only guess, but within the past two to three years. I don't believe it would have been any more recent than that."

The old woman adjusted her glasses once more and began flipping pages. She did not flip back too far and yet arrived at the target date period anyway, suggesting that the store did not sell many books at all. She ran her finger down the pages, looking for something that might resemble the book described to her by this tall ivory man in black.

"A notebook, you say?" she repeated. The Homunculus did not reply. Her finger kept running up and down the pages.

"December 11, 1943," the old woman said, her finger pausing over an entry. "A set of notebooks featuring medical notes and charts, written in English. Yes, I see it here. One was sold on January 11, 1944."

The Homunculus held himself still. "One?" he asked.

"Yes, let me see ..." The old woman continued to slide her forefinger along the pages. "The other one was sold ... yes, here it is, oh, earlier, in November of 1943."

"Two notebooks? There were two of them?"

"They were copies, apparently," the old woman said. She looked up. "At least that's what it says here."

"Were there more copies?"

"No, it appears only two were sold. At least, in our shop," the old woman said.

"Who were they sold to?" the Homunculus asked. "I have come from America for this information, so I hope you understand, this is very important."

"Of course," she said, looking down at the book again. "The copy sold in 1943 was sold to a Henrik Broda." She looked up. "A Jew," she added. "We had to record all sales to Jews during the war."

"And the other?"

She scanned the ledger again. "Let's see. To a Professor Jakob ten Brinken. Or ten Brinke. It's not very legible. But he was not a Jew."

The Homunculus had gotten what he came for, but he said, "I am curious."

"Of what, young man?" the old woman said.

"Why indulge me this way? Why not have your men kill me as I walked in the door? Why give me the information at all? I cannot imagine I was meant to leave this shop alive, after such an obvious trap."

The old woman stiffened, her gaze frozen down at the ledger. Her face, for a moment, was locked in place, her body entirely immobile, as if she had been suddenly paralyzed. But then, her head rose slowly, directly meeting the Homunculus's gaze for the first time. Her eyes, peering over her glasses, bore into his.

"Because I know where the Rabbi is, but I do not know where ten Brinken is. I am relying on you to lead me to him."

The Homunculus's face remained emotionless, as always, but inside, he was running calculations. He wondered if this woman might be working for someone else, someone who wanted him as dead as his two brothers. No, he decided. She was not working for anyone; *she* had set the trap.

There would be no moving as she blinked, because the woman did not blink; she just stared, fearless. Her small frame and crooked back did not appear to give her any pause, any worry that her adversary was twice her size, younger, and clearly more powerful.

Something was wrong here, the Homunculus's mind told him. His scenarios and predictions pointed to a trap, but where would it come from? Someone else must be nearby.

Whereas the old woman did not blink, it was the Homunculus who took his gaze off the woman for a brief moment. He was scanning the room, looking for the assailant who would, no doubt, jump at any moment. But in the split second his eyes moved from hers, she disappeared.

And reappeared behind him.

Her hand grabbed his neck, an iron vise as cold as steel and twice as strong. He felt his windpipe begin to flex inward. "You may not be a man, but you think like a man and underestimate a woman," the old woman said, squeezing tighter on the Homunculus's throat.

His arms bolted upward, snapping her grip away from him, and he prepared to strike back. Again, she was no longer there. She was faster than he, somehow. And stronger.

The Homunculus swung around, his body now in a half-crouch, ready to defend himself from the next blow, but she was nowhere to be seen. Instead, the old woman was clinging, spider-like, to the beams overhead.

"I will not kill you, homunculus," she said. "I need you to

take me to the Professor." She then leaped down, screeching, her hands held like claws, and grabbed the Homunculus by the shoulders. Her weight carried her to the floor, and she expertly transferred her momentum into his body, lifting him and throwing him through the front window. The Homunculus crashed to the dark ground outside, sliding through the mud, broken glass everywhere.

The Homunculus stood, shaking off the broken glass from his coat while he considered the old woman. She was much too strong to be a human. "You're a homunculus," he said, heading back inside the shop. "Who grew you?" he demanded.

The woman, now standing at the center of the bookshop, laughed. "Now you're putting it all together? Very good." She was mocking him.

"Who grew you?" the Homunculus demanded again, entering the shop once more.

The woman did not flinch. "A man who underestimated me and will die for it!" She leapt into the air again, her hands grasping the beam overhead, and then swung her legs at the Homunculus, kicking him with great force. Once again, he was sent flying backward onto the street.

The Homunculus raised himself up more quickly this time, a glint of frustration appearing across his face, a rare escape of whatever passed for emotion in these creatures. Determined to kill this creature, he charged back into the shop, faster than she had expected, and grabbed her by the arm. Swinging her body like a doll, he raised her up and smashed her back down onto the shop's floor. The floorboards cracked and splintered. Her body was smashed; she would not be getting up this time.

And yet, she did. The woman shrugged off the bits of wood plank and, ignoring the lacerations all over her body and face, laughed. Reaching behind her, she grabbed a rack of books and gripped it with both hands. She flung the rack at the Homunculus, sending it crashing into him. Books and wood flew everywhere. "I won't kill you," she repeated. "You will take me to the Professor!"

Buried under the tossed rack and a pile of books, it took the Homunculus a moment to stand once more. In that short time, the old woman was gone.

Ximena met her giant German in the hotel lobby. They had agreed to try a restaurant just one block down the street, which had recently reopened and which the hotel manager insisted had been entirely rebuilt. Thumann was suspicious and assumed the restaurateur had paid off the hotel manager, but a quick walk down the street would settle the matter quickly.

As they walked, Ximena spoke. "Inspector, I did a lot of analysis on the wire reports related to everything in this area, going back about a year. I think things are more complicated than we thought," she said sheepishly.

"Things are rarely easier than we think, young miss," Thumann said. "Don't be afraid to address complexities if they are based on facts."

Ximena inhaled. "Well, I think we are dealing with three crime waves. Perhaps three criminals. Not two."

Thumann stopped walking. It took Ximena a few steps before she realized Thumann wasn't at her side anymore. She stopped and turned.

"Explain," Thumann said.

Ximena strode back to the giant German and told him what she'd found, starting with the Golem attacks and the murders of prostitutes, their wombs removed. "Those are the easiest to track and differentiate since they happen in the north."

"And the third?" Thumann asked.

"The remaining murders in Stuttgart are dramatically different. No prostitutes, just normal, everyday people. But always men. For these, the bodies are found in various states of decay, and — this is important — they are missing blood. Before the prostitute murders branched north, they were all jumbled up, making it hard to distinguish, but I think a third killer is here in Stuttgart, killing men and draining their blood."

"Number three ..." he whispered, more to himself than anything. He was thinking. "Draining their blood?"

"Right," Ximena said. "At least, according to the wires."

Thumann paused further, allowing this information to settle inside the space between his bushy, tangled sideburns. Then he began walking again. Ximena followed.

"Draining blood," he said again.

They arrived at the restaurant to find that the hotel manager was not lying; it was entirely restored, with fresh glass windows, a lovely side terrace area for outside dining, and a well-furnished, immaculate main dining room inside. A well-dressed waiter invited them in and brought them to a fine table lit by candles. The environment was, perhaps, a bit too romantic for Thumann to be sharing with Ximena, but he was too lost in thought to care.

Thumann ordered a bottle of Riesling and glanced at his menu, not reading it at all. He put it down.

"This could be a plot against the Jews," he said solemnly. "The Golem stories present the beast as the hero of the Jews, killing those who persecute them. Someone could be trying to even the score, starting a series of killings that make it look like vampires are at work. The Nazis wanted the populace to believe the Jews were vampires, sucking the blood of innocent Christians."

"But," Ximena offered, "the Stuttgart murders predated the arrival of the Golem."

"Right," Thumann said, though it was clear he had already considered that.

"You didn't think that was the case anyway," Ximena said with a frown. "I see it in your eyes."

"Let's order our dinner," Thumann said. "Enough talk of golems and vampires. I don't believe in any of them."

Thumann wanted to leave Germany, even as the call of crime beckoned him to stay and investigate.

Chapter 7: The Pregnant Corpse

The Golem was unconcerned whether any human creature believed he existed or not. His mind, if you could call it that, was only half-formed. Whereas the Rabbi had put some level of detail into the shaping of the Golem's body, to ensure it was large and strong enough to carry out the dark acts required by the times, he put little thought *into* thought. How much the Golem might "think" was not important. He was a drone, a tool, a weapon; he was simply supposed to do what was demanded of him. His mission was to defend the Jewish people and destroy the Nazis, who aimed to wipe them out. The Rabbi did not believe that any advanced intellectual capacity would be required to perform this function.

The Rabbi, however, had made a number of crucial mistakes. First, he had used the notebook purchased by the suspicious bookseller to augment his own long-researched design. The Talmud spoke of how golems were created, yes, but without sufficient scientific detail and peppered with far too much mysticism. The Rabbi believed that to raise a golem required a balance of science and mysticism. Simply slapping the name of g-d onto his forehead or into his mouth would not work.

By combining components of the notebook's formulas with his own Talmudic studies, the Rabbi was able to raise the Golem. The Rabbi was not aware of the memories and thoughts that were automatically embedded into the creature, however. All homunculi shared memories from the progenitor; this was true for the Homunculus, the Doktor, the Fantôme and, yes, Dr. Cuba. The Rabbi could not have known this.

The Golem, however, was instantly aware of this reality, his limited brain flooded with partial memories, flashes, visions. These clashed with the holy orders of the Rabbi — *kill Nazis!* — and added nuance. Nuance in a half-mind only causes confusion and chaos, and so the Golem was quickly tortured, his mind at permanent war with his commands and instincts.

The Rabbi could not have known that the progenitor's formula also embedded an inclination towards Crime into anything born of it. Having been created for a greater good—told to kill, yes, but for the salvation of the Jewish people—the Golem's programming was corrupted by this embed.

The progenitor's coding told the Golem that Jews mattered no more than Christians or pigeons; all creatures were secondary to the goal of achieving global autocracy and crushing democracy.

And so, the Golem rose and carried out its first missions flawlessly. The ghettos of Prague were cleansed of Nazi filth. The Jews there enjoyed meager freedom, even if it was only block by block. The Nazi Party disavowed any reports of a giant Jewish monster existing, much less actually killing its soldiers, and worked to squash any reporting. Within the ghettos, however, the myth was spreading. A Golem of clay had arisen to save Prague once again, as it had in the 1600s.

The Rabbi would whisper his orders into the ear-shaped structure molded on the side of the Golem's hardened clay head, and the beast would leave the darkened caves and carry out those orders, granted the unusual ability to smell his victims once they were revealed to him. It never wavered, never questioned, never hesitated. Such behaviors did not exist in its being. It would return later that night, covered in blood and with minor scratches and chips that the Rabbi would then repair, to ready the creature for the next day's assignment.

Soon, word of the Golem's attacks spread, and the Rabbi received messages on where Nazis were hiding, to help focus the attacks. Then the Rabbi received a very sophisticated note, sent by an anonymous sender but with absolutely accurate details. This note listed the whereabouts and descriptions of hidden Nazis, along a path downward to the south of Czechoslovakia, into Austria, and then west into Germany. The names listed were known to the Rabbi as important former Nazis, currently being hunted by the Allies, but with little effect.

The Rabbi sat next to his clay beast one night and read the list, line by line, into the beast's mock ear. He would now pursue the path even without the need for the Rabbi to give daily orders. And so, the Rabbi obtained a truck to carry his monster along the route described on the list, sending the Golem out nightly as they approached each target along the way.

But by the fourth week, the Rabbi noticed something was wrong. The Golem froze for a moment before leaving for a nightly attack. Was it hesitation? Confusion? The Rabbi was forced to re-read the order, and finally the Golem rose up, left, and came back bloodied six hours later, as expected.

But what caused that hesitation?

The Rabbi, in his desperation to end the suffering of his people, did not question it further. He loaded the Golem back onto the truck, covered it in canvas, and continued the journey to Germany, where assassinations of Nazis would have a greater effect and where, according to the list, he would find many more in hiding.

Because the Rabbi did not accompany his monster on these sojourns, he did not see another troubling development. In the beginning, the Golem would simply snap the necks of his victims. Later, however, the killing became more gruesome. At times, the Golem would crush his prey's head with one flex of his giant, hardened fist. In other attacks, he would step on his victims, with what appeared to be a cruel smile forming over his carved mouth. And in one attack, he pummeled a Nazi officer into pulp while screaming in terror, as if he—the Golem—were the one being attacked.

The Golem was experiencing empathy, but in a way that would make no sense to any human. And then, as quick as it came, it was gone and replaced by sadistic cruelty.

One night, just inside the German border, the Rabbi heard a rusty scraping sound coming from the back of the truck and pulled over. He pulled away the tarp, and the Golem appeared to be rocking itself, as a sobbing child would. The Rabbi saw what appeared to be wet stains near the Golem's molded, dead eyes. It screamed, a loud, bellowing, metal-and-stone sound that rang across the forest. It was a scream of agony, emotional trauma, all the pain of the Jewish people compressed into a single being, and then forced to share space with the memories of a human progenitor and programming that told him all humans were mere cattle.

Soon after that, the Rabbi himself was found dead. Crushed. The Rabbi could no longer whisper commands in the Golem's clay ear.

And so, the last command remained in effect: to kill the Nazis read to it by the Rabbi from the list. And it did that, continuing to move under its own will, on foot, from town to town, along the path set by the list. Town after town, towards the last on the list: Stuttgart.

As the days went on, the Golem grew madder still. The conflict in his mind saw him become more aggressive. The Golem would occasionally go on a mad rage, killing anyone, anything, even the Jews he had been built to protect.

The myth of the Golem continued to spread throughout the Jewish ghettos, but talk of the beast turning on its people was dismissed as Nazi counter-programming. Jews who learned otherwise rarely survived.

Compounding problems was the fact that officials, such as the remnant German police and their military counterparts, did not believe the stories and took a position very much like Thumann had. This, they insisted, was a set of simple murders exaggerated by a traumatized public and superstitious Jewish poor.

What came next in Stuttgart could no longer be dismissed or ignored, however.

The Golem emerged from the tunnel, having saved little Deborah Abend, with the scent of his prey in the air. Four blood-soaked Nazis were within the area, their prior crimes as fresh on their scent as if they had happened only yesterday. The Golem did not know what crimes these men had committed against the Jews, only that they had occurred ... and were horrible.

They would die, now, yes, in horrible ways.

The beast's giant booted feet crushed everything they stepped upon as he made his way through the debris and fallen buildings of Stuttgart. He moved behind buildings, through abandoned lots, making a small attempt to remain unseen. However, witnesses still saw a dark, massive, stony shape passing by their windows, accompanied by the creaking, scraping sound of the beast's stone limbs moving against each other.

The Golem arrived at his destination within only half an hour. He stood in the backyard of a small house, his giant gray boots crushing the plants in the garden. The house had lost its roof during the war, but now had tarpaulins hastily strung across the holes to keep out the rain. A few of the small curtained windows were lit; music played from a radio inside ... until it did not.

The Golem broke through the back wall — he was far too big to fit through the door — and immediately smelled its targets. Four men sat in a kitchen, playing cards ... until they were not. Giant stone hands came down upon their horrified faces, crushing them in an instant. The scream began, like a lion or gorilla trapped in a cave of stone, accompanied by a scraping of metal from deep inside the thing's massive chest. A young housemaid looked on in terror as the Golem turned to her, his eyes streaming some form of moisture, his face turned to a look of desperation, of pleading. This time, however, the Golem did not stop once his targets were killed.

The pleading face and screaming howl appeared to cry out for help, even as those giant hands smashed the young woman into a wet mass of organs and bones, then continued to flatten the entire house before moving to the next. Within five minutes, it, too, was flattened, its occupants crushed. And then a third house ... a fourth ... and onward down the street.

Police sirens wailed as they approached, but the sound did not stop the great gray creature from his uncontrollable rage. No matter how loudly the beast's stone voice cried out, his body pushed forward. More houses crushed, more dead; German, Christians, Jews. The Golem murdered them all. There was no longer any Rabbi to intercede, no longer a creator to repair his defective creation.

Motorized vehicles began to surround the now half-leveled neighborhood, and soldiers spat out of personnel carriers, carrying automatic weapons. The French military police arrived.

The Golem was in full view, at the head of his path of destruction, allowing the French to aim their weapons with ease. Once again, Stuttgart echoed with the sound of automatic rifles spraying bullets into the air, the sound bouncing off the nearby buildings and wreckage with an endless series of loud "pops."

The bullets had little effect at this distance, striking the hardened creature and merely causing light sparks to zip off him without damage. The beast turned to the French and screamed, the look of pleading now changed to one of fury. His huge hands formed into knotty hammers, and he charged forward, feet thumping into the ground like thunder. Some of the French fled, realizing that they were neither trained nor equipped to battle eight-foot-tall stone monsters. The ones that stayed in place saw their bullets chipping away a bit as the thing approached, but were killed before they could do much more. Heads were crushed, limbs torn apart, entire vehicles tossed into the air.

When the beast finally fled, some sixty-five people were dead, eight buildings destroyed, and several French military vehicles were left in crumpled heaps.

No, this could not be dismissed or ignored.

The dead whore's womb was expanding, her belly now near bursting, but there was no sign of movement. The Professor remained at the corpse's side, waiting for it to give birth, but was now asleep. He had been awake for nearly twenty hours, and the coffee had run out ten hours ago. A book lay at his feet, dropped on its spine when he finally succumbed to his exhaustion.

The Professor's first transemination experiment had resulted in a birth after only nine hours. This time, it was clear that something was going wrong, but the Professor could not know what until a child was either born or spit out, dead. Only then would he be able to investigate his errors.

Nearing the twenty-first hour, there was finally some movement. The dead whore's belly shook, rattling the dirty metal slab it lay on and waking the Professor. Startled, he jumped up, adjusting his glasses and peering at the whore.

The corpse's belly moved, as if an octopus was writhing inside, a shapeless thing that pushed and bulged. And then, it burst outward, breaking through the corpse's stomach with a gushing, slurping noise that resembled the sound of a disemboweling. A dark gray and greenish mass fell to the floor, slimy and heavy, and slid a few feet under its own momentum. The whore's corpse collapsed in on itself, empty. Now, the dead was truly dead again.

The mass on the floor undulated a bit more and then fell still. The Professor knew this was normal; he was ready. Picking the heavy, slimy mass up, he placed it on a large metal tray. The blob was about two feet in length, but shifted its shape as it was manipulated, so any accurate measurement was impossible; it weighed about ten pounds.

The Professor moved the tray to the injector-incubator, a device referenced in the stolen notebook, but for which the Professor had to make certain assumptions about its design. The version built by the Professor had worked before, so he was certain it should work again. He fed the slimy mass into a feed tray at the base of the box-shaped device and inserted a series of needles throughout the mass's volume. Each needle was fed by a tube, which then traced backwards into the odd machine and to two small stainless steel tanks mounted above it. One of the tanks held a copper-colored petroleum mix, and the other was human blood, taken from the corpse-mother's body.

The Professor closed the door to the feed tray and flipped some switches. Inside, the chamber was filled with a mixture of argon and pure oxygen, and the pumps began to pump their contents into the newborn mass. The inner floor of the box, which now held the mass, sat on a piston; as the mass grew, the piston would descend, allowing for more space inside the chamber. It would take another two to three days before the mass was of sufficient formation to be removed from the injector-incubator and laid on a table, to be fed through traditional intravenous means.

Despite the delay in the mass's ejection from its corpse-mother, things were appearing normal now. Perhaps this new specimen might survive after all.

The Professor went to the filthy kitchen of the former butcher shop to wash his hands and prepare a fresh pot of coffee. As he did, however, he saw a figure outside the window.

The Professor froze, refraining even from blinking. He needed to see everything in this moment, hear everything. Even the sound of his eyelids might betray him now.

The shape outside the window wore black. A catsuit of some sort, something dark to ensure stealth, but lithe enough to allow movement. The Professor could not be sure if it was her, come back to kill him, but the physique looked thin, curved, feminine. Who else could it be? The street urchins of Mülheim were not inclined to wear the garb of professional cat burglars.

As silently as possible, he backed up towards the counter of the filthy kitchen, reaching for the knife he knew lay there, his only possible weapon in this circumstance. Grasping it tightly, he turned his body towards the kitchen doorway. The figure was no longer outside. The Professor strained his hearing, but all he heard was the injector-incubator's hissing and clicking.

Uncertain whether he was truly alone or not, the Professor stuck his back tightly against the wall of the kitchen, raising his knife. If anyone came through, he might have a chance to strike before they did.

He waited for what seemed to him to be an eternity before he heard the creak of floorboards. The assailant was in the building. *She* was closing in.

His heart raced, his eyes darted from side to side. He was panicking. He was not built for this sort of thing. Drugging prostitutes and killing them while they slept was easy; fighting a superhuman, soulless creature that wanted nothing more than to shred his body to pieces ... this was beyond his limited abilities. Even if he dared to face such a fight, his fat, weak body would not let him anyway.

He had to change tactics quickly.

The Professor inhaled deeply, then shouted, "Alraune!"

The creaking floorboards fell silent. He had her attention.

"I know you've come to kill me, Alraune. I was a fool to flee. I always knew you would find me here. But I was scared, frightened at what you'd do to me. Come to the kitchen. We must talk! I am your father, whether you recognize it or not. We must talk this out!"

Nothing.

"Think, Alraune! I'm the only one who can fix you if something goes wrong. We don't know what illnesses you might face, what risks there are. I can help you! Only I can keep you alive, Alraune!"

Still nothing.

"Please, Alraune. Come and sit, we can talk ..."

"Who is Alraune?" a voice said. It was not in the other room. It was in the kitchen already, on the other side of the room. The figure stepped forward.

The Professor tried to focus on it, but it stood in the dark. It was not a female. It was not Alraune. Thin, yes, but a man dressed in black. Not an urchin, not a street thief. This was something entirely different. A professional sent to kill him, he wondered.

"Who are you?" the Professor demanded, now holding his knife towards the advancing figure in black.

"Relax, Professor ten Brinken. We are not here to kill you. You can put the knife down."

"W-we?" the Professor stammered, his gaze darting around the room wildly.

Two more figures, also in lithe black catsuits, emerged from the shadows. Also, men.

"Sit, Professor. We will not interrupt your experiment. In fact, we want to see what comes of it. We are only here to ensure you don't leave. Not until he comes to talk to you."

The Professor's heart pounded throughout his entire body, through his neck and up to his eyes.

"Who? Who is coming?" he demanded.

"Dr. Cuba," the man in black answered. "He has many questions."

Chapter 8: The River Leeches

Thumann and Ximena were again in the back of a military vehicle, their coccyxes punished by the rattling jeep suspension and hard metal bench seats. Thumann knew to hold his mouth partially open so his teeth did not rattle; he'd have to teach this trick to Ximena later, as they were already arriving.

They were en route to the site of a Golem attack that had happened only hours earlier. This was why they came to Germany in the first place: to investigate a fresh crime, not one that occurred weeks or months ago.

The jeep pulled to a squeaking stop. As they jumped from the back, both Thumann and Ximena fell into stunned silence. An entire neighborhood had been blasted through, houses leveled, some houses left only with half of their structures intact, their innards exposed to the world. Some small fires still burned, smoke pouring into the air, and everywhere they looked, they saw the muddy tracks of vehicles and huge pothole-like indentations.

Not potholes. Boot prints, they realized. The size of the jeep's tires.

At the far end of the dirt lane were the French military vehicles, crumpled and bent, as though someone had dropped rocks on them from space. More fire, more smoke, more giant boot prints.

What were they looking at? Thumann wondered.

"What are we looking at?" Ximena asked, reading Thumann's mind.

"I ... I don't know," Thumann said, his mouth agape. Ximena had never seen her German in a state of confusion like this. He had seen every type of murder, crime scene, or terrorist case that Scotland Yard could throw at him. The visuals in front of them made no sense. It was like the set of one of those horror movies by that garish director, James Whale, but in the real world, right in front of them.

Thumann's eyes narrowed. "All right," he said, as if trying to steady himself. "Study this." Ximena was not sure if he was talking to her or himself. He pointed in front of him, tracing his finger over the images in front of his eyes. "The damage travels from this end of the street, down the lane, to the French vehicles."

"So, it started there," Ximena said, pointing to the house closest to them. It was a pile of rubble.

"Right," Thumann said, his hand still tracing the path of destruction in their view. "House by house, one by one, until ... there." Thumann pointed to an area near the middle of the street, where much more damage had taken place. The street there was heavily pockmarked with bullets and debris. "The French engaged him there. He managed to survive and then advanced to destroy the vehicles at the end of the street."

"Was the Nazi target in the first house or the last?" Ximena asked.

"I'm not sure," Thumann answered. "I'd guess the first, as he destroyed that utterly."

"He?" Ximena asked.

"Perhaps 'it' would be a better description," Thumann said with a shake of his head. "It appears this Golem does exist. Look at the boot prints. That's not a human foot."

Ximena focused on the indentations Thumann indicated. "I ... I don't believe this," she stammered, unable to wrap her head around the size of what, she knew, were indisputably what Thumann described: boot prints. "That's not possible."

"And yet there it is, young miss. Right in front of our eyes. If we speak to these witnesses, they are going to describe the same thing as the cinema manager, Scheiner. A giant man, wrapped in burlap and ropes, looking as if he were made of clay or stone. We will conduct our interviews, yes, but everything we need to see is right here in front of us."

"So," Ximena asked, eyes wide. "Golems exist? But you said —"

"Never mind what I said. I was angry at my country, angry at how these facts were not lining up neatly for me. But, yes, young miss, golems seem to exist," Thumann said definitively. "We've already met two of them at the pit in South Dakota."

Belknap drove the Homunculus west, out of Berlin and into the countryside. The car was a luxurious 1938 Mercedes-Benz 770, but painted in a medium brown color so that no one could mistake it for a black Nazi officer vehicle. The inside was brown leather and coffee-colored wood, trimmed with shiny silver bits throughout. It was immaculately maintained and bore insignias on the front window to alert military police that this was a vehicle operating with Allied permission.

For Belknap, it was a relief to leave Berlin, which had become difficult to drive through now that the Allies had divided it up. The Doktor's former contacts and influence were still of some use in Germany, but with the Doktor himself dead and such a significant military presence in the city, the criminal organization was suffering.

"Ironic, isn't it?" Belknap said. "We created the war, and now we are victims of it."

The Homunculus, in the back seat, was unaffected. "This is just a phase, and one that was already predicted. The greater effort requires this post-war reflexive gagging, and we planned for it. It would be easier to navigate if my brothers were alive, but the plan remains intact. We are playing a generational game, Belknap. You will not likely see the last move in your lifetime, but your children will."

"I don't have children, sir," Belknap said as he drove.

"That's probably best," the Homunculus said ominously. "How long is the drive to Essen?"

"Six, maybe seven hours. More, if we encounter a lot of checkpoints. Which we will."

The Homunculus settled in for the long ride, pulling a small glass tube out from a leather pocket stitched into the back of the seat in front of him. He unscrewed the cap and prepared to drink. He paused.

Gold and blood and gasoline. One ingredient produced by the earth, another by the human body, and the last by humans themselves. There would be no trips to the maiden for some time, but he would have to wait to ensure his own supply had not been poisoned. He returned the flask to its pocket.

"Do you have an idea of who our adversary is?" Belknap asked. The Homunculus had let Belknap know some of the details of what occurred at the bookshop, but not all. Belknap could be trusted, and he would need to have some idea of the plans for Germany now that the Doktor was not alive to manage things personally. The current reality demanded that the Homunculus rely on lieutenants, at least in the short term.

"One of us," the Homunculus said.

Belknap's head twitched in surprise. "Sir? Is that even possible?"

"Apparently so. Someone else is creating more of us, so it seems likely some of the birth procedures were stolen from Monito Island and sold."

"How were they stolen?" Belknap asked. It was the right question.

"I don't know, and that will be what I have to resolve once this Germany business is over. I don't know how the notebook was copied, but the original is now locked safely elsewhere." The Homunculus was not going to reveal the whereabouts of Snake Island to anyone; not yet, at least.

"Monito is inaccessible. No way to get there by air. One would have to take a ship to the island's sheer cliffs and climb up. Plus, one would have to know there was something even there to go looking for. Sir, it doesn't seem likely that the book came from Monito."

"I agree, and yet someone is creating more of us," the Homunculus repeated. "This Golem creature running around Stuttgart, for example. The Rabbi Henrik Broda must have created it, but then did something very different with it. It's nothing like us, obviously. Then we have the old woman at the bookshop who attacked me. I don't know who created her."

"And this Professor we are going to see?" Belknap asked.

"Our men have him detained in his laboratory right now, and said they think a birth is due any hour now. It should be interesting to see if he is successful, and what emerges."

Belknap was about to ask another question, but saw his strange passenger in the back had raised a hand to stop him. "I must rest," the Homunculus said. "Wake me when we arrive."

Belknap had worked with the Doktor long enough to know he was required to keep his opinions to himself and to mask any facial expressions that might otherwise reveal them. So, with great difficulty, he prevented his face from telegraphing his confusion that the Homunculus needed rest at all. Belknap knew they never rested.

Inside the Homunculus's head, however, the voice had returned, like an incessant drumbeat.

KILL ME.

KILL ME!

Naked, bruised, and covered in leeches, Petra crawled from the river's embankment and gasped for air. Her white skin was now scraped and red, her golden hair a matted, grimy mess, and her lovely, upturned nose hidden behind smudges of river slime. Despite her condition, she was not shivering but did need to find clothes quickly.

Unlike the movies, there was no convenient clothesline nearby. She was in a rural wooded area just outside of Stuttgart, and homes – never mind clotheslines – were not common here. But rural wooded areas did not mean they were not inhabited; Petra scrambled up the embankment until the ground again turned level and scanned her surroundings for any sign of human activity. Where there were people, there was clothing.

Above the embankment, she found nothing, and so Petra pushed on, barefoot, stumbling over roots and rocks and thickets of spiny bushes. The leeches fell from her legs, dead, leaving a trail behind her. This experience was a very different one from the dance hall at Schwetzingen Palace, where she glided as if gravity had no effect on her. Here, gravity was having its way with the Lady Petra.

She walked and stumbled and crawled for at least a mile until she finally smelled smoke. Not fireplace smoke, but cigarette smoke. Someone was nearby; she would find clothes and perhaps even transport to Stuttgart. Following the smell of the cigarettes, Petra decided to move more quietly now, in case whoever she was sneaking up on might make things worse for her rather than better. Closing in on the smoke, Petra soon heard some noise ahead: a small group of people chatting casually. Not in German, however, but ... Romanian? Hungarian? Petra was not sure, but this meant they were not former Nazis in hiding, at least. That was good.

Creeping up slowly, Petra reached a position where the group came into view. She saw three men dressed in dirty hunting clothes, each smoking a cigarette. They stood near a tent and a small fire pit; the fire had already been extinguished. These were simple, poor hunters, no doubt trying to find meat to either sell in town or just to feed their own families. They had simple hunting rifles, and one had a skinning knife on his belt, but they did not appear to be threatening. They were not military men. This was also good.

But Petra knew the consequence of a beautiful, nude woman walking up to such men in the middle of the woods. She had no intention of being raped and simply needed something to cover herself. Quietly, Petra moved in a circular path around the men and their campground to get closer to the rear of their tent. It took half an hour to move around the camp; had she walked normally, she might have traversed it in mere seconds, but Petra recognized that creeping silently meant moving slowly; she resigned herself to take whatever time was necessary to ensure she was not spotted.

When she had finally put the tent between herself and the men, she moved closer, making sure the tent blocked her from view, then slowly lifted the bottom of the tent. No one else was inside. She reached in and grabbed a blanket, slowly slipping it out.

Then, it was just a matter of getting away. For another half hour, Petra slowly crept backwards, ensuring her silence and safety. Once far enough away, she wrapped the blanket around herself and proceeded at a greater pace, back towards the river.

She struggled to listen to the sounds around her, hoping to hear passing cars that might indicate a nearby highway. Continuing her stumble through the woods, she eventually did hear traffic. Petra did not attempt to approach the highway and was not about to hitchhike, since she'd likely meet the same fate dressed in a blanket as if she were naked. Now she could follow the highway from a safe distance while ensuring she was headed towards Stuttgart. If anyone saw her from the highway, they would only see a shambling blanket, and not a beautiful young girl with pearl teeth and an upturned nose. They would just think her a beggar.

Finally, after another hour or two at least, Stuttgart came into view. Petra spotted key points on the city's crumbled skyline and headed toward where her tiny apartment would be. Entering the outskirts of the town, Petra pressed on through the surrounding woods and then onto dirty city backstreets, trying to avoid anyone who might take advantage of her. Finally, her feet scraped and bruised, Petra neared her apartment.

She knew she had to tell Frau Jannings something, but the kindly old woman was a gossip. Petra did not want her reputation sullied by scandal.

Petra peered into the window of the building's back door; inside, she saw Frau Jannings in the kitchen, fiddling with a teapot or something. Petra lightly tapped on the door to get the frau's attention.

"Good lord!" Frau Jannings cried, seeing the filthy, bruised Petra at her back door, wrapped in a blanket. "Dear girl!"

Frau Jannings ran to the door, opened it, and ushered Petra inside. "What has happened, girl?"

Petra remained calm. "I am all right, Frau Jannings. Just tired and a bit scraped from walking in the forest. I was attacked and robbed on my way back from my trip. They stole everything."

"Were you raped?" Frau Jannings asked, partly out of concern and partly, no doubt, out of the desire to have an even more scandalous story to spread around the neighborhood.

"Thankfully, no, Frau Jannings. They only took my clothes to make it more difficult for me to get home quickly."

"This is that Dr. Cuba's gang of villains, I'm sure!" Frau Jannings said. "The radio reports on these attacks nearly every day. People disappearing, robberies, rapes. They say the same inspector who foiled the gang's gold robberies is right here, in Stuttgart!"

Frau Jannings helped Petra up the stairs to the shared bath on her floor. She began to run the hot water.

"Inspector?" Petra asked.

"Yes, they credited him with shutting down the whole Dr. Cuba gang. Now it seems that was premature, and the inspector has come here to Stuttgart. For sure, he is here to capture this Dr. Cuba once and for all."

Petra allowed Frau Jannings to remove the filthy blanket and help her step into the shower. The bottom of the tub was soon covered with dirt, leaves, and blood. The old woman helped gently scrub Petra's back.

"You should go see this inspector, fraulein," Frau Jannings said. "Perhaps he can catch the thieves and return your things."

Petra shook her head. "No, I don't think so. For sure, they are long gone, and I wouldn't want to bother the inspector. I am sure he's a very important man."

"Please keep it in mind, Fraulein Petra. He may be of help to you."

Petra nodded, mainly to satisfy her landlady but also with some level of curiosity about what this "inspector" might have to say about all this business.

Chapter 9: The Butcher's Kitchen

Back at the hotel, Ximena and Thumann sat in the lobby, reviewing what they had seen and what they had learned. The interviews with witnesses in the destroyed neighborhood *did* result in the same account as the cinema: a giant gray golem had leveled the houses, attacked the soldiers, and fled with just minor chips to his stone body.

"Too many witnesses are saying the same thing. This isn't wives' tales or spiritual hoodoo from drunks and old crones. This thing exists," Thumann said, puffing his latakia.

"I'm sorry," Ximena offered.

"Don't apologize. The facts led us to where we are."

"You said we met them?" Ximena asked. "You mean the two Dr. Cuba creatures, at the mine in South Dakota?"

"Yes. There's a connection."

Ximena scrunched her forehead. "I'm sorry, Inspector, I can't see it. What am I missing?" She was frustrated with herself.

Thumann raised a hand to calm her. "You may not have heard everything at the pit," Thumann reassured her. "I was closer. I heard those two devils talking to each other. At one point, the one in black said to his brother, the one named 'Dr. Cuba,' that he could 'fix' him. He said something about correcting his chemistry. As if Dr. Cuba were a laboratory experiment gone wrong."

"A Nazi experiment? On the insane?"

"Dr. Cuba predates the Nazis, I fear," Thumann said, running his fingers through his bushy beard to straighten the knots. "He also said, 'There are no gods. Certainly, none for things that are not born, like us.'"

Ximena scrunched her face further. "What does that mean? These creatures weren't *born*?"

Thumann nodded. "Exactly. The one in black definitely told the other that they were not born. As if they were made in a laboratory."

"But how are men made in laboratories? Is that possible?"

"We both saw the strength of the one in black when he fought Dr. Vines and his men at the island off of Miami. That was inhuman. Superhuman. This could be some new science we simply are not aware of."

"How does this tie into the Golem?" Ximena asked with a frown. It was too much information coming in too fast for her to process.

"If we are dealing with artificial men, such as these two Dr. Cuba creatures, as you called them, then it makes the existence of a Golem creature possible as well. There could be a relationship. Perhaps the arrival of a Golem just after the appearance of these Dr. Cuba things is not an accident; perhaps the same science was used. The Golem is an artificial man in a way, too, after all."

"You think the Golem is a ... a ..." Ximena had never heard the word before.

"Homunculus," Thumann said with finality.

"A what?" Ximena asked. "I don't know that word."

"Few do, even in English." Thumann shoved his pipe into his mouth to free his hand and then reached into his pocket. He pulled out a slip of paper. "I have kept something from you, dear assistant, but it was not intentional. This came to me from America, but only yesterday, and this Golem business did not give me time to show you."

"A telegram?" Ximena asked, recognizing the Western Union logo. "From whom?"

"Our mystic friend in Florida, Madame Blavatsky. Have a look." He handed the telegram to Ximena.

INSPECTOR HEINER THUMANN, INTERPOL

= DR CUBA WAS HOMUNCULUS. BROTHER IS SAME. HE CAME TO STEAL THE GODFREY BOOK. NOW HEADED TO

GERMANY. REASONS UNKNOWN. DO WHAT THOU WILT SHALL BE THE WHOLE OF THE LAW. =

BLAVATSKY

"I am sorry, Inspector, I just don't know what this means," Ximena said. "What is a 'homunculus'?"

"A homunculus is an artificial man, theorized by a Swiss physician named Paracelsus in the sixteenth century. Paracelsus was much like Blavatsky, deeply involved in alchemy and mysticism, but with a background in the science of the time, as primitive as it was. He claimed he could build a miniature artificial man. For centuries later, circus sideshows would display deformed fetuses or mandrake roots in pickle jars, claiming they were dead homunculi."

Ximena waved toward the telegram. "And Madame Blavatsky thinks these Dr. Cuba creatures are ... these artificial men?"

"It would explain much, and we both know Blavatsky is not to be disregarded out of hand. She likely knows much about Paracelsus, homunculi, and the alchemical theories. It's a shame we are here in Germany and not there to ask her. But this also means that the Dr. Cuba in black visited her, and she's lucky to be alive."

"The Godfrey book ... that was the one about the Sunken Gods that Dr. Cuba was obsessed with, correct?" Ximena asked.

Thumann nodded. "Right, so it means this second devil is following up on that whole thing. We don't know why, of course. Nor do we know why he's coming to Germany."

"To find you?" Ximena offered.

"I can't imagine why. He seemed to dismiss me as irrelevant back at the pit in America. But perhaps he has some relationship with this Golem and is coming to try to fix it the same way he did with Dr. Cuba. Golems are artificial men, and the golem myth is the first homunculus story. Perhaps this Golem is a Dr. Cuba homunculus that has also become defective in some way."

"Then we should let him come," Ximena said.

"Well, there's nothing we can do to stop him, so it's moot," Thumann said, puffing again. "But this brings us to the vampire theory."

"The Stuttgart murders," Ximena said.

"Patrol boats off the coast of Venezuela found an abandoned ship, apparently left to sink. It somehow stayed afloat, and the authorities found the crew strung up in the cargo hold, upside down like bats, drained of all their blood. The timing of that ship and the Dr. Cuba business in South America could be a coincidence, but I do not like coincidences. These homunculi may need something as food, but not actual food. Blood, perhaps. Maybe the crew of that ship was their food."

"The homunculi are *literal* vampires?" Ximena asked, not believing the words were coming out of her mouth.

"Not in the Dracula sense or like the movies. We didn't see fangs on any of them. But perhaps they process the blood somehow. I don't know. But it appears Dr. Cuba has some connection to this place, and now, we find out people are being drained of their blood, here in this place. Again, I do not like coincidences."

Ximena simply remained silent, processing this new information.

"There's another coincidence I don't like," Thumann said grimly.

"What is it?"

"Why were we sent here? It seems implausible that we would be sent on an entirely new case that is once again tied to Dr. Cuba. No, that cannot be a coincidence."

"But the remit was granted after a pattern of crimes emerged. To plan a series of crimes all in the hope that it would gain the attention of Interpol, and then specifically to have us assigned to the case, that would be impossible," Ximena said.

She was right, of course. Thumann scratched his whiskers.

"We are missing something."

They sat in silence for a few more moments. Then, Thumann continued. "That second devil said something else back at the pit. He said there were *four* of them. That means two more, other than the two we already met."

"So, the Golem is the third. Who is the fourth?"

"I don't know," Thumann said with a shake of his head. "I don't know if any of this is true yet. But these assumptions currently fit our facts the best. What we can do now is seek out more facts, to turn the assumptions into facts as well."

Ximena nodded. "The pieces are starting to come together," Ximena offered.

"Yes," Thumann said, nodding. "We just don't have them all yet."

"Professor Jakob ten Brinken," the Homunculus said, standing inside the filthy, moldy kitchen of the abandoned butcher shop in Stuttgart. "I've come very far to meet you."

The Professor was seated in a wooden chair; he was not tied up, since doing so would be irrelevant. Aside from the Homunculus, the Professor was surrounded by three of his men.

"You are Dr. Cuba?" the Professor asked, trying to conceal his nervousness. The Professor did not have any idea what this man with poreless ivory skin and dead-black eyes wanted of him.

"I am," the Homunculus said. "But, to tell you the truth, a few of us use that name."

"There are *more* of you? You're an organization, then?" the Professor asked, trying to fill the space with casual conversation, in the vain attempt it might push out the menace in the air.

"Consider it a family," the Homunculus said. "My brother adopted the name but has since died. I have taken it on in his stead."

"I really must get back to my experiment," the Professor said, darting his gaze towards the kitchen doorway, which led to the room where the hissing, clicking injector-incubator continued to do its work on the born mass. "Let's get this over with quickly."

"I don't intend on intruding on your work, Professor," the Homunculus said. "In fact, I want to see the outcome. If you need to attend to your machine, please do so. But until then, you will answer my questions."

The Professor swallowed visibly. "For now, it may run unattended," he admitted. "Ask your questions and let's be done with this."

"Show me the notebook," the Homunculus said.

The Professor did not need to ask which notebook this ivory-skinned man in black was asking for. He also did not need to ask what might happen to him if he did not produce it. The Professor stood and walked to another room inside the abandoned butcher shop; one of the cat-suited invaders followed him. Just to be sure.

Upon returning, the Professor immediately held the book up. "This, I presume."

The Homunculus took it. The cover was a simple, ordinary notebook, but the Homunculus recognized the pages inside immediately; they were copies of the progenitor's original notes, which had been safely stored at Monito Island.

Someone had accessed Monito and photographed the notes.

"You bought this from a bookseller in Berlin," the Homunculus said.

"Yes. An old man," the Professor said.

"That means you knew it was for sale, and where to buy it."

"I did."

"How did you know this book existed?"

The Professor sat again, looking nervous, but clearly willing to tell all to save his cowardly skin. "There were rumors of the book circulating in the underground academic world. For at least a year. Some of us kept in contact with each other through coded correspondence, telegrams, that sort of thing. I received a message that the book had arrived in Berlin. I spent a week going to every bookshop in the city until I found it. I paid a fortune."

The realization that many people knew about the book struck the Homunculus. With that realization came another: there could be even more copies than the two he knew of. This was bad.

"The others in your group didn't try to buy it?" he asked.

"They may have. I got there first," the Professor said.

The Homunculus pointed towards the other room, where the injector-incubator bubbled and fizzled. "And that," he said, "is what you developed?"

"The book only references an injector device of some kind," the Professor said. The Homunculus knew that meant the iron maidens. "It didn't describe them. Presumably, that is in another notebook that was never copied."

"But that machine cannot initiate the fertilization, nor grow the mass," the Homunculus said.

"No, that is the post-birth injector-incubator. For after the mass ..." The Professor's eyes opened wide. "You ... you know how the process works? Wait ... did you write this book?" he asked excitedly.

"No, I did not, but I do know the process. The formula and materials described in that notebook are old, very old. I have since modernized the techniques and improved upon the necessary starter materials."

The Professor stood, completely forgetting his situation in his excitement. "There is so much I have to ask you! The notebook spoke of the anti-womb chamber to trigger the reactions and grow the starter materials into the initiate mass. But it didn't have any details, so I had to improvise."

"How did you improvise?" the Homunculus asked.

"I replaced the anti-womb chamber with a real womb. A dead womb, but with sufficient capacity and properties to act as the substrate and support the transemination and fertilization and then, finally, the trigger reaction."

"Transemination?" the Homunculus asked.

"I'm sorry," the Professor said, stammering. "A word I created. It wasn't in the original text. I used the defined starter materials but augmented them with additional strands and solutions of my own design. I then initiated fertilization with semen and propagated the initiate mass growth with various different explorer enzymes to act as catalysts."

"Semen?" the Homunculus asked. "Yours?"

The Professor appeared horrified at the suggestion. "No! Of course not. Of a dead man. A hanged man, if you must. But that was only a sort of nod to the —"

"The *Mandragora* myth," the Homunculus interjected. "You thought you could create a homunculus from impregnating a prostitute with a mandrake root and the semen of a hanged man?"

"No," the Professor said, shaking his head. "But the formula needed a spark, a fertilization trigger. Semen seemed the likely answer. Using the semen of a hanged man was just a ... a flourish."

"Did you use mandrake, too, then?" the Homunculus asked mockingly.

The Professor shook his head; he was not about to admit that, in a moment of desperation, he had. "No. The explorer enzymes I tried were all plant-based, yes, but the one that proved successful was *wañuchiq saphi*, from the Andes region of South America. All attempts thereafter failed, and I believe it was because I did not use the *wañuchiq*. That mass," he said, pointing to the other room, "is the second attempt with the *wañuchiq*. I have high hopes it will succeed."

The Homunculus strode into the adjoining room, standing next to the injector-incubator. He noted the stains on the floor, no doubt where the mass had landed after its "birth."

"Your semen is killing it," the Homunculus said definitively.

"What?" the Professor said. "I said, it's not mine ..."

"Any semen, Professor. The addition of semen is killing the mass before it can become viable."

"But the first experiment *was* viable! She grew, she matured!

The bookshop crone! The Homunculus hid his concern, but his thoughts raced. This man had actually completed the process and created a homunculus. He turned to the Professor. "The sperm in the semen of your first experiment must have been sterile. That is the only reason it worked. You are right, and the killer root is a key ingredient. You deserve some respect for having worked that out. But your childish belief in this *mandragora* myth, of semen and mandrakes, of prostitutes and hanged men, is keeping you from repeating your success. If you try again, without any male essence at all, you will likely succeed."

Then, without warning, the Homunculus struck the injector-incubator, breaking a small round glass viewing window near its front. As the Professor looked on in horror, the Homunculus reached in, grabbed the mass, and squeezed.

"You'll kill it!" the Professor screamed, lunging at the Homunculus. Two cat-suited operatives grabbed him and held him in place as he struggled against them. "You will kill it!" he screamed again.

"It is already dead, Professor," the Homunculus said. "Your machine is causing some cellular replication, yes, but only in the same way that hair cells continue to grow for a short while after death. You must start over, but without your foolish *mandragora* myths and with only pure science. No male essence. None."

The Homunculus removed his hand, then took a handkerchief and wiped off the black, oozing slime of the dead mass. He then folded the dirty handkerchief and placed it back into his pocket.

The Professor continued to look on, horrified. The Homunculus turned and stood directly in front of him. "I'm not going to kill you, Professor ten Brinken. I am going to help you.

You will have another chance at creating your homunculus. But we have to keep you alive so that you can do that."

"What do you mean?" the Professor asked, shaking.

"Someone *is* trying to kill you. They set a trap for me at the bookshop, with the intent that I would lead them here, to you. For certain, they followed me and are watching right now."

"Alraune!" the Professor cried. "The witch has found me after all!"

"Alraune?" the Homunculus asked.

"Her name. The first viable mass, grown into a woman. She was normal, kind, loving, even. Until she was not. She turned cruel, sadistic, murderous! She tried to kill me. I fled here to continue my experiments in hiding. Now you've brought her here!"

Homunculus nodded, thinking of the homunculus he'd encountered at the bookshop. "I believe I met your 'Alraune.' An old hag. She is strong, but I am stronger."

"A hag?" the Professor said, appearing confused. "No. She is a lovely creature with auburn hair and a plump face, no older than twenty. I designed her specifically to appear that way."

The Homunculus paused at that. The woman he'd met was certainly not young. He wondered if the Professor had created more viable masses than he realized, or, more likely, if this female homunculus could alter her appearance, as could the males.

"Nevertheless, you have my men to protect you so long as you stay under my care. We will move you to a safe house, and you can restart your experiments. We will see how successful your approach is when stripped of the extraneous mythology."

"I don't understand. Who are you? Why do you even care about these things?" the Professor asked.

"I am a homunculus."

The Professor, predictably, gasped.

"A first generation, in fact. To date, all attempts at creating a second generation have failed. My brother, who first adopted the name Dr. Cuba, was one such failure. If your Alraune is already mad, then she, too, is a failure. So, you can see, I have an interest in seeing your work's success. It is my legacy as much as yours."

As he left the room, the Homunculus motioned for one of the operatives to follow. Whispering, he ordered, "Have resources spread throughout Stuttgart. I want word as soon as this Golem appears again. It's time I see this other creature with my own eyes."

Chapter 10: The Bastard Beast

The scent of Nazis was strong in this small, blasted-out section of Stuttgart, which had formerly been home to numerous prosperous industries. The Allies assumed the factories had been converted to military production and focused much of their bombardment here. The resulting damage was severe, and now much of the area was nothing more than piles of rubble sitting twenty, thirty feet high. Entire smokestacks had been reduced to dust and brick-bits, factories melted into glass, homes converted into mounds of stone and bones.

Despite the pervasive ash, charcoal, and charred debris, the Golem could smell his prey with complete clarity. There were four former Nazis hidden here, likely underneath the rubble in a fortified hole or abandoned wine cellar. They were not deep below the ground, but relatively close to the surface, making them easier to sense. The Golem's huge form clambered over the piles of debris, crushing brick and wood below his huge, booted feet. He did not care if they heard him coming, as it would do them little good. Even if they escaped, he would find them later. As long as they smelled like Nazis, the Golem would eventually find them and kill them. He could pursue them for centuries; clay never dies.

Homeless men clambered about the rubble, searching for something they might sell or trade for food. Still others rummaged for things to turn into firewood. A few children could be seen playing, displaying their enviable capacity to ignore the horrors of war and find ways to create games even in the path of ruin. The Golem stomped and crunched his way through the rubble a good distance away from the others, but a few did see his massive silhouette moving like a performer's shadow puppet against the gray skyline behind him. Those who saw him ran.

Finally, the Golem neared the four men. Now he could not only smell them but hear them as well; they were speaking in low voices with upper-class German accents, most likely playing cards at a table in their makeshift underground hideout. The Golem winced; or, he would have winced, had his hardened face allowed such a range of expression. The initial minutes of approaching his victims were always the most difficult; for those few minutes, the Golem was flooded with the crimes of his prey, and now was no different. Impressions, emotions, images, horrors.

This beast was cursed not only with the ability to smell his victims, but also to feel their minds inside his own. The Golem's crude, noise-filled psychic sensing ability was not something the Rabbi had even intended to grant his monster. Without any ability to communicate his pain to the Rabbi, the Golem's creator could take no action to alleviate it.

Now just steps away from his targets, the Golem could not bear the onslaught of images he was getting from these four. Each time it was worse, and this time was the worst of all. He could see the atrocities they committed. The flesh they burned, the women they raped, the people they killed. He screamed. The vast pile of rubble that was once this section of Stuttgart heard the roar of wind running through stone, iron scraping gravel, a lion and a tiger battling in a cave.

The Nazis, in their spiderhole, also heard it. Now there was a rustle of fabric, the snapping of gun bolts, muffled anxious whispers.

It did not matter. The Golem's great hands came crashing down, smashing the boards and beams that had been clumsily erected as camouflage. The men below shouted, and as the dust cleared, they came into full view: four men, in plain clothes, huddled near the far end of a hole dug into the ground, aiming their weapons at the great, stone beast in front of them. The hole contained a small table, now smashed to kindling, and some rudimentary cooking gear. The Nazis had likely been living here for months, trying to wait out the Allied occupation, perhaps hoping for a rescue.

The Golem, screaming from the horror in his head, the pain in his body, the conflicted programming, knew only to kill these monsters that lay cowering beneath him.

"Za-beem-myeh!" he screamed, if the sounds could at all be considered words. It was a sound he had groaned so often to the Rabbi, but which the old man never understood. The Rabbi had dismissed it as the sound of an animal; to him, the sound was merely the gravelly scraping of air arising from the stone pit of the beast's chest. The Rabbi could not be blamed; indeed, no one would have recognized it as an actual word.

Now the beast screamed it. *"Za-beem-myeh!"*

"Der Golem! Er ist real! Er ist hier!" one of the Nazis screamed, firing his rifle. The poor German only had four bullets, and all of them bounced lazily off the hardened clay body of the towering, bastard beast.

"Za-beem-myeh!"

With just two more paces forward and down, the Golem reached the four men; all of them had exhausted the little ammunition they had. Now they raised their arms to cover themselves as huge, boulder-like fists came falling down upon them. The cave, once covered entirely in dirt and ash, was now covered in blood and viscera.

For a brief moment, the sounds stopped. The emotions left, the images disappeared. The Golem's screaming stopped; his own pain subsided. A small moment of peace.

Only a moment.

A new feeling took over. A new scent. No, it was the same scent, from a new direction. More Nazis, these about four kilometers away. The curse would not let him stop.

He would rest, as he always did after a killing, and then move forward. There were always more.

"What are you trying to say, beast?" a voice said. The Golem rose up from his crouch, hands bloodied, and turned. "What is that? 'Za-beem-myeh.' What is that?"

The Homunculus stood above on a pile of rubble, looking

down on the Nazi's spiderhole. As before, he wore his black cloak, black gloves, black hat with red headband.

"Are you trying to speak? Is that it?" he asked. "I want to help you." The Homunculus had recognized something in the sound the creature was making. It was not so much that the rasping scrape itself formed a word, but that something else, something inside the Homunculus' mind, suggested it was a word.

The Golem stepped forward and up, climbing back out of the hole, and then further upward to the top of the pile. The Golem now stood in front of this daring, black-clad man with ivory skin, towering over him. His fists were still shaped like boulders, stained with Nazi blood. This creature before him, this man with a hat, did not smell like a Nazi. He should not die.

"I think you and I are related. We may be brothers, of a sort, beast," the Homunculus said fearlessly. "Come with me. I can help you. I need to know where your creator is."

To the Golem, the sounds coming from the man's mouth were just that: sounds. He could not interpret the sounds; he did not recognize them as communication at all. The only communication he had ever known was the commands issued to him from his creator, the Rabbi. And the images, emotions, and horrors of his victims right before he destroyed them. Nothing more.

The Homunculus came to understand. "I need you to take me to your Rabbi, your creator. Henrik Broda. The Rabbi. Where is he?"

The Golem did not respond.

"You don't understand me, do you?" he asked of his giant clay counterpart. "I wonder if you can hear at all."

Suddenly, the Golem screamed again, raising his hands to his head as if in pain. *"Za-beem-myeh!"* the creature roared.

At the same time, the Homunculus was struck by the voice of Dead King Skyx. The voice he first heard at that pit in South Dakota, the voice his Brother-Son insisted was there, pushing him to awaken the Sunken Gods by injecting pure gold deep into the earth. The voice that the Homunculus insisted was not there, as he tried to convince his brother that this madness was just a result of his malformed growth, something that he, the Homunculus, could fix if his brother would just return to Monito for proper examination.

As much as the Homunculus denied the presence of that voice, it was now stronger than ever. A rushing of waves, crashing of white sound, and the low murmur of two words spoken in perfect English.

KILL ME!

But now, in front of this beast, the voice was growing louder still, clearer still. There was no mistaking it for a trick of the wind or some medical condition of the inner ear. Now, the words formed more clearly, became louder, drowning out the background white noise until only they remained.

KILL ME!

KILL ME!

The Homunculus raised his hands to his own ears to stop the sound. The voice was hurting him now, too much auditory information for a limited biological construct, the voice of a god blasted at full strength into the body of a man. A false man, yes, but a man, nevertheless.

KILL ME!

And all while, the great gray giant screamed, *"Za-beem-myeh!"*

Not a coincidence. Not a trick. Not the voice of Dead God Skyx! The Homunculus looked up, facing his stone counterpart, realizing the Golem was speaking Czech, or at least trying to. The Golem was possibly hearing the same thing the Homunculus was.

"What is that?" the Homunculus shouted, trying to hear his own voice over the one inside his head and the metallic, stone roar of the Golem in front of him. "What does that mean? Kill me? Why do we both hear this?"

The Golem struck without warning. Whether it was out of madness or a random lashing out for whatever pain the beast was experiencing, his boulder-like fist unfurled and reached out to grab the Homunculus by the arm, flinging him sideways like a child's wooden toy. The soulless Homunculus landed on his back, fifteen meters away, crashing down onto the pile of rubble. The voice in his head was lower now, not as loud, not as painful. And the only thing that had changed was his distance from the Golem. It was a form of signal feedback, he thought.

His thoughts would have to wait. The Golem charged now, crashing his giant boots over the rubble and broken wood pilings to attack the Homunculus a second time. This time, the Homunculus was prepared. With lightning-fast movements, he thrust himself upward just as the Golem reached his position, rotating his body in mid-air and cartwheeling so that he landed behind the giant gray monster.

Knowing that any more attempts at communicating with the Golem were pointless, he took the only action left to him. The Homunculus formed his own fist and sent it forward, into the back of the creature. It hit solid, hardened clay with a shuddering crunch. Beneath the covering of burlap, the Homunculus could feel bits of the beast's back chip away from the impact.

The Golem turned while swinging a giant arm backwards. His massive fist connected, once again sending the black-clad figure flying into the rubble. The Golem no longer screamed, and the Homunculus no longer heard the voice. So long as the Golem was not screaming, the Homunculus heard nothing. It was in that moment that the Homunculus realized they were not hearing the same thing.

He was hearing what the Golem was thinking. The rasp was just that, a scraping of stone. The Homunculus only understood the sound as the Czech words "*zabij mě!*" because of a silent, psychic signal between them.

He was connected to this big, gray beast.

In that moment, even as the Golem charged once more, the Homunculus understood. The progenitor's formula allowed his memories to be duplicated into each homunculus created by it; Dr. Cuba and the Homunculus shared the exact same memories because they were duplicates of the Father-Father's real-life memories. In the same way, somehow, this bastard creation, this Golem, was sharing not just memories, but thoughts in real time.

The Rabbi had no doubt infused qabalistic qualities into his beast, something the other homunculi did not benefit from. But there would be time to explore this idea later.

The Golem struck again, pounding the ground near the Homunculus with both fists, sending gravel and rock and timbers flying. The Homunculus barely dodged the blow, pulling away at a speed no normal human could have mustered. Using his momentum, the Homunculus flipped his body over itself, landing in a crouched position.

The Homunculus grabbed a metal pipe from the ground and lunged, hoping the metal could do more damage to the beast's stone hide than his fists. He landed on the thing's shoulders, and he swung the pipe downward onto its sculpted head. Clay chips gave way, but the head had been reinforced with a heavy layer of thick, hardened stone, a sort of helmet in the shape of a Dutch bob. A single blow with the pipe did little damage, so the Homunculus repeated ... again ... again. More chips, more dents, but nothing to stop the Golem's frantic rage.

The Golem reached up and grabbed the Homunculus, one giant hand grasping his legs and the other his arms. He held the black-clad devil high before bringing him down to the ground with impossible force. The Homunculus hit the stones below him and heard cracks. His bones were shattering. Pain, unlike anything he had ever felt, shot through his body like lightning.

The Homunculus fell limp as major nerves began to fail. He was not yet paralyzed, but another blow like that would either immobilize him or kill him. And he had no weapons to stop this

Golem. Though he knew nothing less than a bazooka, fired at close range, would work. Even if he were able to land a lucky blow of some sort, he had no strength left. He had nothing.

But his brain.

The Homunculus closed his eyes and focused. The Golem, above him with hands raised for the killing blow, froze. And then screamed.

Realizing the two shared a telepathic connection of sorts, one which strengthened with proximity, the Homunculus flooded his own mind with pain and horror, and thus imparted it back to the Golem. Within just a few seconds, the Homunculus could ascertain what types of thoughts did the most damage: scenes of horror, violence, physical pain, and torture. Fortunately, this devil had many such memories to pull from, having committed each of these acts many times over.

The Golem screamed, his gravel-pit roar becoming high-pitched as he once again grabbed at his own head, trying to pull the thoughts and feelings out of him. The Homunculus pushed even more horrible thoughts into the beast's brain, forcing him to relive terrors that made Nazi tortures seem kind and forgiving.

Instinctively, the Golem began to run. Whether he realized the damaging signal would weaken with distance or whether he simply felt the urge to flee was irrelevant. The beast was now headed away, and thus the Homunculus might survive this fight after all.

The Homunculus crawled to a toppled post and used it to lift himself up. One leg was crushed, but he had enough strength left in him to drag himself along. Finding another pipe on the ground, the Homunculus used this as a sort of staff to hold himself up as he began what would be a long journey out of this toppled section of Stuttgart.

He would not survive without repair in an iron maiden, but no such maiden was available in this city. He would have to somehow make it back to the Stuttgart safehouse and arrange transport back to Berlin—and survive the trip there.

Chapter 11: The Killer Root

Professor Jakob ten Brinken was amazed at the facilities within the Berlin safehouse. The Dr. Cuba organization was clearly well-funded; the equipment within the underground laboratory was relatively new, and the older pieces were well-maintained. There was a relatively good supply of chemicals, elemental powders, and test equipment.

For the reactions prior to incubation, the Homunculus told the Professor he may use his preferred methods: a dead woman's womb as the fertilization substrate and spark environment, in place of of the Homunculus's mechanical anti-womb chamber, and his injector-incubator as an initial growth chamber before transferring the mass to one of the strange iron maidens for post-incubation nutrition and a stable, inert growth environment.

The Homunculus had his doubts about using a real womb, however — dead or otherwise — but the only working anti-womb tank was back at Snake Island, and the Homunculus did not trust the Professor enough to take him there. The Homunculus could also not deny that the use of a biological womb might have special advantages. Perhaps this sweaty, twitching Professor was onto something.

The Professor selected a female corpse from the bunker's small morgue and dragged it onto a wheeled cart. He then rolled this into the laboratory, where he would begin his seventh attempt to create a new Alraune. The transemination formula was ready, with the appropriate amount of killer root included—and no semen or mandrake, per the Homunculus's direction. The Professor now simply needed the host womb and trigger reaction.

The Professor was certain this time would work, and he could not hide his anticipation at the thought that she would be his and only his.

As he prepared the corpse's womb, he thought of how she would worship him the way he deserved. And if she did not, he would destroy her and make another. There was no shortage of possibility now that he had working equipment, and the secret to success.

Inside one of the copper-clad iron maidens, the Homunculus was left to his thoughts and total, calming silence. The blood-gold-gasoline mixture was pumping into him, restoring his body. It was a mixture of his own making, quickly blended to ensure he would not be poisoned. His crushed leg was knitting itself together, his bruises healing, his back repairing. There was no pain associated with the process, but an itch of cells and bones and tissue reconnecting, growing.

He wondered if the homunculi had been able to telepathically communicate all along.

His Brother-Son, Dr. Cuba, had revealed that they could alter their appearance by manual manipulation of facial bones and skin, an ability that neither the Homunculus nor his Brother-Brothers had known of even though they were the first generation. Now, this Golem revealed that not only were memories transmitted through the genetic fabric of a homunculus, but thoughts could be shared between them, as well.

This created tremendous advantages. If the telepathic link could be improved, the homunculi might well be able to communicate over long distances without the need for coded radio transmissions or telegrams. Security concerns would be solved once and for all.

For now, it was clear that the ability required close proximity to function well. The Homunculus had first heard what he had assumed was the voice of Skyx all the way in America, and yet the Golem was likely still in Czechoslovakia. That signal was impossibly weak, with barely any comprehensible words. At Snake Island, he could discern the phrase "kill me!" but it was still muffled, buried under telepathic static. The telepathic noises became much clearer, if more painful, only when he was within a meter or two of the Golem.

Distance and signal fidelity would have to be improved. While the slovenly Professor worked on his Alraune variant of the homunculi, the Homunculus would focus on this new development. At least for the next few days, while he regained his full strength.

He still needed to find the Rabbi, and he knew he would likely have to destroy this Golem. Like his Brother-Son, Dr. Cuba, he could not allow a defective homunculus to roam the world.

Thumann once again sat in the dining room of his modest hotel, but this time sipped his coffee and pecked at pastries without his young assistant, Ximena. He was concerned about her disappearance — this was not like her — but he also knew she was beginning to have cabin fever, stuck at his side all this time. She was young and independent, he knew, and the poor girl needed some time on her own. Hopefully, the French occupying force would protect her.

Still, the coffee and pastries did not taste as good as when they were accompanied by thoughtful conversation with the young Chilean. All Thumann had to accompany himself now was his own labored breathing and the sound of his chewing. Thumann ate the pastries anyway, of course.

His thoughts turned to the investigation. He desperately needed to speak to Madame Blavatsky. Thumann knew little about "homunculi," and since Blavatsky had been helpful in some of his past cases, he realized she could be of help now as well if her theories were correct. She was a lunatic, but a clever lunatic; Thumann was never quite clear on how much of her crazed persona was handcrafted and how much was the product of her various peculiarities and drug habits. For Thumann, however, she was reliable; when she said something was a fact, it usually ended up being proved as one.

But Blavatsky was in her Florida swamp, far from Stuttgart. Telegram communication would not be proper for such a detailed conversation, so Thumann was stuck. He'd have to make do with the resources he had in front of him. He suspected Ximena had gone out on her own to do some fact-digging, so perhaps she would come back with something to help move this case forward.

Today's plan was to visit the site of a particularly devastated part of Stuttgart, where locals said another Golem attack had just happened the day before. Thumann was not thrilled that he was yet again a day behind.

However, when Thumann overheard a young woman asking about him at the front desk, his plans changed. She was about twenty-five years old, thin, with blonde hair, pearl teeth, and flawless skin. She was radiant, and she immediately drew the attention of everyone in the lobby and dining room.

Thumann saw the desk clerk point towards him. He brushed the sugar and pastry flakes off his chest and stood as the young lady approached. She seemed to float across the floor.

"Hello," she said in a mild voice that simultaneously signaled innocence and strength. "My name is Lady Petra. Are you Inspector Heiner Thumann?" She extended her hand.

Thumann nodded and lightly shook her hand, grasping only the fingers. "I am, Fraulein. May I invite you to sit? I can order you a coffee, and you can help me finish these pastries."

Petra sat but shook her head. "I've already eaten, but thank you. I am here at the prodding of my landlady, who heard on the radio that you were in Stuttgart."

Thumann sat now, sliding the plate of pastries towards the young woman. She again declined, smiling politely. "I hadn't realized I was the subject of radio reports," Thumann said. He was fibbing; he was well aware the news had mentioned his presence in the city and was privately proud of it. "How may I help you, then?"

"I was attacked while leaving Berlin to return to Stuttgart. I thought it nothing more than the usual thugs or street criminals, but my landlady, the dear Frau Jannings, says there is a wave of such crimes. She said they may have something to do with that horrible Dr. Cuba."

"What happened?" Thumann asked, concerned for this young woman's predicament while also anxious for any new leads. "Were you injured?"

"Only superficially. They robbed me of my jewelry, purse, those things. They stripped me and left me to walk back naked." Petra said this last part without any hint of concern over who might overhear her. She was surprisingly confident, despite her frail and delicate appearance.

"Were you ...?" Thumann trailed off.

"Raped? No, thankfully. They appeared only interested in my money and jewelry. I ended up with only scratches. I believe they took my clothes to slow down my return to Stuttgart."

"This is a blessing," Thumann said. "But this also means you may well have encountered Dr. Cuba's gang, as they rarely use rape as a weapon."

"So, this is true?" Petra asked. "Dr. Cuba was not killed in America? The news reports were wrong?"

Thumann shook his head. "No, Dr. Cuba was killed. I saw it with my own eyes. But we believe another figure has risen up and adopted the name. There are many similarities between what happened under Dr. Cuba's crime waves and what is happening again here in Germany."

"So, Frau Jannings's advice was good, then. I am glad I am speaking with you."

"I am glad, too. Are you sure you won't take coffee, at least?"

"No, thank you."

Thumann sniffed in mild frustration. He wanted to eat and drink his coffee, but was too polite to do so if she was not joining him. His stomach rumbled. "I came here to investigate what we believed was an unrelated series of crimes. You have probably heard of these so-called 'Golem' attacks."

"I don't pay much attention to the news, but I did hear something," Petra admitted.

"Some madman running around in a circus outfit, causing terror," Thumann said, not wanting to alarm her with the truth. "But then we uncovered a series of murders. Two, in fact. We aren't sure if we are dealing with three separate crime waves or some larger conspiracy."

"Frau Jannings told me about the murders, yes. Bodies left bloodless or some such thing."

Thumann raised an eyebrow. A remarkably steady young woman, he thought. "Yes, exactly. Very unusual, but Dr. Cuba's gang has used forms of fright and terror to create environments amenable to their ends. It could be this reconstituted group is using new tools, serial murders and bloodsucking, or ... Oh, I am sorry, dear lady," he said, stopping himself from any further garish descriptions.

Petra raised a hand. "I am not as delicate as I may look, Inspector. I know the world is filled with terrible things."

Thumann's mustache twitched. "Well, nevertheless, I will refrain from explicit talk. But we are struggling to connect these crimes, and we may well discover the attempt to do so was in error. They might simply be different madmen doing different mad things."

"I see," Petra said, appearing disappointed. "I wonder if I might have something that could help you, however. A clue, as they say?"

"Do you?" Thumann asked, leaning forward.

"Most of the men who attacked me were unremarkable. As I said, street thugs. Just dirty men wearing dirty clothes."

"I see," Thumann said, finally relenting and sipping his coffee.

"One, however, stood out. He was tall, well-dressed. All

black. A black overcoat, a black suit, a black fedora hat."

Thumann froze, the coffee cup hovering in front of his bushy beard. "The hat. Describe it?"

"All black, with a red hat band. He just seemed entirely at odds with the appearance of the others. As if he were the leader, and they the henchmen."

Thumann put his cup down. "Did he say anything? What did his voice sound like?"

"He didn't speak, no. So, I don't know. He just stood and stared. He had black eyes, very black, and skin as pale as mine. Although I believe I carry the color better than he does," Petra said, smiling a bit.

Thumann missed the joke entirely, too busy marveling that she had seen the black-clad devil. Thumann's mind raced. Recognizing this, he slowed it down. Now was the time to absorb information and process it, not let adrenaline take over.

"You've described a man who is known to me," Thumann said, lowering his voice and pulling a map of Germany from his pocket. "He is part of Dr. Cuba's organization, yes. I knew he was headed to Germany, but didn't know when he might have arrived or where, specifically, he is. You may have just provided that proof. Can you point to where you encountered this man?"

Thumann unfolded the map and laid it on the table. Petra examined it. "The main highway that comes down from Berlin," Petra said, pointing to a line on the map. "It was very busy, lots of cars, military trucks, all that. And, again, this was before the checkpoint, still within the city limits."

Thumann pointed to the highway leading from Berlin to Stuttgart. "That would be here."

"So ..." Petra thought, aiming her finger over the map. "About here." She pointed to a more specific spot within the Berlin city limits.

Thumann studied the map, but his mind raced once more. If this was the red-fingered devil, Thumann wondered why he was performing common highway robberies. Surely, he had amassed a fortune and did not need this woman's necklace or earrings. Something did not sound right, and Thumann was again worried he was trying desperately to tie Dr. Cuba into a series of crimes that may have nothing to do with the group.

But she did see the devil, he thought. This could not be denied.

"Then it appears I head next to Berlin," Thumann said.

Petra looked into Thumann's eyes. "I wish I could join you. I would like to get my valuables back. But I am sure that's not possible."

"No, I'm afraid not. It may be dangerous if we encounter this devil. But, more likely, it will just be boring police work. How may I contact you if we find anything?"

"I rent a flat about two kilometers from here," Petra said. She produced a small pen and paper from her purse and began writing. "Here is the address. I'm afraid there's no telephone. Send a note to Frau Jannings, and she can ensure I get it."

She slipped the paper to Thumann, who took it, looked it over, and put it in his vest pocket.

"Thank you, Herr Inspector. I think I will leave you now," Petra said, standing. "I hope this has been helpful."

Thumann stood and shook the Lady Petra's delicate hand gently. "It may come to nothing," he said, "or it might be very important. Either way, thank you very much, fraulein."

He then watched her float out of the dining room, through the lobby and out onto the street.

Unable to understand German or French, Ximena headed towards a part of town that was more likely to have English-speaking people in it.

Ximena knew she should not have come to this part of the city alone, but wanted to have a bit of independence. Throughout her time in Germany, she had relied on her German mentor for guidance, escorting, and translation. This was a level of reliance that made Ximena uncomfortable. She felt a bit like a daughter to Thumann and appreciated his care and protection, but to be entirely dependent on another person twenty-four hours a day was beginning to wear thin. Even daughters have their own lives, after all.

While there, she hoped she might strike up some conversations with locals to learn more about the killings she felt were not related to the Golem: the "vampire" killings of seemingly random people, left drained of their blood. They needed more evidence to tie these murders to Dr. Cuba, if Thumann was right.

Ximena had found a hotel that catered to Americans, with a mix of US soldiers as well as immigrant businessmen and the wives of both. Most had not been in Stuttgart very long, but eventually she found one English-speaking German, a man named Hutzler, who was more than willing to chat. The hotel was relatively fancy and had a pleasant bar on the first floor, where Ximena sat to talk to Herr Hutzler.

"Yes, this Dr. Cuba name has been popping up in the local rumor mill for a few weeks now," Hutzler said, sipping a cola. He was a kindly man of about fifty, thin, with wireframe glasses and a modest-looking suit. He claimed to be in banking, but did not appear wealthy; a lower-level clerk, perhaps. But he had been in Stuttgart even before the surrender and knew its people well.

"What sort of crimes have been attributed to Dr. Cuba?" Ximena asked.

"Robberies, a few murders. The usual. In the beginning, the name was just being thrown into news reports to sell papers. The Dr. Cuba scandal in the Americas affected us in Germany, too, since we had gold stolen by that villain. I think the newspapers were a bit disappointed when your boss caught the man."

"But you think that more recent crimes were the work of Dr. Cuba?" Ximen asked. She removed a pad from her pocket and began jotting down notes with a small pencil.

"I do," Hutzler said, nodding. "There is something different about these. It was not the newspapers assigning blame to Dr. Cuba. The locals are doing it now. They started hearing things. Whispers. Rumors. Just like they had back when the gold was being taken out of Berlin bank vaults a year ago. Even years before that. Going as far back as at least twenty years ago, Germany was plagued by this villain known only as 'the Doktor.' This latest crime wave is more like that. More familiar, less artificial. Not just to sell newspapers, I think."

Ximena sipped her own drink, a simple water with lemon. She wrote "the Doktor" in her notes. "If Dr. Cuba is dead, and these crimes remind you of this 'Doktor,' why would you think this is the work of Dr. Cuba then?"

"Some say Dr. Cuba is a group, like the Sicilian Mafia. I have my own theory."

"What's that?" Ximena asked.

"Dr. Cuba did not die in America. The real Dr. Cuba was here in Germany, operating as the Doktor. Your inspector may have seen someone die in America, but not Dr. Cuba. Now that peace is returning to Germany, he's back and rebuilding his criminal enterprise. That's what I think." Hutzler seemed quite sure of his theory.

Ximena knew better, of course. The original Dr. Cuba *was* dead, sprayed with molten gold and sunk, like an idol, into a lake. His so-called brother, however, the red-fingered devil in black, was alive, and probably using the "Dr. Cuba" name for his own ends. But there was no reason to believe he was operating in Germany, and certainly not as far back as 1926.

But Ximena recalled the Interpol wires of similar murders in German and France, long before her trip with Thumann. What if Hutzler was onto something?

Thumann said he overheard Dr. Cuba and his black-clad brother say there were "four of them." Four homunculi. Dr. Cuba, the black-coated devil, and two others. Could those other two have been the Doktor and another in France?

If so, then the Golem of Stuttgart — or, more accurately, the Golem of Prague — was a *fifth* homunculus. If, of course, Thumann was right and not chasing ghosts.

"These other murders," Ximena asked.

"The bloodless bodies?" Hutzler asked, reading her mind.

"Yes. I am curious as to why the newspapers haven't reported much about them."

"There is so much happening in Stuttgart right now," Hutzler explained, "I think the reporters are stretched thin. The news publishers are struggling simply to get ink and paper to print the newspapers, and they have perhaps less than half the staff they did before the surrender. Now, combine that with all these strange happenings in Stuttgart, and it's simple: not everything can get reported."

Ximena nodded. That made sense to her. "What is your theory about those killings? Are they Dr. Cuba, too?"

"Probably," Hutzler said, sipping again. "There were reports of bloodless bodies found in Berlin during the height of the Doktor crime waves. So, yes, it could be."

Ximena looked at her watch. "Well, thank you very much, Herr Hutzler, you have been very helpful."

Hutzler stood, an old-fashioned gesture that Ximena very much appreciated, even if she never quite understood it. "I am happy to help the great Inspector Thumann and his exotic assistant," he said, extending a hand. Ximena shook it, managing to keep a straight face, though she was disappointed to see even this man did not take her seriously.

"It was a pleasure to meet you. If the inspector has any questions for you, I will have him drop by the hotel."

Ximena headed towards the door and bumped into a tall man wearing a suit much finer than that of Hutzler. "*Drecksau*!" the man grunted, turning to face Ximena. Switching to English, he sneered, "You're the little whore sitting with that idiot banker, aren't you?"

The accent was German, aristocratic, strong. The man's posture was haughty, one used to power. If anyone was a former Nazi, this man was. Whoever he was, those in the hotel lobby did nothing to stand up to him; if anything, they looked afraid of him.

"You're a filthy pig. Get out into the mud, pig!" the man shouted, pushing Ximena out the door. "How dare you touch me. Go back to your jungle in the Amazon or wherever you come from, pig!"

With that, he shoved Ximena out past the street and into the mud.

"Germany is for Germans!" he shouted as he left Ximena.

Ximena saw the man turn to leave and decided it was best to remain face-down in the mud until it was safe to stand up. She did not want to be knocked down again.

When the German turned a corner and fell out of view, Ximena tried to stand but slipped in the wet mud, falling once more. After another attempt, she managed to stand and tried to wipe as much of the mud from herself as she could, but she was covered, her dress ruined.

With a sigh, Ximena looked back toward the hotel. She could see Hutzler sitting inside, staring down at his table, afraid to look up.

Surrender, she realized, did not mean a sudden, overnight change in German culture. The country was still filled with hate and fear.

Chapter 12: The Spider Crone

The Golem rested.

He had found a place in a wooded area near the border of Stuttgart to hide, away from checkpoint police and wandering military patrols. With his great stone hands, he dug a hole and buried himself with the dirt, leaving only a bit of his face resting on the surface, uncovered. From a distance, he was now entirely invisible.

The voices and emotions had stopped for now. The Golem was at peace, but his clay brain was damaged. There was no pain, but there was also no direction. Something was happening; he was losing his sense of purpose. He was also having difficulty smelling his next victim's scent in the air.

Something was changing, and it was not for the better.

The Golem closed his eyes and rested, and the wind soon covered his exposed face with dry leaves.

Thumann's heavy feet clomped the floorboards of the hotel lobby as if they simply could not be bothered to recognize the carpeting. He was furious.

He stormed up to the front desk, cutting in front of a married couple trying to book a room. "I'm here for the Nazis you are hiding!" he shouted loudly, so the sound of his voice would echo through the walls. The front desk clerk looked at him with terror. Thumann's height made him look like a tree, his fists the size of pumpkins. "Nazis!" he repeated.

The clerk froze. Thumann was not going to waste time. He turned and shifted the direction of his wrath to the adjacent dining room. There, the tables were filled with French and American patrons, along with some upper-crust Germans. Herr Hutzler sat there as well, sitting once again at the same table he had been at when Ximena met him.

"I am Inspector Heiner Thumann!" the giant German shouted, getting everyone's attention. The dining room fell silent. "Yesterday, my co-inspector was here talking to some of you and was accosted by some punk. He threw her into the street. You are going to tell me who that man is and where I can find him!"

Faces went pale, and heads turned to look at each other. Everyone remained silent.

"I have an unusual remit," Thumann continued, beginning to pace slowly around the dining room, weaving himself through the tables. Terrified eyes stared at him. "I have international authority, meaning the French soldiers out there can't stop me if I am on official business. And I am on official business. So, I am going to stand here and ruin your breakfast and very possibly your ability to swallow it until someone tells me who it was that threw my assistant into the mud!"

Now Thumann clomped from one table to the next, staring down each person at each table, being sure his burning, white-hot gaze met the eyes of each of them, one by one. What he said about the French military was not particularly true, but Thumann realized many years ago that if he raised his voice loud enough, he could get away with quite a bit of truth-stretching.

"Who was it??!!" he boomed again, pounding a fist on one of the tables. Teacups scattered and crashed, as if running for cover.

Thumann came to the table of the cowardly Herr Hutzler and burned his eyes into the thin man. Hutzler's eyes darted to the left. In his rage, Thumann almost did not notice and began to walk to the next table. Then, he stopped. He looked back at Hutzler, who again darted his eyes to the left. He was signaling.

Thumann looked away and continued stomping through the tables. "Who?" he boomed again. Now, however, he had a destination. Making it appear random, so that he did not give away Hutzler's role in this impromptu investigation, Thumann clomped around Hutzler's table until he was conveniently facing towards the thin man's left. A table of aristocratic German men, none more than thirty years old, sat staring. One in particular glared at Thumann with anger, not fear.

Thumann raised his hand and pointed. One giant, sausage-like finger was aimed at the man. "You," Thumann said. "Was it you?"

The young German stood. "Don't bring your filth to this part of town, *volksverräter*!" the man said defiantly. "Or I will throw you into the mud, too!" His hand reached into his coat pocket and produced a military pistol, aimed directly at Thumann.

Thumann did not flinch, moving towards the young man as if he did not even see the gun pointed at him. With only a few steps, he was in front of the man. Thumann swung his arm, knocking the pistol from the young man's hand with a loud *thwack*. The man's eyes widened, and now his face was not as defiant.

Thumann's other hand swung around and grabbed the man by the collar, lifting him off the ground. The man was thin and weighed little, allowing Thumann to carry the man through the dining room, through the lobby, and out to the street, to the shock—and delight—of many watching. "Are you a Nazi?" Thumann asked. "Tell me you are a Nazi, you bastard, so I can beat you to death and get a reward afterward!"

The man struggled to get free of Thumann's grip, to no avail. Thumann pushed his arm forward and let go, sending the man into the mud. He slid about a meter before coming to rest, looking up at Thumann with absolute terror. He did not answer.

Thumann advanced, now standing over the man. He leaned over, pointing a finger at his face yet again. "When I am doing an investigation, the city is mine," he said, his forehead red. "And right now, I am investigating Stuttgart, so Stuttgart belongs to Thumann now. If I want to bring in an army of cockatoos to help my investigation, I will, and you'll be covered in birdshit while keeping your mouth shut and nodding your head like a good little boy. Do you understand?"

The man nodded, like a good little boy.

"The Golem!" Thumann heard from behind. He stood up straight and spun around.

"What?" he boomed.

It was a small child, pointing to Thumann. "The Golem, he's real! He's come to kill the Nazis!" he said.

Thumann looked around in confusion at first. A crowd had formed, and he was the center of it. They stared at him with fear. This had not gone as he had planned.

Thumann turned back to the young German in the mud. He started to say something but hesitated; anything he could say now might be misinterpreted ... or, worse, interpreted exactly as he intended it. It was best to retreat.

With a frustrated huff, Thumann turned to storm off, whispers of "The Golem!" following behind him.

The Professor decided it was time to celebrate his newfound luck in being granted protection by this strange Homunculus. He left the safehouse without any problem, which should have alerted him, but, in his euphoria, he did not notice. The Homunculus's men followed him, not about to let their new scientist out of their sight, but the Professor remained entirely unaware he was being followed.

Heading to a nearby bar, the Professor threw a hand into his pocket to feel the Reichsmarks there, if only to reassure him he was, for the moment, wealthy. Opening the door to the pub, the Professor was greeted with thick cigar smoke and loud German music. There were only a few soldiers — Americans, by the look of them — and quite a few pretty German girls. He strutted to the bar and waved down the barmaid. She was busty and outgoing; he very much liked the former attribute, but the latter, not so much. But he knew she had a job to do, so he would overlook her crude behavior.

"Beer, and a big one," he shouted. It was as if he were announcing himself to the entire bar. Nevertheless, no one noticed him.

The barmaid produced a large stein of fresh beer, with a huge frothy head, and charged him an exorbitant fee. The economy of Berlin was still in shambles, and pricing of luxuries like beer was based on whatever one thought they could get from the sucker standing in front of them. The Professor did not care and happily tossed some Reichsmarks on the counter, hoping to draw attention to his own newfound wealth.

It worked. Within just a few moments, the ugly and unpleasant Professor Jakob ten Brinken was surrounded by three lovely young women, all of whom were also busty and outgoing. He decided to drink his beer, stare at their breasts, and hope they would eventually shut their mouths. He knew very well they were just after his money—or, instead, the money given to him by his strange benefactor—but he did not care. If he could attract these three tramps within a few minutes, maybe with enough time, he might find one who was worthy of his attention. A woman with the perfect shape and perfect submissive nature.

The three girls continued to fawn over him, their acting abilities poor by any standard, but soon realized they would not get anywhere with him, no matter how much cleavage they showed. After only a short time, they became fed up and left him alone once more. The Professor sniffed arrogantly at them as they retreated, happy to resume his beer in privacy. He wanted attention as an important figure of standing, but not from whores.

One beer led to a second, and eventually a third. The Professor's eyes soon began to focus inward, his head spun, and his inhibitions faded away. As he moved through the pub, occasionally changing his seat to get a better view of the crowd as well as any new women who might walk in, he was now bumping into the people around him more frequently. The Professor was too drunk to notice that the patrons were losing their patience with him.

The fourth beer proved too much. A pretty American soldier entered the bar, in uniform except without any hat, revealing her blonde hair. Her figure was nothing remarkable, but the way she carried herself was enough to enrage the Professor. He had now been in the pub for at least two hours and had not met a single woman who interested him; the only ones who approached him were clearly sluts. Now, as if mocking him, a female "soldier" arrived and was receiving attention from the other men in the room.

"Whore," he said, a bit too loudly. One man, standing next to the Professor, turned.

"What?" the man said.

"Whore. She's a whore. That so-called soldier. Whore." The Professor's words were melting together and coming out with a fair amount of spittle.

"You should keep that opinion to yourself, mate," the man said in a British accent. "Those American boys won't like you insulting one of their women." He pointed to the US soldiers in the corner.

The Professor stood. "I don't care!" he shouted, drawing the pub's attention. "That woman is a whore!" He pointed at the young soldier.

The woman's eyes opened wide for a moment and then settled back into a neutral position; she had heard this sort of thing before. She turned and resumed her conversation with the other Americans.

"I said you're a whore!" the Professor repeated, louder this time. "You can pretend that you're a man, but you will never be one! You're only in that uniform because a man put you there. We make you! *Men* make you! Without men, you are worthless. A worthless whore!" The spittle was reaching a significant distance.

The Americans stood up. The woman motioned with her hand that they should leave the matter be, but they were not in agreement. They shoved their table aside and approached the Professor.

"Say it again, *kraut*," one of the Americans said. "Say it again, and I'll make you swallow your own teeth." He raised his fist, ready to bring it down with significant force. Two more Americans stood behind the first, fists also raised.

"Professor ten Brinken, you are under arrest!" A new, male voice called from the corner of the pub. Two men emerged, dressed as French military police.

The Professor, a bit too drunk to know what was happening, prepared to stand toe-to-toe with the Americans. The MPs positioned themselves between him and the soldiers, cutting off their ability to throw any punches.

One of the MPs turned to the Americans. "This man is wanted for abuse of a child. We have orders to bring him to the French sector."

The Americans lowered their fists, seeming quite pleased with this development. "You hear that, pig?" one of the Americans said. "You'll be going away with these Frenchies for a long time!"

They laughed.

The Professor was handcuffed and hauled away, his body pushed and tossed about like a bag of onions. The bar patrons, happy to be rid of him, cleared the way towards the door for the MPs.

Once outside, the Professor was thrown into the back of a French military truck and driven around the city for about twenty minutes. When it was deemed safe, the men drove back to the Homunculus's safehouse, removed their French MP uniforms, and put the Professor back to bed.

"This man has problems," one of the operatives said. "And it's not just that he can't hold his liquor."

"Inspector, I did not need your protection," Ximena said as courteously as she could muster. "You might have been killed or arrested over nothing."

"You are the one who could have been killed," Thumann said, defending himself. "They could have done all sorts of horrors to you. You don't know what men are capable of."

Ximena smiled, just a bit, to try to calm her mentor. "But I *do* know, Inspector. I do. I am a woman, and I experience it far more frequently than you do. And more directly. For all the things you only imagine, women actually experience."

Thumann snorted, pipe smoke coming from his mouth. "They need to know you are protected by me, Inspector Thumann!" he boomed, saying his own name as if it were, itself, a weapon to be feared.

"No, sir," Ximena countered, "they do not. Men should treat me with respect because I earn it, and because it is the way we should behave as a society. Loud men should not behave only because they fear another, louder man."

Thumann snorted again, this time just grunting.

Ximena gently took his hand. "I know you meant well, Inspector. And I appreciate it. Sometimes. But I need to become a proper inspector, and that means not having my giant German to hide behind."

"The fraulein speaks the truth," a feminine voice said from the doorway. Thumann and Ximena turned.

"Lady Petra," Thumann said, recognizing the waifish blonde beauty. "Might I introduce you to my co-inspector, Ximena Alejandra Torres Orellana." Thumann mangled the pronunciation of Ximena's name, but it represented the first time he had tried to utter the entire thing.

Ximena extended a hand; Petra took it, but ever so lightly. The two could not have been more different: Ximena, a black-haired Latina with dirt under her nails, carrying a leather shoulder bag, and Petra, an elegant, Aryan nymph in a pink and white dress.

Petra smiled. "Very pleased to meet you. I have, of course, read of your exploits, although only recently. My landlady told me of Inspector Thumann and his investigation into the Dr. Cuba matter in America."

Ximena was at a disadvantage. "And how do you know the

Inspector?" she asked.

Thumann interrupted. "Lady Petra sought me out after hearing about our investigation on the radio. She was accosted by someone who fits the description of our black-coated devil from South Dakota."

Petra cut Thumann short now. "With regard to what the fraulein said, Inspector, and with all due respect, you should allow her to defend herself. She is obviously old enough to work as an inspector, so you should respect it when she says she may not need you to chase down bullies on her behalf."

Thumann scowled. "Neither of you knows what men are truly capable of," he muttered again, more to himself than to anyone else. His thoughts were not on these two ladies, however. They were on Hilda. His beloved wife had not known the horrors of men—until she had.

Ximena and Petra both sensed the tension in the room and simultaneously attempted to defuse it, each in their own way.

"Perhaps we should be off, then," Ximena said. "Our car is outside."

"I came to bring you sandwiches for the ride," Petra said, patting the large purse at her side. "And to wish you luck and safety."

"Thank you, Fraulein," Thumann said, accepting the bag of sandwiches. "I am sure we will enjoy these greatly."

"I hope to see you when you return," Petra said before floating out of the lobby.

With Petra gone, Ximena touched Thumann's sleeve. "Inspector, there is one more detail I need to discuss."

"What is it?" Thumann asked. He was still a bit irked.

"The reason I was in that hotel restaurant is that I was doing my own investigation. I now believe that there may be five homunculi, not four."

"Five?" Thumann asked with a frown. Now he was focused purely on the case, and not his bruised feelings.

"Five," Ximena repeated. "Dr. Cuba and his brother, but also the Doktor from Germany. In checking the old wire reports, many of the crimes in France of that period were attributed to someone the press called 'the Fantôme.' As I see it, their crime waves go back to at least 1910 or earlier."

"I remember hearing about this 'Fantôme," Thumann said. "They would be in their sixties, then."

"If they are men, yes. But what if they are not, as you suggested?" Ximena answered.

"They don't age?" Thumann said, considering this new possibility. "They don't age," he said, allowing the idea to settle in his head.

"They might not. So, the Devil, the Doktor, and the Fantôme worked together, in secret, while Scotland Yard treated them as different cases. But in reality, they were always a single organization."

"This Dr. Cuba, then, the fourth homunculus?" Thumann asked. "Where does he fit in?"

"He represents what you call an 'outlier,' I think? In English?"

Thumann nodded. "An outlier, yes, that's the right word."

"You said the brother was trying to bring Dr. Cuba back to fix him. This suggests that something went wrong. Dr. Cuba came later, after the first three. So, the Dr. Cuba gold heists were not part of the plans of the original three homunculi. They also did not match. Dr. Cuba's crimes were bold, brazen, and attributed to him. The crimes of the three originals in America, France, and Germany were hidden, subtle."

"The Devil needed to stop Dr. Cuba. He was drawing attention to their existence," Thumann surmised.

"Yes, that is what I think," Ximena said. "So, the Golem would be the *fifth* homunculus, and likely another outlier."

"And the black devil has come here to investigate him,

perhaps stop him, just as he did with Dr. Cuba," Thumann said as it all clicked into place.

"Claro que si, eso es exactamente lo que esta pasando ahora," Ximena said, falling into Spanish. She was getting excited. "I mean, sorry, yes. That is it, exactly."

"Then the bodies found without blood may be because of the black-coated devil. He was spotted in Caracas around the time that ship was found with its crew exsanguinated."

"What?" Ximena asked, her forehead creasing in confusion. "Oh, *desangrado.* Their blood drained."

"Yes, um, des… desangrado," Thumann said, trying his Spanish once more. "And the Lady Petra saw him in Berlin. For sure, we will find more such bodies there."

"But the telegram from Madame Blavatsky was just from a few days ago, and she said he was in Florida at that time. If he's in Germany, he has only just arrived. The vampire killings happened before then."

"True, but perhaps this villain's gang was gathering a supply of blood for him in anticipation of his arrival."

"Like Renfield, from the book," Ximena said.

"You read *Dracula*?" Thumann asked, his bushy eyebrows raised.

"Yes, recently. Renfield was Dracula's advance scout. For sure, these homunculi have similar agents around the world."

Once more, a woman's voice interrupted them, but this time not from behind them, but from above.

"Not quite right, Inspector," the voice hissed.

Thumann's head snapped around and then upward. There, in the beams of the hotel lobby, a woman crouched upside-down, stuck to the ceiling like a spider. She appeared to be about seventy, with gray hair and a sneering, wrinkled face. Her clothes were tattered, filthy.

"You're a fool, Thumann!" she shouted, her voice hissing

like a gas leak. "And if you go to Berlin, you will die!"

The creature crawled along the ceiling, nearly silently, but now everyone in the lobby was staring at her. With a single, deft movement, she fell to the floor, landing as a cat, in a crouched position. Thumann reached his hand into his pocket, grasping his brass knuckles. Ximena froze in place.

The old crone stood, her back bent with age, and yet she still moved with surprising grace. She pointed a finger at Thumann. "If you go to Berlin, you will die, Thumann. And your little bitch, too!" Her finger moved to point to Ximena.

Showing no fear, Thumann began walking towards the crone, his fist now pulled from his pocket and ready, armed with his Celtic knot brass knuckles. "I think you had better come with me for an interview," he said, knowing that the request would be ignored.

It was. The old crone leapt up, reaching a height of nearly three meters, only to come down on Thumann like a vulture landing on its prey. She scratched at his face, hissing.

Ignoring the pain, Thumann pulled the crone off of him and threw her into the far wall with little effort. The pictures fell from the wall, crashing down on the ground, their frames splintering. The crone seemed entirely unaffected, leaping to her feet quickly and scrambling towards a side door.

Ximena raised the small pistol she now held, aiming it at the fleeing crone, but could not get a clean shot; there were too many people in the lobby. Thumann reached out and pushed Ximena's arm down; he did not want to risk someone getting shot, either.

They rushed after the old woman, but she was not on the street. They circled around, searching for her. A boy across the street pointed upward. "There, on the roof!" he shouted. Thumann snapped his head upward; the crone was scattering along the rooftop. There would be no way to pursue her now.

Thumann's hands fell to his side, and Ximena pocketed her pistol. "*Pucha, se escapó*," she said, frustrated.

"Six," Thumann said, breathing heavily.

"What?" Ximena asked, looking at him.

"Not five. There are six," Thumann answered. "That creature was a homunculus, too."

Ximena gasped, her gaze flying to the rooftops again. "Of course! If so, then she is the one draining the blood of victims in Stuttgart."

Thumann snorted. "Which means that black-coated devil may be here to find her, too. Or she's working with him."

"That old woman wanted to stop us from going to Berlin," Ximena said. "Why didn't she kill us here and now?"

Thumann's cheeks puffed out. He finally realized he was winded and needed to breathe. "Something is wrong here. There are traps within traps. You are correct, young miss; if she really wanted to stop us, she could have. No, this is a feint. A trick. Someone wanted us to come to Germany. And now this creature wants us to go to Berlin."

"So, what do we do? We stay here?" Ximena asked. "What about the other homunculus?"

"No, we go. But we go knowing it's a trap. The only way to find out who has set the trap is to step into it."

Chapter 13: The Enochian Queen

The flight from Berlin to London was difficult, but not impossible. The Allied forces tightly controlled all air traffic and had placed drastic limits on civilian flights. The Homunculus instead relied on his German predecessor's network of underground resources, most of which had remained remarkably unaffected by the war. It was, after all, a war he had helped orchestrate.

The Homunculus boarded a small two-seat single-prop aircraft and directed the pilot, a trusted operative of the now-deceased Doktor, to chart a flight path that would avoid Allied towers and spotting stations. With a refueling stop at a secret location in Antwerp, the plane landed in London just ten hours after takeoff from Berlin. False papers ensured the British suspected nothing. From the airport, it was a half-hour drive to his intended destination, a members-only club known as the Enochian Queen. Thirty minutes would be enough for the Homunculus to change his face.

The Enochian Queen was located in the wealthy Mayfair district, set up behind an otherwise ordinary tailor's shop on Bond Street, but accessible only through a nondescript, unmarked door positioned away from the shop's main entrance. The Homunculus, now bearing the face of a man of about fifty-five, rapped on the door with a gloved hand. One of the door's wooden panels flipped open, and a portion of a man's head could be seen moving within; he was wearing a black hood that left only his eyes visible.

"As above," the hooded man said. It was a passphrase.

"So below," the Homunculus countered. He sighed silently at the amateurish theatrics.

The wooden panel snapped shut, and the door opened. The Homunculus entered, greeted by a thin man in a very well-made suit, a crisp necktie, and white gloves. Once the door closed, he removed his hood; the man was only about thirty, with dark hair and a well-manicured, curled mustache.

"Welcome to the Enochian Queen," he said. "May I have your appellation?"

"Fotheringay, the Soulless Beast," the Homunculus said, affecting a formal London accent.

The mustached man wrinkled his brow. "With respect, kind sir, that appellation is not known to me."

"And yet," the Homunculus said, drawing himself closer to the man so that he towered over him, "I am here bearing it."

"Are you a player, then, sir?" the man asked.

"I am," the Homunculus said firmly. "My concern is that the men in this club are not. Or, at best, have long since forgotten the rules."

This put the younger man at some discomfort as the Homunculus was suggesting that the club had lost its knowledge of how to play Enochian Chess, the very thing they purported to be founded upon. In reality, there were layers to the deception, none of which were particularly complex: the tailor's shop hid the Enochian Chess club, the chess club hid the occult order, and the occult order hid the fact that the members were just an assortment of bored and powerless simpletons with a desire to imagine themselves as part of something mystical.

The young man silently wondered if he was now facing someone who truly knew the game and, perhaps, what was going on behind it all. For the protection of his own membership, he opted to simply pass the matter on to someone higher up. "Let's go into the salon, then," he said, gulping nervously.

The Homunculus removed his overcoat and hung it, along with his fedora, on a rack in the hallway, and then followed the young man through a corridor along the side of the tailor's shop to a larger space built behind it, unobservable from the street and lacking any windows. The room was bathed only in gaslights and candles, decorated with dark wood panels, dark wood furniture, and two large dark wood fireplaces. Books lined the walls, and elegant chairs, sofas, and divans were scattered about. In one corner was a well-stocked bar.

There was not a single chessboard anywhere in sight, Enochian or otherwise.

"If you will make yourself comfortable, I will summon the Day Master," the man said, indicating a set of chairs near one of the fireplaces. "You may also help yourself to the bar. You must serve yourself, as we do not have a barman."

The Homunculus sat and crossed his leg, waiting. His posture exuded someone who was here with deep authority and even deeper self-confidence.

The Day Master would be the club's highest-ranking member present at the moment, likely tasked with dealing with things such as unannounced visitors or ensuring the bar was restocked. Today, an older man of about sixty emerged, wearing a decidedly out-of-style suit and needlessly pompous cravat. He clearly wanted to appear as if he had just stepped out of the 1890s, but instead looked much like a fool.

"I am Lord Commander Dreyfuss, bearing the appellation King of Swords. And you are ... ?" he demanded.

"Fotheringay, the Soulless Beast," the Homunculus said.

"I know of no one by that name nor title, sir," Dreyfuss said indignantly.

"I won't waste your time, Dreyfuss," the Homunculus said, dropping the theatrical pretenses that this club seemed desperately to require. "I am here to speak to Mr. Edwin Blacke, who I understand spends much of his time in this club. I ask that you produce him for me. If you require some level of understanding as to my knowledge of what you do here, we can arrange partners and play a round of chess. I warn you, however, that I will win."

Enochian Chess was a four-player variant of traditional chess, similar to Indian chaturaji, created by the original occultists of the Hermetic Order of the Golden Dawn, which had included members such as William Butler Yeats and Aleister Crowley. The Golden Dawn had fallen apart decades earlier, and only the most serious adherents remembered how to play the game; it was unlikely anyone in the Enochian Queen were among them. The Homunculus knew that not only would Dreyfuss be unable to find two other men to fill the seats behind the chessboard, Dreyfuss himself probably never learned how to play. Boasting about his prowess, the Homunculus only intimidated the man further.

"No need," Dreyfuss said, predictably. "I will see if the Silver Prince is available."

As Dreyfuss left, the Homunculus shook his head at the ridiculously childish names the club required. Eventually, Dreyfuss re-emerged with another man in tow. Blacke was about fifty years old, of medium build and serious demeanor; hints of gray decorated his temples, and his beard was trimmed in a contemporary style. "I am Blacke," he said as he entered. "Who are you?"

"Fotheringay," the Homunculus answered.

"Your real name, please," Blacke said. "There is no Fotheringay in this group."

"True enough, but I do not have a name. I have an appellation I use, however, and you may have heard it outside of these walls. Dr. Cuba."

Dreyfuss and Blacke froze; they knew the name well and had never expected it to be said out loud within the walls of their secret club, much less admitted to by someone standing in it.

"Dr. Cuba is dead," Blacke said after a moment's hesitation. "Killed in America, the papers say."

"And yet I stand before you, apparently with breath in me yet," the Homunculus said, maintaining authority through absolute confidence.

The men remained frozen until the greater coward, Dreyfuss, fled. "I'll leave you to it, then, Blacke," he said, scurrying towards a curtain that led to a back room.

"I'm sure I don't need to tell you not to call the police, Mr. Dreyfuss," the Homunculus said, calling after the man.

"What do you want with me?" Blacke asked nervously.

"Just information. Something straightforward, in fact."

Blacke was shaking, the color bleaching from his skin. "What information could I possibly have?"

"Relax, Mr. Blacke. I have no intention of killing you. Some of the crimes attributed to me in the newspapers are exaggerations," he said, raising a hand to calm the man. "But only some."

Blacke was not calmed.

"You were the secretary to Israel Regardie, were you not?" the Homunculus asked.

"Yes, for a short time," Blacke answered. "While he was at the Stella Matutina and for a time after that."

The Stella Matutina was an occult offshoot of the Order of the Golden Dawn. However, it was deemed a fraud by Regardie, who had studied under the Golden Dawn's original co-founder, MacGregor Mathers. In much the same way that the members of the Enochian Queen were play-acting at being occult chess players, those in Stella Matutina had been play-acting as prominent occultists. The only good to come of the Stella Matutina was the book Regardie wrote on their rites, which allowed insight into the older rites of the Golden Dawn itself.

"During that time, a man named Henrik Broda was a member of the Stella Matutina," The Homunculus said. "He was a Rabbi, but one with occult interests."

"I remember Broda, yes," Blacke admitted. "He was not particularly remarkable. But as you likely know, Mr. Regardie is Jewish and maintains connections with that community. Especially Jews with an interest in the occult, such as himself."

"I need you to tell me where Broda may be living now. I suspect he moved to Prague, and more recently, Germany. He likely maintained some correspondence with someone in the Stella Matutina, perhaps with Mr. Regardie himself. Tell me what you know, and I will leave, and you may continue to pretend to play chess and drink Scotch for the rest of your days."

Blacke's eyes darted nervously as he tried to remember something. Anything. "Umm, yes ... he ... I think there was a telegram. Perhaps a year ago, maybe less. From Germany, not Czechoslovakia. Yes, from Germany."

The Homunculus's gaze bore into Blacke's. "Do you have it?"

"No, Mr. Regardie would have discarded it. But I think I can remember the name of the city he sent it from. Let me think ... this was some time ago. Kirchdorf, I think."

"Kirchdorf am Inn, near the Austrian border?" the Homunculus asked.

"I think so, yes. The telegram was about some ritual or another," Blacke said. "Raising of the dead or some such nonsense."

The Homunculus held up his hand. "The content of his discussions is irrelevant. I need merely to find the man."

Blacke shivered slightly. "It's all I know of Broda's whereabouts. There were no other communications from him after that."

The Homunculus turned to walk out of the salon and back down the entry hallway. "It is sufficient. I leave you in peace."

Blacke remained frozen but called after his strange guest. "Are ... are you really Dr. Cuba?"

Blacke did not receive an answer.

Thumann did not want to be in Berlin. It was here that the Nazis took his Hilda from him, to return her only to heaven, and not to him.

Perhaps he *was* a Golem. Maybe he should embrace this role and spend the rest of his days hunting hidden Nazis, punishing them for what they did to his Hilda and for the ruination of his life, and frightening small children with his thundering steps. Perhaps if he died with the blood of a hundred murderous Nazis on his hands, he could finally sleep.

But he was Inspector Thumann, not Nazi Hunter Thumann. He was a cop, a flatfoot. His days of soldiering were long gone, his ability to chase things and run about was fading. He could only do what he had forever done: police work. This would have to suffice.

And, he realized, perhaps stopping this Dr. Cuba business could prevent a new movement, worse than the Nazis.

The Lady Petra—Thumann was skeptical she was truly a "lady"—had been helpful, and happily, the spot she had pointed to on the map was in the American occupation zone. The American government had, for the moment, taken a positive view of the nascent Interpol, and Thumann's papers would be generally well-received at any US-manned checkpoint. Thumann also enjoyed a small amount of celebrity in the US since the Dr. Cuba business. There would undoubtedly be less friction in this zone than there might have been had they been forced to poke around the French or British or, God help them, the Russian zone.

Once more, Thumann and his co-inspector would find themselves checking into a hotel and meeting in a lobby to discuss their next moves. Once again, Thumann would sleep on a slim mattress and brush his teeth over an alien sink. Once again, he would be reminded that he no longer shared a home with Hilda and had become a soulless nomad.

Checked in and unpacked, Thumann and Ximena met again in the lobby for an early dinner. This particular hotel had no dining room, so they walked across the street to a restaurant that was open for business, but simultaneously undergoing restoration. Half of the place was brand new and gleaming, but only a few feet away, the other half was still missing a roof. Ironically, the restaurant was called Das Eichendach, or "The Oaken Roof."

A waiter approached. As expected, he treated Ximenawith dismissive haughtiness. Thumann, meanwhile, did not notice; he was, again, distracted.

"Wine, sir?" the waiter asked.

"Gewürztraminer, if you have it," Thumann told the waiter.

"We do not, sir. We do have an Alsace Riesling," the waiter responded. "But German, not French."

Thumann snorted. "Fine." As the waiter left, he turned to his companion. "To find this devil here will be a task. With the Lady Petra's help, we have at least narrowed our search area. But nevertheless, this will still be like finding a needle in a haystack, if the haystack were buried in a cave."

Ximena shook her head. "We must draw him out."

"Exactly right," Thumann said, pointing a finger at Ximena. "If this is a trap, and the old spider crone really wanted us in Berlin, we need to turn the tables. We need to set our own trap. Traps within traps, but at least one of them will be ours."

A look of consideration crossed Ximena's face. "We make ourselves the bait?"

"Or," Thumann said, turning his finger around so it pointed at himself, "at least make me the bait. We will leak to the local newspapers that the famous Inspector Thumann is in the area searching for this Dr. Cuba gang. That may be enough to bring the devil out of hiding to confront me. If my name doesn't do it, the name 'Dr. Cuba' will certainly work." Thumann sat back in his chair.

The waiter brought the bottle of Riesling to the table and uncorked it. He poured two glasses and promised to return with menus for today's dinner offerings.

"Too sweet," Thumann grunted, after sipping the wine. "Too damn sweet. If I wanted a damned Auslese, I would have asked for it."

"You like a drier Riesling, I know," Ximena said. "What do they call it? Kabinett?" Thumann realized she was learning her mentor's taste in wine.

"We go to the newspaper tonight, after dinner," Thumann said, his nose still wrinkled from the oversweet wine. "Perhaps I will agree to a radio interview. We must move quickly."

"We must not cause a panic, however, Inspector," Ximena added. "If Berlin thinks Dr. Cuba is back, that could put pressure on the local authorities to investigate, and that would push him further underground."

Thumann shook his head. "I met that red-fingered devil. I looked him in the eye and spoke with him. He will want to meet me. I know it. Besides, the local authorities are too busy trying to rebuild Berlin. They don't have the police force here to investigate crimes, they are too busy re-bricking the police stations and hiring new recruits."

Ximena scrunched her brow. "Inspector, did that old woman have a red finger?" she asked.

"I did not see one," Thumann said, "but everything happened so fast. I cannot be sure."

"I wonder if it is a reliable way to spot them," Ximena pondered.

"Probably not," Thumann surmised, sipping his wine again. "Nothing is predictable about these creatures, except their sense of superiority. We must remember that and use it."

The Professor was no longer allowed to leave the safehouse after his fake arrest by the Homunculus's operatives. He was now guarded day and night, and errand boys would run to buy him supplies or anything else he needed, such as beer. He could get as drunk as he liked, but only in his room.

The Professor was not happy about this arrangement.

"Where is your superior?" he demanded. "I want to speak to him immediately. This Dr. Cuba or whatever he calls himself!"

Standing before him was the head of the deceased Doktor's security operations in Germany. Brentley was a Brit, a tall and stocky man with a bald head and long beard; he never smiled, and was not smiling this time, either. "No," Brentley said curtly.

The Professor stamped his foot like a schoolboy. "I demand to see him! I am not to be kept as a prisoner here!"

Brentley simply raised an eyebrow at him. "You've proven

you can't leave the safehouse without drawing attention to yourself. That means whoever is trying to kill you will have an easier time of it. Frankly, that would please me just fine; I'd have less work to do. I don't like babysitting. But I have my orders."

"I don't give a damn about your orders!" the Professor shouted, poking a finger in Brentley's refrigerator-sized chest.

Brentley grabbed the finger and twisted. "You are a sick man," Brentley said as the Professor cried out in pain. "I don't know what women did to you to make you hate them, nor why you can't seem to keep your mouth shut about them and avoid starting fights in bars. I had a wife and daughter once, and I can see you have a sickness. I should probably shoot you myself and be done with it. But the boss needs you for something, so I'll keep you alive until he gets back. If that means I have to chain your fat sausage leg to the bed, I will do it. Now, shut up and do whatever work you've been ordered to do. Do I make myself clear?"

The Professor nodded, unable to speak as his finger was twisted back on itself.

He glared at Brentley, realizing the man was like this *because* of his wife and daughter. They did this to him, the Professor thought. As far as he was concerned, women ruined everything they touched. They were bitches, all of them. But the Professor would make proper women. Good women. Not whores.

Chapter 14: The Two of Swords

Thumann returned, alone, to his room. He was exhausted, both physically and emotionally. For the past day, he had been trying his best to remain unaffected by the atmosphere of Berlin and the memories that the city rained down upon him. In front of Ximena, Thumann knew he had to remain Thumann; he could not be anything but the clomping, determined German inspector.

So much of it was an act, however. So much of Thumann's behavior during the car ride from Stuttgart, during the dinner at the Oaken Roof, was pretense. He was sure Ximena noticed his skills were off, ever so slightly, but she likely did not realize how much energy Thumann was expending trying to keep himself together.

Now, alone in the room, he let go. A combination of rage and grief flooded him. It did not matter how many years passed; now, nearly a decade later, he had not forgotten Hilda. He could not stop imagining what they must have done to her in Dachau. He could not stop replaying her horrors in his head. It would not stop.

Thumann fell to his knees, and his fists, clenched into mighty hammers, pounded the bed. His face turned red, then his neck, then his arms. He wanted to scream.

After a few moments of rage, he calmed. He remembered there was peace to be had after all. There was a way to bring himself back to a time when he was not tortured with these thoughts, these flashbacks.

Thumann reached under the mattress and pulled out the pistol; he had brought it with him to Germany.

One bullet in the chamber. It was enough.

He placed the gun on the bed and sat in the chair. The chair was close enough that the gun was in arm's reach. He let his breathing fall to a shallow rhythm and let his pulse slow.

There was a peace to be had, if he had the strength to take it. Thumann had sat in this position, with this pistol, many times before, in his apartment in France. He quietly wondered if, this time, here in Germany, he would have the courage to do what came next.

"Inspector Heiner Thumann, I believe you wanted to speak with me." Thumann jumped out of his chair and turned.

The Homunculus stood at the open door of Thumann's hotel room, his head reaching the top of the doorway exactly. Thumann was not entirely clear how the door had opened itself. His hand instinctively reached for his jacket pocket to produce his brass knuckles before he realized his jacket was slung over the chair at the opposite side of the room.

"I'm not here to hurt you, Inspector," the Homunculus said. "But you clearly went through some effort to summon me, allowing yourself to be named in the local press, so here I am."

Thumann lowered his hands and sat back down in his chair. He would not give this devil the benefit of sensing any fear in him. "Come on in, then," Thumann said gruffly.

The Homunculus entered, standing tall over Thumann. As always, he wore a black overcoat, black suit, black gloves, and black fedora with a red hatband. He slowly took off his gloves to reveal his bright red forefinger. "Just in case, for some reason, you think I am an impostor," he said.

"You may sit," Thumann said, indicating the chair across from him.

The Homunculus loosened his coat, removed it, and placed it neatly on Thumann's bed. As he sat, he nodded towards the gun. "By the looks of it, if I wanted you dead, I simply might not have shown up at all."

Thumann glanced at his gun with a frown, wondering how the devil knew who it had been meant for. Shaking his head, Thumann dismissed it as a simple guess.

"I was cleaning it, nothing more," Thumann said, though he admitted he did not sound convincing. "But never mind that, you are correct. I did summon you, and here you are."

Thumann clearly wanted to assert dominance, as if he were pulling the Homunculus's strings. The Homunculus shrugged; the ultimate sign of dominance was not caring about it in the least. "I hope this will be a friendly visit. I assume you have questions that you want answered."

"You and your gang attacked that poor girl from Stuttgart. Are you resorting to common crimes now?"

The Homunculus's face remained stoic. "I don't know anything about that, but I would hope you want to discuss something more important."

"Well, then," Thuman said, moving on; he did not believe him, but could press this devil on that point some other time. "Dr. Cuba. I want to talk about Dr. Cuba." He pulled out his pipe and pouch of tobacco, thinking it would demonstrate that his guard was lowered.

"Dr. Cuba is dead. You saw it. Your assistant saw it. Sunk to the bottom of a lake, sprayed in gold. Fitting, actually."

"A bit on-the-nose, if you ask me," Thumann snorted, lighting his pipe.

"Destiny can seem that way, for those who believe in it," the Homunculus countered. "But yes, I understand the question. If Dr. Cuba died at the Homestake Mine in South Dakota, why is he still very much alive in the criminal underground? And the newspaper headlines?"

"Exactly," Thumann said. "I think you're profiting from your ... your ... your 'brother,' is it? From his network."

"My Brother-Son, to be accurate," the Homunculus said.

Thumann had no idea what that meant, but he elected to stick to his line of questioning. "You've adopted the name 'Dr. Cuba.' Back in South Dakota, you said I could refer to you by that name. You said you didn't have one of your own."

"True."

"So, you have restarted his criminal enterprise? You are responsible for the latest crimes in Germany, France, and around the world?"

The Homunculus crossed his legs, resting his arms on the armrests. "The press attributes everything to me now. The vast majority of these crimes are simple post-war contractions. Thugs, criminals, rapists of the most ordinary stock. Not my people, not my organization."

"You work in the shadows. That is why you had to stop your brother."

"Correct," the Homunculus said. "He had become a risk. I wanted to help him, but, as you saw, he refused."

"You said you wanted to *fix* him," Thumann said. "What did you mean?"

"For the answer to that, you will have to open yourself up to believing things you never thought possible," the Homunculus said.

"Just tell me," Thumann said impatiently, blowing smoke at his guest.

"As Blavatsky probably alerted you by now, I am a Homunculus. I was born—well, *grown*, in fact—in 1870, along with two others."

"The Doktor in Germany, the Fantôme in France," Thumann said.

The Homunculus nodded. "Very good. Yes, they are my Brother-Brothers. I advanced my creator's formula and created an updated batch of homunculus masses in 1928. None survived, except for the one who adopted the name Dr. Cuba. For this reason, I refer to him as my Brother-Son."

"You're all marked with a red finger," Thumann said calmly. "I noticed that on both of you."

"It's a means of uniquely identifying each of us."

"It's good to know that your kind will be limited to ten, then," Thumann smirked.

The Homunculus pointed a finger at his feet, as if to say, *"Not necessarily."*

"So, your Brother-Son was defective somehow?" Thumann asked.

"Yes. He was not grown under proper laboratory conditions, but grew on his own instead. I am not entirely clear how. Nevertheless, he developed various defects, including an obsession with an obscure religious cult. He believed he could raise ancient gods by injecting pure gold deep into the earth, and they would grant him godhood. That was why he raided so many gold depots and vaults, and why he was running that equipment in South Dakota. In short, he was mad and had to be stopped."

Thumann put his pipe down. "But you and your brothers, the two in Germany and France, had your own criminal organizations. These predate that of Dr. Cuba."

"Correct. And they still operate."

"So, you and I were only on the same side by chance," Thumann said plainly. "Dr. Cuba may be dead, but I am now tasked with shutting down your remaining operations. These vampire murders and Golem attacks, for example."

"Those are not our operations," the Homunculus said. "We are *still* on the same side. I mean to stop these other two homunculi just as I sought to stop Dr. Cuba."

"Two?" Thumann asked.

"The Golem and the old crone," the Homunculus said. "Or hadn't you pieced that together yet?"

Thumann remained silent, not wanting to reveal anything to this devil.

"A notebook containing my Father-Father's formula and some equipment descriptions was stolen, copied, and sold at a bookstore right here in Berlin. At least two men purchased a copy each. A rabbi named Henrik Broda has one copy, and with it, he created the Golem creature. His methods are of interest to me, since he appears to have combined our homunculus formula with ancient kabbalistic mystical practices."

"You mean the occult?" Thumann asked. "That may be too

much to swallow, even if I accept the rest of what you are saying."

"Not the occult, per se," the Homunculus responded. "If I were to guess, Rabbi Broda found a way to take a homunculus birth-mass and insert it, somehow, into a body molded by him, thus animating it. I am as interested as you are in finding out just how, exactly, Broda accomplished this. I'd like you to help me in this."

Thumann frowned at that. "Help you?"

"Yes. Rabbi Broda was last seen in Kirchdorf am Inn, near the eastern border of Germany. I'd like you to use your skills to find his current whereabouts."

"And why would I do that?" Thumann asked. He was not usually in the business of helping criminals.

"Because if Broda has a formula to make one golem, he can make more. And you've seen how much chaos just one can cause."

Thumann thought for a moment. "Why don't you go to Kirchdorf, then?" he asked.

"I'm occupied with the crone. You see, a professor named Jakob ten Brinken purchased the second copy of the notebook and created a female homunculus, but he added some flourishes that have proven to be dangerous." The Homunculus grew introspective for a moment. "I think, but cannot prove just yet, that the hag is his homunculus. The Professor grew her as a beautiful young thing, but something has gone wrong."

"So she would be your Brother-Sister, then," Thumann said.

"I hadn't really thought of it until now."

"Then, both are defective. The Golem has gone mad and is killing randomly, and the hag is draining people's blood to stay alive," Thumann summarized, attempting to appear that he had the whole picture.

He did not.

"Wrong, Inspector. They may be defective, but they are not mad. The Golem was told to take revenge on the Nazis and defend the Jewish people. He is carrying out that order within the limited capacity of his brain, or whatever mechanism drives his body. The hag is attempting to kill the Professor, out of revenge for having abused her. For now, I have him under my protection. But neither of these homunculi is killing indiscriminately. Both have their motivations."

Thumann straightened in his seat. "You have this Professor?"

"I do. In a safehouse. He is well guarded."

"I'd like to speak to him," Thumann said. "He would be crucial to my investigation."

"I'll consider it, Thumann. Later."

Thumann had not expected the creature to hand over the Professor for questioning; he likely knew too much about the Dr. Cuba organization to allow him to blab to an Interpol inspector. But he had to ask.

"If I find this Rabbi Broda, you will want him, too, then?" Thumann asked.

"Ideally, yes," the Homunculus answered. "But it is more important that the golem problem is contained. Obviously, you won't be in a position to give him to me, I'm sure."

Thumann puffed his pipe.

"We both need this spread of homunculi to stop, although for different reasons," the Homunculus continued. "At this point, you really should just come work for me, Thumann. You are essentially doing that already, just without the benefit of having me pay you for it."

"Don't be confused, sir, you and I are enemies, and I will bring you and your brothers to justice," Thumann said, brushing off the devil's attempt at temptation. "If I'm right, you and your brothers are responsible for shifting entire economies, possibly enflaming social unrest, and even provoking war. I could arrest you now and possibly end the Dr. Cuba organization in one move. Why would you possibly tell me all this now?"

"In the short term, Inspector, we share the same goals," the Homunculus said. "Neither of us wants to see the homunculi run loose. My brothers are no longer a factor. The Doktor and the Fantôme were killed. I am here in Germany to find out who killed them, and why. I assume it was the hag, but I cannot be sure. The only other homunculus that I know is the Golem, and he's not subtle enough to have killed my brothers."

"That you know of," Thumann repeated. "Perhaps more copies of this notebook were sold."

The Homunculus stood, once again towering over the seated Thumann. "We should hope there are no more copies, no more homunculi. That is why we must work together, as we did in South Dakota. It will prove more useful, I'm sure, than being at each other's throats."

"And after? What is your grand plan for Dr. Cuba? What will I do with you then?"

The Homunculus pointed at an invisible spot in the air in front of Thumann. "You've found the limit of my transparency for today. I have no intention of telling you my larger aims. But, yes, we will be on opposite sides when that time comes. Let us enjoy the fact that, for now, that is not the case. And," he added, "there's something else."

Thumann stood now, nearly matching his guest's height. "What?" he asked.

"When this is over, I may have a great gift for you."

"A bribe?" Thumann said, his forehead creasing in consternation. "Please don't be so obvious."

"Not a bribe. A *gift*. Something my Brother-Son had prepared for you. Originally, it was an insurance policy. I thought it crude and boorish, and now I see it's something you need. But if I were to give it to you now, you'd lose your focus. No, we should wait until this is over, and I can give it to you then."

Thumann leveled a long look at him, wondering what this devil was on about. What could this creature possibly have for him?

The Homunculus gathered his coat. As he did, he picked up Thumann's gun from the bed and aimed it at Thumann's chest. Thumann froze, though his heart began to race in fear. The Homunculus paused, and then turned the gun around, handing it to Thumann by the barrel.

"You see? You're not ready to die, after all. And we're all friends here," the Homunculus said.

Thumann took the gun and pocketed it. The Homunculus turned and headed for the door.

"Do me a favor, Thumann," he said.

"What?" Thumann asked with a growl.

"Don't kill yourself. The Nazis win if you kill yourself." With that, the Homunculus turned and headed out of Thumann's room, down to the lobby, through the front door, and out onto the streets.

As he left Thumann to his thoughts, the Homunculus did not notice the creeping spider of a woman crawling across the rooftops above him, watching.

Getting into the car, he told Belknap to take him back to the safehouse. Belknap did just that and, to the best of his knowledge, drove in a manner that should have prevented them from being followed. He kept his eyes on the rear and side-view mirrors, looking for headlights that might be pursuing him. He checked each intersection, traffic light, and construction zone for signs of an ambush. He randomized his route, circling back, turning, pushing forward, doubling back, all to keep any pursuer confused. Belknap had been driving this way for over a decade, and he had no reason to believe he had suddenly lost his ability to keep his passenger safe and hidden.

Belknap's expertise, however, had not prepared him for the possibility that he might be being followed from above.

Had anyone from the street been looking up, they might

have seen a shadowed figure with silver hair and hunched back leaping from roof to roof, clambering over bombed-out structures, always just one block behind Belknap's car. But it was dark, very dark, and even if someone had looked up, they would have only caught a quick flash of a wild, jumping crab-woman scurrying against a dim, crescent moon behind her.

Belknap's car disappeared down a side alley that appeared to have no exit, but the crone could see it had made a sharp left turn into a hidden garage door. Her inhuman speed made it easy for her to drop down and scurry under the door before it closed. Looking around, she found no guards at the upper end of the ramp. Slowly she crept downward to the next level, and then further down to a second; this is where the underground car park had been constructed. There were no guards here, either, but there were men milling about, working on a handful of the ten or so vehicles parked there. A few were just cleaning and polishing the cars, while others were performing engine maintenance. If anyone had stumbled upon the hidden door and secret ramp, they would have only found an innocent-looking parking garage filled with entirely uninteresting cars. Nothing suspicious at all.

From a dark corner, she watched as Belknap's car pulled to a halt and the tall, black-clad Homunculus stepped out. He strode towards an elevator door while Belknap remained with the car, chatting with the other men in the garage. For much of the garage's length, she could remain hidden by passing behind the vehicles, along the dark wall. But if she were to reach the elevator and follow her prey down even further into the bowels of this safehouse, she would have to cross into visible light.

So, the homunculus hag did the only thing she could do, given the circumstances. She killed all the men.

Leaping silently to the garage's ceiling, the crone hurried along the pipes until she was above the first man, then dropped down, landing with almost total silence, and snapped his neck before he even realized anyone was near him. The man made an audible gurgling noise, however, raising the attention of another mechanic nearby.

"Hey!" the second man shouted, just before he, too, had his neck broken. It was enough to alert all the men.

The crone jumped to the next man, instantly thrusting his head into the window of a nearby car and pushing down to slice his throat on the broken glass.

Shots rang out, echoing through the cement garage, but they could not hit the jumping, scrambling creature. Within another thirty seconds, two more men were killed, left spurting blood on the floor.

Only four men remained, Belknap among them. Belknap pulled a pistol from his pocket but did not try to aim it at their assailant. Instead, he ran towards a phone near the elevator door. By the time he reached it, two more of his fellows were dead, one impaled on his own shotgun.

"Attacker in parking garage!" Belknap barked into the phone. "Send more —"

Belknap never finished his sentence. He was struck sideways with the now-dead body of the only other remaining mechanic. The hag lifted the body of the mechanic like a doll, bringing it down to smash onto Belknap. She repeated this move, over and over, flinging the mechanic's body upward and then swinging it back down, until Belknap and the mechanic were both essentially pulp.

The hag saw the elevator had already begun to descend, no doubt to collect more reinforcements, forced open the elevator shaft doors, and threw herself down, landing on the roof of the elevator car. When the car came to rest, the crone could hear the door open and men dash in, unaware their opponent was merely above them. The hag quietly climbed off the roof and into the space between the car and the elevator shaft's interior wall. Conforming her body like an octopus, she was able to straighten herself flat, so as the elevator began to rise again, it passed her without any harm.

With the elevator car now ascending above her, the crone stepped across the gap and forced open the shaft door. She found herself inside the safehouse proper, in what appeared to be some sort of locker room for the homunculus's henchmen. For the moment, it was empty — all of the men were headed up to the garage, allowing her to proceed further into the underground complex.

Listening for any sign of approaching enemies, she made her way silently forward, finding a hallway with various offices and meeting rooms, all empty. She moved ahead further until she heard men ahead of her. Ducking into an office, the men ran past her, each carrying a shotgun or rifle. Once they passed, she emerged once more and pressed on.

The elevator buttons had indicated she was on the only other floor apart from the garage; Professor ten Brinken would be here, on this floor, somewhere. She continued to search, only ducking into the shadows one more time, as another group of men rushed past, ready to join their fellows.

The hag next found herself in a large oval room, sterile and clean, much of it lined with stainless steel. Three odd, coffin-sized chambers, standing upright with a glass viewing port near the top and connected with tubes and wires, lined one wall. The hag looked at them curiously. These did not look like the Professor's devices — the "injector-incubators," he called them — but were similar. The hag assumed these were also used to birth or repair homunculi.

"The iron maidens," a voice said behind her. She snapped around.

The Homunculus.

"We use them to revive," he said, walking towards her casually. He slowly removed his coat, readying himself for the fight that would ensue. "You're welcome to try one, if you like. I'd have to seal you up in it, however, and I cannot guarantee I would let you out again."

The hag hissed and leaped, but this time the Homunculus

was ready. He snapped his body to one side, turning slightly, offering her nothing but his left shoulder. She grabbed him, but he pulled her off of him immediately and flung her into the air, towards a side wall, where she struck the cold steel wall with tremendous force.

The crone was unaffected. She quickly rose up again and leaped once more. This time, the Homunculus picked up a metal table and blocked her in mid-air. She clung to the table, and the black-clad devil flung it downward, smashing her into the steel floor. Red blood, though not quite human blood, splattered against the floor and walls. It was viscous and shimmering with a slick of what looked like engine oil.

The hag hissed again, then struck the Homunculus from below, knocking his legs out from under him. He fell back and, despite his own speed, could not move away before the screaming beast was on top of him, pounding his body with clawed fists. Despite her petite frame, each blow was the equivalent of ten men, and the Homunculus could barely catch his breath.

Finally seeing an opportunity, the Homunculus timed a return blow in between those of his opponent, knocking her slightly sideways. It was all he needed to right himself and kick her body away, sending it scattering across the floor into one of the iron maidens. The force dented the copper-lined chamber, and a tube snapped, sending a spit of gasoline into the air and onto the floor. The hag struggled to get up now, her body slipping on the gasoline, giving the Homunculus yet another advantage.

He strode over to her, grabbing an electrical cable from the wall and yanking it free. Blue sparks shot from the exposed wire. He held it towards the hag, intent on electrocuting her.

But, once again, the Homunculus underestimated his opponent, perhaps because she was just a second-generation, female version of his superior, first-generation self. The hag slipped to one side and brought her legs around with great force, once again knocking the Homunculus to the ground. This time, she did not rain down blows upon him but grabbed the exposed electrical wire and shoved it downward, into the gasoline. It sparked and ignited, setting the Homunculus on fire.

The hag leaped away from the blaze as the Homunculus kicked and rolled, trying to put the fire out. The movements only made things worse, as the gasoline splashed onto more of his clothing, spreading the fire over his body rather than extinguishing it. He did not scream, but his movements were desperate, flailing, and entirely ineffective.

Not waiting to see if he'd either die or put out the fire, the hag ran from the room. She didn't come here for the Homunculus, after all. She did not have to look far; right outside the doorway of the strange laboratory stood Professor ten Brinken, having come to see what the noise was about. Upon seeing the hag, he froze, his eyes wide.

"Who are you?" he demanded. "Get back!" The threat was meaningless, as the Professor was unarmed.

The crone crept closer.

"Who are you?" he demanded again. "What do you want?"

"I want you, Professor," she hissed, her cragged skin pulling against her pearl white teeth. "I've come to retrieve you."

With another burst of lightning-like speed, the hag jumped forward, grabbing the Professor and throwing him over her hunched shoulder as if he were nothing more than a blanket. She headed down the hallway, back towards the locker room and elevator, still smelling the burning fire from inside the lab.

The Professor struggled and kicked, but to no avail; the hag's grip was too firm. The air rushed past him as she ran at impossible speed through the facility. The men were now piling out of the elevator, having returned from the parking garage and the dead bodies of their colleagues. As they saw the hag, they aimed their weapons, until one man shouted, "Wait! Don't shoot!"

The crone froze, realizing how she would escape this after all. She flipped the Professor's fat, weak body until it was in front of her; a human shield. "Yes," she hissed. "Your superior wants this man alive. You dare not shoot."

She was right. The men knew that the Homunculus had wanted the Professor kept alive at all costs, for some reason, and they could not risk killing him here.

"Let her go," one of the men said. "If the boss wants, we can track her down and get him back later." The men lowered their weapons.

The hag, still holding the struggling Professor, moved towards the elevator. "No! Don't let her take me!" he screamed in a panic.

The crone slipped into the elevator and closed the door. She felt it begin to rise, but only about midway to the next floor, when it stopped. The men below had used the elevator car as a trap and cut the power to the elevator.

The Professor laughed nervously. "You're trapped, bitch! You can't escape. You have to let me go!"

Ignoring him, she threw him over her shoulder again and held him in place with her left arm, as if he were strapped in a steel band. With her free hand, she punched into the side wall of the elevator car, smashing it open. Still holding the Professor, she climbed out onto the top of the car with her free hand. The Professor continued to kick, with little effect, as the crone grabbed the elevator cables and, using her feet and free hand, ascended the cable like an acrobat at a circus show. The Professor closed his eyes tightly, sure they would soon fall back down to their doom.

They did not. The crone successfully scaled the remaining height of the shaft. When they reached garage level, she gripped the cables with her legs and ripped the door from the shaft with her free hand, revealing the garage.

Within just another minute, the homunculus hag had jumped into the garage and fled the safehouse with her victim, the Professor, on her shoulder.

Chapter 15: The Iron Maiden

Alraune was beautiful, of course. Not quite the innocent, silvery wisp of a girl like Petra, but beautiful in an entirely different way. Her hair was auburn, medium length, and framed a slightly round face with plump lips and an elegant nose. Her figure was curved, with dimensions of such perfection that it would seem she had been designed, not born.

Which is exactly what she had been. She was beautiful because the Professor enjoyed abusing beauty. Alraune was perfect in every way, except that upon her birth, she immediately hated Jakob ten Brinken.

Now she stood over him, smiling. The Professor often told Alraune to smile, but the smile he now faced was not the kind of expression he sought. Not at all.

"Wake up, Professor," Alraune said. "Do wake up."

The Professor was most certainly awake — and terrified. He was tied down to a metal slab that leaned against a wall in a dark room. The room was so dark that the Professor had no idea how big it was; the slight echo that accompanied Alraune's voice suggested it was large. A warehouse, he thought.

"Alraune," he rasped. He was exhausted from his abduction by the hag and dehydrated. "You hired the hag to kidnap me! What do you want with me?"

Alraune paced slightly, her figure only partly visible in the darkness. "A reunion, I suppose?" she asked, as if questioning herself. "Or is all this just another result of your programming?"

"What do you mean?" the Professor asked, barely getting the words out past his throat. He needed water.

"You built me to be dependent on you, to need you. Perhaps I could only remain away from you for so long before a chemical instinct rose up and forced me to seek a reunion." She stopped to glare at him, the promise of death in her gaze. "Do you think it is that, Professor?"

He did not.

"Do you intend on killing me?" the Professor asked. "I remember you screamed something to that effect when you left me."

Alraune stopped pacing. "I was emotional," she said calmly. "You had just finished burning me, remember. And, of course, you know we women get emotional under such circumstances."

The Professor recognized none of her sarcasm. "I was teaching you," he said. "You needed to learn."

"Of course, Professor. I was a very uneducated young girl. I was not aware of the ways of the world." The Professor nodded in agreement, as much as he could, as he lay tied to a slab. "For instance, that time you severed my foot because the milkman looked me in the eye. I could not have known such a thing was forbidden, but you taught me."

"You regenerated. I always made sure you regenerated," the Professor said. He was not pleading; he was stating what he thought should have been obvious, unaware it was not helping his situation.

Alraune paced again. "Thank goodness for your laboratory! Of course, I — as a woman — saw it only as a torture chamber. I suppose I could not possibly hope to understand the underlying science of it all."

"No, you could not," the Professor said, without a quantum of irony. She was mocking him, and he remained stubbornly ignorant of it.

"I recall a time you burned me with a cigar simply for looking out the window," Alraune said.

"You were mine," the Professor protested. "You were not for anyone else, whether through a doorway or a window. But your nature led you astray."

"My nature?" Alraune asked.

"Even if I created you, you were still sufficiently infected by natural female aspects. As pure as you were when your birth-mass emerged, you soon gravitated towards your natural state. A whore."

When she did not respond, the Professor continued. It was not that he was unconcerned for how his words were being interpreted; no, it was that he did not imagine that the woman standing before him could possibly disagree with him. He may have felt it impossible that she *could* even fully understand him. "You were my first, but you will not be my last. I will continue to pursue my work and create the perfect woman. I don't care how many attempts are necessary. I will succeed. At least you can revel in your small part in this great effort. You were a failure, but a necessary failure. The next set of masses will create women without the inclination towards filth. They will be innocent, compliant. Loyal. Obedient."

Alraune remained silent and still.

"I can only improve my efforts by making more masses. You are imperfect and will remain that way. Your nature is fixed. You cannot change. The next generation will be better. Perfect in every way."

Finally, she spoke. "I am afraid you are no longer in your laboratory. Let's consider this damp, dark place as *my* laboratory. And here, it will be me doing the experiments."

There was a pop, and then a crack. Subtle, like someone cracking their knuckles. Nearly inaudible. But then, more came. Cracks, snapping, twigs breaking, bones crunching.

The Professor felt nervous once more, unsure of what he was hearing.

"I am not fixed, Professor," Alraune said, her voice odd. "Most certainly not."

The Homunculus survived the hag's attack, but only barely. Had he not been mere feet away from a functioning iron maiden when it occurred, he would most certainly be dead.

Instead, he was able to shed his burning clothes and stumble, naked, into one of the maidens and begin his rejuvenation.

His body was charred, but would be healed with the proper amount of time. Allowing his brain to set aside the sensation of pain — a skill the Homunculus and his Brother-Brothers had learned decades ago — he slowed his breathing as the maiden's door closed and the steel injectors shot into his abdomen, flooding him with the chemical mix.

Given the damage done to his body, the Homunculus knew this would require at least twenty-four hours inside the maiden, if not more.

With much time to think, the Homunculus resigned himself to one disturbing fact: these two new quasi-homunculi — the Golem and the hag — were stronger than him. In both confrontations, the Homunculus had been badly beaten. The hag was decidedly more agile and faster. The Golem was a being of brute strength, likely as strong as three or four first-generation homunculi.

Each must have a weakness, though. For sure, the hag could be damaged by fire, as he was. Any final defeat would require some trap involving immolation to ensure she was permanently destroyed; that could be planned for. The Golem, however, would not succumb to fire, not with his birth-mass encased in stone. Something entirely different would need to be planned to destroy the bastard beast.

There was a way both could be destroyed at once, if they could be lured into the exact location at the same time. The Father-Father had learned, decades ago, that his homunculi creations were sensitive to radio waves at the extremely high frequency band of thirty gigahertz or higher. Such waves were not in everyday use, and producing them generally exceeded the current capabilities of the day, so they presented little risk to the Homunculus himself in daily life. But could this type of radio wave be fashioned into a weapon? Indeed, there existed laboratories with equipment capable of generating such signals, but certainly none in post-war Stuttgart. But none of this was practical; there would be no way to work this weakness into any effort to stop the two quasi-homunculi.

There were still so many questions unanswered. The Homunculus still did not know who killed his brothers, the Doktor and the Fantôme. Was this hag somehow responsible, as he suspected? She had the physical strength to do it, yes, but the two brothers were poisoned, not attacked. Was she also capable of more subtle techniques? If so, what was her motivation? She seemed fixated on getting her revenge with the Professor, not with the Dr. Cuba organization. But few others knew of the sustaining solution used by the homunculi, much less how to taint it into a toxic mix. The hag certainly would have known this.

That led him to Rabbi Henrik Broda, the one other person the Homunculus knew had knowledge of the solution. That man might be able to answer many of his questions, but there had been no evidence of his movements since entering Germany, many months ago.

Professor ten Brinken was a key to much of this, and now even he was gone. Where had the hag taken him? Would she kill him? Keep him alive as a souvenir? What was her true intention?

The Homunculus's visit to Thumann's hotel served two purposes: to potentially align their efforts in this drama, but also to sniff out what Thumann might know that he, the Homunculus, did not. The Homunculus left that meeting thinking Thumann knew precious little. The great German Brain was slipping, no doubt falling into a well of depression due to memories of his wife. Thumann might not be the help the Homunculus had hoped for.

In the relative silence of the iron maiden, surrounded only by the light clicking of pumps and switches, the Homunculus could once again hear the voice of the Golem in his head. Faint, but present.

Kill me.

The bastard beast was still alive, of course, but he had gone silent for a time. Whatever he was up to, he was thinking again, but distant, given the weakness of the telepathic signal.

Could he, the Homunculus, strengthen it?

If this were a signal of the mind, then perhaps the mind could attune it. Telepathic waves were likely a wave like any other, with a frequency and a wavelength. Like a shortwave receiver tuning into an AM signal, could he tune his brain to fix on the Golem's signal?

The Homunculus exhaled, a slow breath; a technique he had learned many years ago from monks in Bhutan. His muscles faded away, and his skeleton followed. Soon, he no longer had a body, or none that he could sense, anyway. All focus fell upon his breath.

In.

Kill me.

Out.

Kill me.

Next, he allowed the breath itself to fade. As he had done in the cargo hold of the *Eustis*, he stopped his heart and his breathing. This technique enabled his meditation abilities to surpass those of any Bhutanese monk, who would constantly be distracted in some small way by the required rising and falling of their lungs. The Homunculus could kill himself, for a short time, and end such distractions entirely for the duration, even longer in the iron maiden, which kept him functionally alive.

Kill me.

The words were clearer now, for sure. Not louder, but *clearer*. As if, with a shortwave radio, one was simply adjusting the squelch, but not necessarily increasing the gain.

If he could receive a signal, perhaps he could send one.

Listen to me.

Nothing. No response, but still, something had happened. The faint voice of the Golem had fallen silent. He was certain the beast had heard him.

Listen to me.

Again, there was silence—until a response came, loud and

distinct, without telepathic static or propagation. Pure, crystal clear, and undistorted.

Healed, have you, Homunculus?

But it was not the Golem, the Homunculus realized in shock.

It was the hag.

Thumann and Ximena found themselves waiting at the Berlin airport, a place they had not expected to be. A telegram had arrived from Thumann's Brühl, forwarded from his hotel back in Stuttgart, and Thumann was not happy about its contents.

INSP. THUMANN

= YARD SENDING SHRAKE. MEET HIM AT BERLIN AIRPORT. GIVE HIM COMPLETE COOPERATION. =

BRÜHL

For some reason, Scotland Yard's Inspector Andrew Shrake was added to this case. Brühl, always eager to ensure the world's police agencies knew the ICPO was open to their assistance, was bending over backwards to accommodate the Yard. Or did Brühl have some other motive? Thumann was not sure.

Shrake was Scotland Yard's "Golden Boy," although at age forty-five, he was hardly a boy. He was, however, astonishingly handsome: fit, blonde with silver streaks, with a short-cut beard and armed with the voice of a radio news announcer. Shrake was also an American, one of the only Yanks at the Yard. He had reportedly had a promising career in the US and relocated to London to chase a woman, or so the story went. The Yard snatched him up quickly, not wanting his abilities to go to waste. Shrake was a favorite son, yes, but he did not lack skill when it came to policing, and he had caught his fair share of villains over the years.

There was very little wrong with Andrew Shrake, which drove Thumann absolutely mad.

Now, Thumann's irritation was palpable. He did not enjoy the idea of babysitting Shrake.

"I met with the Homunculus," he told Ximena, hoping to distract himself from his thoughts. "Our bait worked, and he found me at my hotel."

Ximena looked shocked. "Did you arrest him?"

"No," Thumann said matter-of-factly. "For now, I need to leave him on the loose. But we made an arrangement, of sorts."

"An arrangement? Of what sort?"

Thumann nodded. "Once again, dear miss, we find ourselves working on the same side as this villain. But only for now. He is after the same thing we are, and we may yet help each other."

"How?" Ximena asked.

"Later," Thumann said, pointing ahead of him. "The Golden Boy is upon us."

Inspector Shrake approached Thumann and Ximena with a calm and confident stride. He was dressed smartly, in a Saville Row suit and elegant wool overcoat; his blonde hair was fitted with some chemical or another to keep it in place, and his blue eyes reflected the sun shining in from the large airport terminal window. With such features, he fit right into both pre-war and post-war Germany, although on which side was anyone's guess.

"Inspector Thumann," Shrake said, offering a hand. "It's good to see you again."

"Inspector Shrake," Thumann said, shaking his former colleague's hand. "You know my co-inspector, Ximena Torres Orellana."

Shrake gently shook Ximena's hand. "How do you like your new post at ... what do they call it?" Shrake asked.

"ICPO," Ximena answered with a neutral expression.

"Although the name 'Interpol' seems to be catching on." Thumann might not have had any love for the Golden Boy, but Ximena's opinion of Shrake was a complete cipher to him, at least.

"Co-inspector Torres will be joining you on your trip back to Stuttgart. We have word that another vampire killing occurred, and the crime scene is fresh."

"You're not coming with us to Stuttgart, then, Heiner?" Shrake asked.

"No," Thumann said, and Ximena's gaze snapped to him in surprise. "I head to Kirchdorf am Inn."

"Inspector?" Ximena asked. This was news to her, as well.

Thumann raised a hand to stop her from asking anything else. It was clear he did not want to speak in front of their guest. "I'll join you as soon as I finish my investigation there. Meanwhile, Miss Ximena can update you on our progress so far."

"Perhaps I should follow you to Kirchdorf, Heiner?" Shrake asked. "For the sake of efficiency?" It was clear he felt he was being sidelined by following Ximena.

"No, I will only be there briefly and can rejoin you immediately after. Kirchdorf is only a four or five-hour drive from Stuttgart." Thumann seemed fixed on this decision, and Shrake knew not to press.

"Very well, Heiner. I will take good care of your co-inspector," Shrake promised.

Silently, Ximena recoiled. It was more likely that she would end up taking care of him, she thought.

"Thank you, Inspector Shrake," Thumann said, then turned to Ximena. "Dear miss, a moment." Thumann nodded slightly to the side, indicating they should step away from Shrake. "Just a moment, you understand," Thumann said to Shrake, as if reassuring him. The Golden Boy nodded, as if giving Thumann permission to speak privately with his own colleague.

Thumann brought Ximena out of earshot.

"Inspector?" Ximena asked, raising her eyebrows in concern. "Shrake will want to know why we're not including him."

"To blazes with Shrake," Thumann said gruffly. "We have a job to do, and babysitting the Yard's Yank isn't one of them."

"Should I give him all the details of our investigation to date, then?" Ximena asked. "Are we keeping anything from him?"

Thumann shook his head. "No, go ahead and tell him everything. He won't believe it anyway. He will report back to the Yard that Thumann has lost his mind, the Yard will report this back to Brühl, and Interpol will call us back to Paris. By then, I hope to have this wrapped up."

"And your meeting with the black-coated creature?" Ximena asked.

"You were correct. The Doktor and the Fantôme were also homunculi. The tall devil says he does not know who killed them. But his allegiance to his own kind is blinding him from the obvious."

Ximena was lost. "I don't know what you are saying, Inspector."

"The *hag* killed his brothers. She killed the Doktor and the Fantôme, and now wants to kill the Homunculus himself. But he is too arrogant about his position as a first-generation homunculus. He thinks he can repair them or, if he can't, he will destroy them. He can't imagine a scenario where these later generations might want to kill *his* generation."

"Did you tell him this?" Ximena asked.

"Of course not. He wants me to help track down the creator of the Golem, a Rabbi Broda. While I do that, these villains appear to be fighting each other. We need merely to wait, watch, and see who is left standing. They could destroy the entire Dr. Cuba organization for us."

"So, this was a trap after all."

Nodding his head once, Thumann said, "It was a trap for him, not for me. The hag probably followed me, hoping the

Homunculus would meet me."

"And he fell into it."

"He did. We can't know for sure what will happen next on that side of the board, but we still have pieces to put together on our side.

"To see how the Golem fits in with the other two," Ximena said.

Thumann nodded once more. "I have to go to Kirchdorf to find the Rabbi who created him. The Golem itself is just a beast running wild. The Homunculus wants to try to repair him, as he had tried with the original Dr. Cuba. Failing that, he will likely try to destroy him. It certainly looks as if all these creatures are headed for a collision, with humanity in the middle of their battle."

"A fight for supremacy?" Ximena asked.

"It may be more complicated than that. Each piece may have its own motivations. For now, we can't know them all."

"What can I do, then?" Ximena asked.

"Let us use Shrake to our advantage. Be more aggressive in your pursuit of these vampire murders, find out more about the hag. See if she really is responsible for those killings. If she reappears, it won't hurt to have the Yank on your side."

Military police had reported a body strung up upside down and without blood. The newest in the rash of "vampire murders." Ximena hired a private car to take her and Shrake to the site, but the car had not arrived. Ximena could not be sure why, but she assumed it was likely due to the influx of military personnel into Berlin and the relative lack of private cars to drive them around.

Shrake, for his part, showed patience, at least. As they stood on a Berlin street corner waiting, he asked to be brought up to date on the facts of the case. Ximena efficiently revealed what Thumann knew so far, weaving a tale of homunculi grown in laboratories, a crazed megalomaniac sinking like a golden idol in a lake in South

Dakota, and plots to invoke a change in the global order through a massive criminal enterprise of untold power and secrecy.

To Ximena's surprise, Shrake showed little disbelief and appeared to take everything she told him at face value. More than once, Ximena wondered if none of this was new to Shrake.

With the facts out of the way, Shrake shifted the subject entirely. "You seem to have done well here, Miss Ximena," he said, pronouncing her name wrong. "I'm surprised."

Ximena looked up, her gaze narrowing on him. "And why?" she asked.

"You've learned quickly under Thumann," Shrake said, not answering her question.

"Why is that a surprise, Inspector Shrake?" she asked. She was not going to let his comment sit unanswered. "Why should I not learn quickly?"

Shrake bit into his bread. "You replaced Bernard Gentleman. He had worked at the Yard for years before he was assigned as Thumann's, well, 'handler.' Gentleman had a distinguished career already established for himself. You, quite frankly, did not."

"Gentleman was not a police officer," Ximena corrected. "He was an office assistant with a focus on bookkeeping. He had as much police training when he joined Thumann as I did."

"He had years at the Yard, however, and years of experience working with the police. With their procedures, their methods, even if he never had a badge." Shrake looked at her shrewdly. "You were ... what? A translator? From Chile?"

"That's right," Ximena acknowledged without a shred of shame. She was proud of her background. "And one that speaks multiple languages, opening up new capabilities for the Yard."

"I'm afraid you might not be familiar with the map of Europe, miss. Scotland Yard is in the United Kingdom, and one of our neighbors is Spain. They invented the Spanish language in Spain. Spain is certainly closer than Chile."

Ximena did not flinch. "But the Dr. Cuba investigation was not in Spain, was it? It was in the Americas. South and Central America, to be exact. I do recall there being an entire ocean between Spain and the 'New World,' as they call it. And more to the point, the two languages are not identical."

Shrake huffed; he was becoming irritated. Ximena was forcing him to say what he truly meant.

"You're a *woman*, miss," Shrake said bluntly.

"I can confirm that, yes," Ximena said, holding her ground.

"Police work is men's work. It's upsetting to morale to have you waltz into Scotland Yard as though you are some sort of equal to a man like Gentleman, who worked for years to get into his position."

Ximena raised an eyebrow, not backing down one bit. "Then, thankfully, you need not worry any longer since I am not at Scotland Yard," she countered.

"The ICPO chose you over more qualified men at the Yard and police agencies around the world. That's worse."

"Inspector Thumann asked me to join him," Ximena said.

"Of course. And were it not for a man, you would not have all the opportunities you have now. You're riding Thumann's coattails. You should remember that."

"It seems, Inspector Shrake, your problem is not with women at all, but the men who help them," Ximena said casually, remaining unaffected by his ire. "You should take your argument to Inspector Thumann, then, and see how far it gets you."

Shrake smiled at that, which only raised Ximena's suspicions. The man was clearly up to something, trying to provoke her.

A car drove up, breaking the tension, but a military car, not their hired car. A young, fresh-faced soldier emerged.

"Inspector Torres?" he asked.

Ximena nodded.

"Priority telegram."

Ximena took the telegram, and her eyes widened.

"What is it?" Shrake asked.

"Another drained body found, but not in Stuttgart," she said.

"Where?" Shrake asked.

"Here in Berlin. But this one was more gruesome. The man was strung up and forced to drink his own blood."

Ximena and Shrake stood silently for a moment. Shrake spoke first. "I'll go. We will need to split up now. Let me check on this Berlin killing while you investigate the scene in Stuttgart. We can all regroup there by the time Thumann returns from Kirchdorf."

Ximena nodded. She was not thrilled about letting Shrake go to Berlin alone, but he was right. They simply could not be in two places at once.

The soldier turned to Ximena. "I can make this car available to you if you need a ride to Stuttgart, miss," he said.

"Thank you," Ximena said. "But my associate will also need a car," she added, indicating Shrake.

Shrake shook his head. "It's fine. I have a car here in Berlin I can use."

Chapter 16: The Five Shields

Shrake had a reason for not offering Ximena his own car, which had already been flown into Berlin. He was not quite ready to let her see the Scarlet Phantom.

Shrake walked many blocks away from where he had left Ximena, wanting to be sure that, should she come back for some reason, she would not find him. He ducked into a hotel, asked to use their telephone, and made a quick call. Within fifteen minutes, the car arrived.

The sleek Rolls-Royce Scarlet Phantom growled like a panther in heat. Only ten such models were made in all the world, and Shrake had his unit repainted in solid, dull black. The original bright red suggested by Rolls would not do for his line of work.

The car looked like a more modern version of Rolls-Royce's Silver Wraith, but with a lower overall height and longer frame. A rear passenger compartment could fit four, with two leather bench seats facing each other, the front driver compartment separated by an ornate teak wall with gold flourishes. The interior was strewn with luxurious details, including a bar, reading lights, and a small bookshelf under the seats. The extended rear of the vehicle hid Shrake's specific modifications: a heavy mass of electronic equipment that added a host of capabilities not available in any other car on the road.

The driver, a short Russian named Vulgar Annie, emerged to open the rear door for Shrake. He bore a stern face and crisp driver's uniform. The Five Shields gave the short Russian his name because calling him "Anatoly from the Volga" was too complicated. It was also intentionally ironic: despite his rough appearance, Vulgar Annie was so professional he'd be loath to tell a dirty joke even at gunpoint.

Ignoring the gawks of the passersby, Shrake quickly dipped into the car and allowed the Russian to shut the door.

Inside, one such piece of special electronic equipment was

a powerful radio system that included a scrambler. With the door shut and no one able to see inside, Shrake opened a hidden latch behind an opal-lined clock mounted in the teak wall. A small shelf folded down, revealing a transceiver/receiver set. As his driver slid onto the highway towards Berlin, Shrake wound a small crank to power the radio — it was kept isolated from the car's battery system by intent — and spoke into the transceiver.

"Goro, confirm," he said.

A voice crackled from a speaker on the receiver unit. "I'm here, Shrake," the man said.

"I'm heading to you, meet me at the Royal Swan bar on Südendstraße. I assume you know of the murder there?"

"Correct. We have been monitoring it and can update you when you arrive. Did the Phantom arrive intact?"

"She's running as smoothly as ever. Thanks for having it shipped."

"You owe Mozart a tenner, remember," the voice crackled.

"Mozart owes *me*. I'll remind the bastard when I see him," Shrake said, smiling. "Shrake over and out."

Shrake put the transceiver away and folded back the hidden panel. He adjusted the hands on the opal clock slightly to ensure the time was accurate versus his wristwatch, then settled in for the long drive.

Now, Inspector Shrake had time to think about his meeting with Thumann's co-inspector, Ximena Torres Orellana. Yes, he *was* testing her. Her employment at Scotland Yard had been brief, since she was so quickly hustled away to Interpol with her giant German mentor. But in the time that she worked at the Yard, she had managed to attract attention, and Shrake was watching. Much of that attention was of the more uncivilized kind — smug male Yard bureaucrats and seasoned police officers turning their noses at the idea of a young Latina woman daring to share the same space as them. But a few in London had also begun to recognize her abilities. It might have shocked both Thumann and Ximena to know that

Andrew Shrake was one of the latter.

Shrake was handsome, yes. He was fit, bronzed, and rugged. He was intelligent, and he was successful. This brought two forms of attention down on him, as well: fame and jealousy. Thumann, having come from the murder beat on the dirty streets of pre-war Berlin, had little interest in fame and those who won it, and so he let his jealousy of Shrake blind him to the man's actual abilities. In many ways, Shrake had earned the fame he enjoyed in the States and at the Yard, but Thumann would never admit it. Thumann simply resented Shrake.

And so, Shrake recognized that he and this young woman from Chile shared a common burden: both were underestimated and shunned by at least some of their colleagues. Yes, Shrake had overcome much of this and was left only with a few disgruntled critics like Thumann, while Ximena was nearly drowning in them. But Shrake could see the future that awaited Ximena once she, too, overcame the jealousies and suspicions of her critics. He was convinced she could become a great detective, but, for now, simply lacked the proper training and years of experience. All of this would come.

Ironically, Shrake knew that Thumann was the perfect mentor for Ximena and would hasten Ximena's rise through the profession. Shrake did not return Thumann's resentment in kind; he respected the giant German, both for his technical competence as a police inspector and for having survived great personal tragedy.

Shrake also had a secret that no one in Scotland Yard knew. He was the founder of the Five Shields, a tiny group that worked to protect world democracies in complete secrecy. Shrake named it so based on the creation myth of the third-century faith, Manichaeism. In their myth, the universe was initially divided into Light and Darkness. A great Father ruled the world of Light, accompanied by five "Shekhinas," individual expressions of pure light. They fought against the Darkness by sending a human, called the Original Man, to battle along with five shields. These shields were the manifestation of the five Shekhinas on the human plane. Shrake thought "Five Shields" an apt name for a secret organization meant to protect humanity.

So secret was the Five Shields organization that only Shrake and his four companions knew of its existence, yet together they had foiled assassination plots, coups, and terrorist attacks on four continents. Shrake's role at Scotland Yard was merely to ensure the Five Shields had access to crucial information that could help them uncover such plots and take action to stop them. The other four members — Goro, Puño, Motley, and Mozart — each held similar positions with access to crucial information.

The Five Shields was never inclined to take up criminal cases, no matter how sophisticated or widespread the criminal organizations might be. The group left such matters to bodies like Scotland Yard and instead focused only on political crises. As a result, Shrake and his colleagues had ignored the crime waves of the Doktor, the Fantôme, and Dr. Cuba, treating them as nonpolitical. It was only after Thumann had begun to string together the crimes and suggest that the Dr. Cuba entities may have been working to shift global powers that Shrake took notice. The higher-ups at Scotland Yard ignored Thumann's mumblings, and Shrake was aware that Brühl at ICPO was also dismissing them.

Thumann, according to Ximena, had pieced together an odd theory, taken from snippets of information given to him by the "devil" Homunculus, what he overheard in South Dakota, and by a henchman named "Doctor Vines" during an encounter in Florida. Ximena herself listened as Vines lectured them on Dr. Cuba's theories of Crime as a force of nature, and Thumann had come to believe the homunculi were plotting some larger-scale, decades-long, perhaps even centuries-long, plan to shift world power.

His logic was compelling, and Shrake, unlike Thumann's superiors, had not discounted it. But Shrake could not reveal his interest in Thumann's theories, lest he expose the mission of the Five Shields. So Shrake continued to pretend to be aloof, haughty, and disinterested, all while paying careful attention to Thumann and his investigations.

This was what prompted Shrake to join Thumann in Germany. He could easily pretend that Scotland Yard needed someone to take up the Dr. Cuba case on its behalf, now that Thumann was working solely for Interpol, so getting the assignment was the easy part. Getting Thumann to trust Shrake, however, was proving difficult. Thumann had traveled alone to Kirchdorf am Inn, and Shrake was handed off to be escorted by Ximena. Shrake had wanted to be at Thumann's side the next time he encountered a homunculus.

Still, he was learning much of the case history and facts from Ximena, as fantastic as they seemed to be. Homunculi grown in labs, clay Golems come to life, a madman trying to raise ancient "Sunken Gods" by injecting gold into the earth's core ... it would sound insane to anyone.

Shrake knew it was not insane. He'd already begun to piece together decades of crimes conducted by these strange "homunculi" that Thumann spoke of and saw the patterns. Or, more accurately, Mozart of the Five Shields had seen them; Mozart was the genius of the group and could flush out conspiracies before anyone else.

So, Shrake was here now, in Stuttgart, to see spot connections between these strange occurrences and the re-emerging Dr. Cuba organization. In just twenty-four hours with Ximena, he was doing just that.

No. Shrake had not been provoking Ximena. In truth, he was not testing her, either.

He was *auditioning* her.

Fully healed, the Homunculus pressed the necessary switch, and the iron maiden opened, hissing as the interior vacuum sucked air from the laboratory. The steel needles extracted themselves from his torso as the door opened, and the Homunculus stepped out onto the cold floor. The lab was still partly destroyed from the hag's attack; it could be cleaned later.

In addition to healing his body, the time inside the maiden proved useful. The Homunculus overheard a few details in his experiments with telepathing. From the Golem, the Homunculus gleaned that the beast was revived and readying for another attack in Stuttgart. The clay creature continued to operate from the Rabbi's programming and had identified more Nazis in hiding.

From the crone, however, he learned less, but not nothing. Her telepathic signal had originally been clearer than the Golem's, but now it was more heavily polluted with propagation after their first contact. Was she scrambling her own signal because the Homunculus might be listening in? It was a possibility; she did know the Homunculus had discovered his hidden power.

Whether she was scrambling or not, the Homunculus nevertheless learned that the hag was also on the move to Stuttgart. He suspected that she, too, was going to confront the Golem. Apart from internal voices, the Homunculus was now able to pick up emotions in the telepathy signal. The Golem was filled with rage, confusion, loss, and shame; the beast wanted desperately to die, but suffered under the knowledge that it might never. The hag was filled only with hate, and that hate was clearly aimed at the various homunculi and their creators. If this were true, then it was even more likely that the hag *had* killed the Doktor and the Fantôme.

But why would Alraune want to destroy the homunculi if she, herself, was one of them? Her wish to kill the Professor made sense; he had abused her mercilessly, treating her as a thing built only to please him. But did her self-loathing extend to her entire species? Was her burden so great that she wanted to wipe out *homo homunculus* entirely?

And with the Professor now stolen out from under his protection, the Homunculus no longer served a purpose for the hag, so he — and the Golem — were likely next. If they were all converging on Stuttgart, then that is where he, too, would go.

There was another matter, however. Deep inside the telepathic signal was the hag's voice, repeating one message.

COME TO ME.

COME TO ME.

The Homunculus could not be sure if she intended this for him or some other recipient. But he did feel a compulsion building in him. Was it curiosity? Or could the homunculi's telepathic abilities compel someone to follow a command?

He would go to Stuttgart to find out.

Shrake arrived precisely on time; Vulgar Annie was always punctual.

Outside the Royal Swan, Goro already stood waiting in a fine wool overcoat, stylish tailored suit, and a fedora that reflected the most recent taste of fashion from Tokyo's Ginza district. Had he been dressed poorly, questions might be asked of a Japanese man hanging around post-war Berlin, but a rich Japanese man would be given deference. Like each of the Five Shields, Goro would dress however his mission called for him; but he most definitely preferred to look smart.

Shrake stepped out of the black Scarlet Phantom, ignoring the looks the car inevitably earned him from passersby. Goro did not ignore them, however, and smirked. "You really should learn to travel without that beastly thing," Goro said, pointing to the car.

"And you should travel without that god-awful cologne," Shrake said, slapping his friend on the arm. "I could smell you all the way from Potsdam."

Goro adjusted his tie. "Then we'd best hurry, if the bachelors of Potsdam can smell me. It won't be long before they descend in numbers."

"Where's the body?" Shrake asked.

Goro pointed across the street and down about one block. "Warehouse. But this is an odd one. I've invoked our special powers to keep the locals out of it."

"Special powers?" Shrake asked. "Do we have those?"

"I made up some story about being sent from the Central Intelligence Group and reporting directly to Rear Admiral Souers. This area of Stiglitz is under American control, so for now, they bought my American accent."

"You do a good Yank, that's true. That ruse won't hold for long, though," Shrake said.

"No, but you're here now and can flash that Scotland Yard badge," Goro countered. "Trust me, we don't want the Americans walking around in there yet."

The two headed down the street as Vulgar Annie parked the Phantom in a less conspicuous side alley. Parts of this area of Berlin were heavily destroyed, while others appeared untouched. Such was the fickle effect of gravity on bombs.

Shrake and Goro entered the warehouse and were greeted by three other men already inspecting the site.

"What the hell?" Shrake said in surprise. "This seems a bit much."

All five of the Five Shields had gathered there. The squat, bulky Puño stood beside the elegantly dressed Black butler, Motley. The impossibly tall African, Mozart, completed the assembly.

"This may be worth our collective time," Mozart said, a crisp British accent covering over hints of both French and his mother tongue, Jula.

"It's never a great idea for all of us to be in one spot at a time," Shrake reminded them. Few knew of the Five Shields, but some of those who did would want them dead.

Motley sniffed in agreement. "The travel costs alone are absurd." He maintained the group's finances and often reminded them of this fact. "I'm not amused we had to fly that damned car of yours here, Shrake."

Goro directed Shrake further inside. The warehouse had

been repurposed, apparently over some time, to suit a particular need: the draining of human bodies. A series of overhead rails had been installed, with straps to hold a victim's feet, allowing the body to hang head-down. Below the railing, along the ground, were copper or brass collection vessels, each of which was then connected via a series of black rubber hoses. The hoses came together into a single, wound snake that led to a larger piece of equipment. This was a large metal chamber, box-like in shape, large enough to fit an average human inside, standing.

"Any idea what all this is?" Goro asked.

"Whatever it is, it's run by gasoline. Look," Puño said in a deep, gravelly rasp. He stood next to a fairly typical tank, with hoses that also ran into the large metal chamber.

"This is all very bizarre," Shrake said, taking it all in. "Also, sophisticated. Not shoddy, nor built haphazardly. Someone had the time and means to do this." He turned to Motley. "What would something like this cost?"

"I'd estimate a few thousand dollars before the necessary hand labor," he said. "Perhaps more."

"Built before the war?" Shrake asked.

"No," Motley said. "This equipment is too new for that. Likely during the war, perhaps only two or three years ago."

"It looks abandoned," Shrake noted. Other than for the strange chambers, the space was nearly entirely empty.

"It does," Goro agreed. "Except this fella is a more recent addition." He pointed to a body, still fresh, hanging upright, not facing downward. His body was held aloft with straps under the arms and waist, and there was no collection vessel beneath him. Instead, tubes were connected to needles inserted into his arms and ran back up into the man's mouth.

"Gruesome," Shrake said. Ximena had mentioned the victim had been force-fed his own blood, but seeing it in person was a horrifying thing even for Shrake.

"He would have died slowly," Motley said. "Somebody had

a grudge."

"Do we know who he was?" Shrake asked.

Goro nodded. "Whomever did this, they took care not to have this location found before now," Goro said. "But it seems now they wanted it found and, more importantly, they wanted us to know who the victim is." He reached into the jacket pocket of the dead man and pulled out a wallet. Goro handed it to Shrake. "His papers are intact."

Shrake took the wallet and removed the identification papers. "Jakob ten Brinken. Of course."

"Of course?" Goro asked.

"Thumann's assistant, Ximena—the one I told you about—she told me one of the homunculi is a female. She was created by this fellow here, Professor ten Brinken. He abused her, and she fled, but only to get herself healed enough to spend her days hunting him. He was on the run for a few years, supposedly, but it seems his creation caught up with him."

"Then, there's this," Motley said. He pointed to the Professor's left hand; the forefinger had been painted red.

"Another message," Shrake said.

"Meaning what?" Goro asked.

"Thumann claims these homunculi each have a red finger. It's some way of distinguishing them. The homunculus from America has a red forefinger," Shrake answered. "This scene wasn't left for the police to find, after all. It was left specifically for Dr. Cuba."

Motley sniffed. "All this supernatural hocus pocus, I don't like any of it."

"I thought you'd be used to it by now," Mozart said.

"Let's wait," Shrake said. "Thumann is smart and relentless. His assistant has talent and a keen mind. Together, they may resolve this for us."

"So, you will head back to Stuttgart?" Goro asked.

"Yes, to let Thumann know what's happened here," Shrake said. "As for you fellas, I suggest you disappear before anyone starts asking questions. Let the locals chalk this up to their 'vampire killer' headlines."

Petra heard male voices on the first floor, coming from Frau Jannings's parlor. The frau was not inclined to have visitors in her home, much less men. But the tone of the conversation seemed light, as if the frau knew these men.

Petra opened her door to listen, but could barely make out what they were saying; they were not whispering, but they were also trying not to be overheard. She crept towards the staircase, and then downward just a few steps, until she could make out bits of the conversation. From the clinking of cups, she knew Frau Jannings was serving the men tea.

Petra began to piece together portions of the conversation.

"... to the north ..."

"... Bremen and then further on?"

"... the ships won't wait forever ..."

Petra frowned. It was a plot, most certainly. These were men making plans, with the help of her elderly landlady. To what end, though?

Petra dared to drop down a few more steps. The door to the parlor was cracked, still blocking some of the sound, but she could make out more of the discussion now.

"The route is long. Through the English Channel, out to open sea. Then many days. Many days."

"The crew, they speak Spanish?"

"I presume. It flies under an Argentine flag."

"I cannot speak Spanish."

"You can learn once you get there. You will have to."

"This will not be easy."

"Better a difficult life than no life at all."

Petra had heard enough. She quietly snuck back upstairs, into her room, and closed the door.

Frau Jannings was helping Nazis flee to South America.

Chapter 17: The Buried Box

"We are here," Ximena's driver said. It had been an agonizing fifteen-hour drive to Stuttgart, primarily because of a long wait to refuel about midway from Berlin. Germany was still suffering fuel shortages, and Ximena had not realized how lucky she and Thumann had been so far with fuel. That changed with this trip.

The military driver was pleasant enough and filled the time asking Ximena many questions about South American culture, music, and food. He seemed genuinely thrilled to meet someone from another continent, and Ximena enjoyed talking with him.

Ximena wondered how Thumann was faring with his trip to Kirchdorf am Inn. For sure, he would need a few more hours than she had.

The car had pulled up to an address given to the driver by radio. As Ximena exited the vehicle, she saw she was now standing outside an old, bombed-out meatpacking plant. The building had no roof, and only three of its brick walls remained standing; the interior was a pile of rubble. It would appear an Allied bomb had made a direct hit.

Ximena was met by an American military police official who introduced himself as Corporal Williams; he had the face of a thirteen-year-old, but the voice and carriage of a far older man.

"I'm instructed to give you full cooperation in this matter," the corporal said. "Where is Inspector Thumann?"

Ximena extended her hand. "I am Inspector Thumann's co-inspector, Ximena Torres Orellana," she said, shaking Williams's hand. "Inspector Thumann was called away to another crime scene. Can you take me to where you found the body?"

"Three bodies," Williams corrected. "We found three."

"We only heard of one," Ximena said with a frown.

"I believe when we first notified Interpol, that was true. We found two more since then. The latest two are still strung up in there," Williams said. "It's not pleasant to look at, ma'am," he added.

"I will be fine," Ximena reassured. In reality, however, she was still getting accustomed to crime scenes; the work she had done with Thumann in the first Dr. Cuba case was mainly related to gold heists, not violent deaths. Since then, she had studied murders and related evidence, such as photos, but had not yet spent much time in the presence of cadavers. She steeled herself for what she was about to see, not about to telegraph any jitters in front of this corporal.

The two headed into the building, climbing over piles of brick and fallen wood supports. Inside, there was little evidence remaining of the original meatpacking operations. Nearly everything had been turned to black ash and debris. What must have once been overhead rails to carry cow carcasses through the plant were now crumpled and lay on the ground, like some sort of twisted trainyard pattern. There was no particular smell, however, as the stink of burning wood and ash had long since faded.

"Apparently, the killer used this spot more than once," Williams explained. "Through here, but watch your step." He pointed to a section that was still surrounded by a few half-standing walls, hiding whatever was inside. Someone could certainly use this spot for nefarious activities without being noticed.

"How were the bodies discovered?" Ximena asked.

"I believe the original report said some scavengers found them. Probably looking for copper or metal to trade," Williams answered.

They passed into the interior area, and Ximena gasped. There, hanging on a half-collapsed wall, were two bodies, strung upside down. Their color was inhuman, as if they were some sort of poorly made imitation of a human. They were pale gray, without a hint of color.

"Are you all right?" the corporal asked in concern.

"I am fine," Ximena said, pressing onward, cursing herself

for reacting in front of this man.

"Do you know who they were?" she asked.

"No," Williams answered. "They didn't have identification papers on them, and without a family around to identify the bodies, we may never find out."

Ximena pointed to the body on the left. "He was rich," she said. The corpse was well dressed, in what was likely a relatively new suit, despite some dirt now dusting the body. The man appeared to have been about forty-five, with dark hair that had flecks of gray. "There may be people looking for him."

"We notified our partner offices throughout Germany, so hopefully we will hear of something," Williams said.

"The second body," Ximena said, pointing to the corpse on the right, "is dressed entirely differently. Much poorer. These two were of different social statuses."

"Is that important?" Williams asked. He was an MP, not a criminal detective.

"It suggests the murderer isn't a typical serial killer, targeting a certain type of victim. It suggests the victims are chosen at random. Or perhaps as opportunity allows it. Where is the third body?"

"Back at HQ, on ice," Williams said. "But the condition is identical. No blood. If you look, there is some sort of puncture mark at the neck of each body. The murderer apparently hung them upside down and drained the blood into a bucket or some other container."

"All men?" Ximena asked.

"Yes ... yes, now that you mention it. None of the victims was female. Is that important?" the corporal asked.

"It might be," Ximena said, though she knew it was.

It *was* many hours later when Thumann reached Kirchdorf am Inn. As tiring as Ximena's trip to Stuttgart was, Thumann's trip was worse. He wished he had taken an aeroplane, but private flights were simply not available for anything but the most serious military missions.

The Inn River was beautiful, and as Thumann's car passed the uninhabited spaces between the small Bavarian towns of the region, he almost forgot that Germany had been at war. The water here flowed cleanly, briskly, and the banks of the river were green instead of gray. As they approached Kirchdorf proper, the land appeared essentially flat, dotted with trees and livestock farms. It was a tranquil scene.

Upon reaching Kirchdorf am Inn itself, there was likewise little evidence of any disaster or horror sinking its fangs into the small town. Unlike its namesake town in Austria, the German Kirchdorf had seen minimal wartime conflict and controversy and remained, apparently, peaceful.

Thumann knew that had Rabbi Broda been moving along the roads through Germany, not only as a Jew but as one transporting a giant clay monster, he would likely have kept to the side roads and slept in safe places. And, so, Thumann questioned the locals for the location of any Jewish ghettos or gathering areas for nomadic groups. For the first hour or so, Thumann received no firm answers, and a good number of dirty looks; some suspected this suited, fat German was seeking Jews for some nefarious reason, while others were conditioned to never answer any question about Jews, under any circumstances.

Finally, however, he was directed to the eastern edge of Kirchdorf, near Lake Waldsee. Here, he was told, he would find a motley spread of tents and wagons, where nomads would rest along the lakeside before moving further into Germany or into Austria. The locals called this *vergessenes feldlager,* or "forgotten field camp," and Thumann was told he could expect to find a mix of "Jews, refugees, and criminals" hiding in the fetid array of ratty lean-tos.

Within another fifteen minutes, Thumann's driver brought them through a field to the field camp; there was no missing it, as it was exactly how the locals had described. Fires were lit in both metal drums and makeshift firepits, and Thumann counted about fifty tents and simple shelters made of sticks and tarpaulins. A few horse-drawn wagons peppered the scenery, making the entire place look like it had been picked up from one hundred years ago and plopped down again in front of Thumann. The poverty and desperation here were indisputable; the people were a collection of the poor and the near-dead.

Thumann's driver pulled a pistol from his glove compartment. "This may be a dangerous place for someone with an automobile, sir," he told Thumann.

Thumann clasped the brass knuckles in his pocket. "I will be fine," he said, stepping out of the car and making his way across the muddy field towards the encampment. Immediately, he spotted the suspicious eyes scanning him. The people living here could never be sure who might be coming to cause them problems: military personnel, local police, or politicians wanting to clean up the countryside of its forgotten human detritus. Thumann could not fault them for their suspicion.

Positioning himself in the middle of the camp, Thumann stood tall and shouted. "I am Thumann. I am not a Nazi, but my wife was killed by them. She was sent to Dachau to die in a camp far worse than this one. Now I seek the Rabbi Broda to know how he may help me. Who here has seen this Rabbi?"

It was a gamble. The people here might not believe Thumann's story or, more likely, they might not care. But Thumann was left with few other options, and the clock was his enemy. Soon, he thought, Brühl would recall him to stop this investigation entirely.

There was a long period of silence; no one wanted to speak. Thumann stood his ground. To indicate he had no intention of leaving, he reached into his coat and withdrew his pipe. He lit it and waited still more.

"Broda is dead," someone said, from Thumann's right. He turned slowly to face the source of the voice and saw an old man, hunched and emaciated, standing over a fire made of logs and sticks.

Thumann walked towards the man, adopting a pace that telegraphed calm and patience. "Dead, you say?"

The old man nodded. "Killed by his beast," the man said.

"The savior of the Jews, you mean?" Thumann said.

The old man nodded again. "He could not control it."

Thumann stood in front of the man now. He saw him trying to cook a pot of water with a few crude potatoes thrown in. "What do you mean? Why would the Golem kill his creator?"

It was another calculated risk; by naming the "Golem" out loud, he risked terrifying the people in the camp. On the other hand, if they were largely Jews, as Thumann suspected, they might hold the beast in their hearts as their protector. He aimed to show reverence to the clay giant.

The old man kept his gaze downward, at his pot and potatoes. "The thing returned, bloodied. No doubt it had killed many of the evil scum. But the toll on its own soul was too great. The Rabbi had not counted on the beast having a godly morality of its own. It went mad."

"It killed Broda?" Thumann asked.

"It did. We found his body, smashed to bits. After that, the great beast disappeared. We have since heard it is elsewhere in Germany. Still defending us, but confused. Lost."

"Can you show me where Broda's body was found?" Thumann asked.

"There," the old man said, pointing to a small patch of trees near the outer edge of the encampment. "Rabbi Broda kept himself there, away from the rest of us. But always protecting us."

Thumann thanked the man and held open a palm with some Reichsmarks in it. "Are these worth anything here?" he asked, making it clear he knew his offer might be pointless in the underground economy of the discarded and destitute.

The man took the coins. "I can make use of them," he said.

Thumann tipped his hat at the man, turned, and headed towards the trees. He had suspected Broda was dead and would have been surprised to find out otherwise. Had Broda been alive, he would likely have been in Stuttgart, to direct the beast's activities. Was the old man correct, and the beast simply turned on his creator out of madness? Or was it simply a beast and nothing more, and killed the Rabbi much the way a circus lion might turn on its trainer?

Thumann turned to find the old man had followed him, watching from a distance.

The old man appeared to have told the truth. Thumann did find a small camp within the patch of trees, and the Golem's huge footprints were clearly visible. A tent had been strung up from a robe, tied between two trees, but the wind had since tossed it aside. In fact, much of the Rabbi's camp was tossed about, scattered, and covered in dirt. To Thumann's surprise, however, it had not been ransacked; apparently, the people within the *vergessenes feldlager* held the Rabbi in such regard that they kept his belongings untouched, even after his death. Thumann wondered how many Nazis the Golem had killed in this part of Bavaria to earn this reverence.

This reverence may have also explained the lack of Broda's body. There was no sign of blood at the campsite, but everything had been covered by dirt, and such signs would likely have been covered up long ago.

Thumann turned again to the old man. "Where is the body?" he asked. "Did the people bury him?"

"As required by the Law," the old man responded, referring to Jewish custom. Thumann realized the man was following him to ensure he did not disrupt the site.

"And the beast?" Thumann asked.

"Into the woods, and never returned," the old man said.

"Has anyone else come here?" Thumann asked. "From the outside, I mean. Strangers, but with bad intent?"

The old man shook his head. "You're the first stranger, I think. We would not let a non-Jew here."

Thumann was not sure what to do in response to that. Clearly, the people had assumed Thumann, himself, was Jewish, after announcing that his wife had died in Dachau. If he corrected the man now, he would be thrown out ... or worse.

He asked Hilda to forgive him for the deception. He was certain that if the people knew how much he loved her, they would forgive him, too.

Thumann crouched to examine the site a bit more closely. His eyes scanned the area, searching for something. He knew that the Rabbi had a thing of great value, which he would have hidden as well as he could. But where?

Thumann gently and reverently lifted some of the fallen fabrics and junk that lay strewn across the ground. He moved slowly, patiently, all while keeping the old man in the corner of his eye, to make sure he was not doing anything the man might view as desecrating. This might not be holy ground, but to the people of the *feldlager*, it was likely very close to it.

Slowly and deliberately, Thumann began passing his hand over the ground, clearing the top layer of dirt and clearing away the debris.

"What are you looking for?" the old man said.

"Something dangerous. Something we must not let anyone else have, or it would rain destruction down on this field camp, if not all of our people." It was not, technically, a lie; the old man might have interpreted "our people" as being the Jews, when in fact Thumann was referring to everyone in Germany and elsewhere.

Again, he hoped Hilda forgave him for the deception.

"There are no bombs here," the old man said.

"Not a bomb," Thumann said. "Something far more deadly. The Rabbi was keeping it safe. If we don't find it, everything he did will be for nothing."

The old man came closer now, crouched, and began to help. He, too, moved slowly and with reverence, patting his hands along the ground, unsure of what he was looking for. For many long minutes, perhaps half an hour, the two men gently searched the Rabbi's last resting place.

Then, Thumann heard a thud.

The old man's hand hit something solid in the dirt. Something wooden.

"A chest," the old man said. "Here."

Thumann crouch-walked to the spot and knelt. He helped the man uncover the small box and lift it ever so gently out of its hiding place. It was made of thick wood, about the size of a shoeshine kit, but not particularly heavy. It was kept closed with a single metal clasp, but without any lock. For sure, the Rabbi had little need for any stronger security when he had a Golem to defend him.

Thumann slowly unclasped the latch and flipped the box open. There, beneath some papers and old photos, was the notebook.

Petra steeled herself, inhaling deeply before tapping on Frau Jannings's door. This was going to be a very uncomfortable conversation.

The elderly German woman opened the door and smiled broadly at seeing her favorite lodger. "Fraulein Petra! You've come to visit me! I am so pleased." She opened the door fully, inviting Petra to cross the threshold into her parlor.

Petra stepped in, appearing nervous. "Do ... do you have tea?" she asked.

Frau Jannings's eyebrows lifted. "You never ask for tea, dear! I always invite you, but you never accept it. Whatever is the matter?" she asked. She indicated Petra should sit. The furniture was old, musty, and smelled of damp. It was, Petra knew, the best Jannings could manage in this economy.

She sat as Jannings moved into the kitchen to put a kettle on. She returned quickly, eager to know what was bothering her young, pretty lodger. "Are you well, dear? Did the inspector find your things and return them to you?" she asked, sitting next to Petra.

"No, he did not, I'm afraid. But it's fine. It was nothing valuable," Petra said.

"What is bothering you, then, dear?" Jannings asked.

"Please don't be cross with me, Frau Jannings," she pleaded.

"Never, dear girl!" Jannings replied, taking Petra's hands into her own.

"I overheard your conversation with those men, I'm afraid. And I daresay I understood the overall context." Petra stopped speaking, waiting for Jannings's reaction.

The old woman stiffened. Her face fell slack, the kindly, concerned look of an elderly landlady slowly dissolving and turning into the expression of a woman with a secret that she most certainly had not wanted to be revealed. She released Petra's hands and sat back a bit, putting a small amount of distance between them.

"And what was the context you think you understood?" Jannings asked stiffly.

Petra pushed on. "They were German officers, in hiding, and you are helping them escape to Argentina. As a result, I would guess that you are, yourself, either a Nazi Party member or a supporter of some kind."

Jannings's face remained stiff. "And tell me, girl," she said, no longer feigning kindness, "what will you do with this information?"

Petra inhaled slowly, choosing her words carefully. "Frau, you must understand, I have no intention of reporting you. I am not that kind of person. In fact, quite the opposite. I admire your bravery. It must be challenging living with such a burden, in these times."

Jannings remained stoic but continued to measure her young lodger's response.

"But this is irrelevant," Petra continued. "This is no longer about people reporting on each other, who is a Jew, who is a Nazi. Frau, you must understand, you are in another danger altogether!"

"What danger?" Jannings asked. "What danger is greater than war?"

Petra inhaled again. "The Golem, Frau. This creature is hunting Nazis and those helping to hide them. It's killed two dozen or more in Stuttgart alone, perhaps hundreds since it entered Germany. It will come here, to your house, for you. This is not something you can escape, Frau!"

Jannings' smile returned, the facade of the elderly, kind woman restored. "Dear Fraulein Petra, please don't worry. That dirty piece of clay won't bother with an old woman like me. Everything will be fine. Now let me get you that tea." Jannings stood and left for the kitchen.

Petra had accomplished what she intended: to warn her loving landlady of the coming danger. There was nothing more she could do, and she decided to quietly leave at that moment.

This was, without Petra's knowledge, a wise decision. When Frau Jannings returned from the kitchen, holding a loaded shotgun, Petra was already gone.

Chapter 18: The Black Pact

Thumann rejoined Ximena and Shrake as soon as he arrived back in Stuttgart. Not wanting to discuss their findings inside the hotel, lest anyone overhear, he suggested they stroll by a lake.

"I found nothing new at the murder scene in Stuttgart," Ximena admitted. "A few more bodies, strung up and drained. All men, as expected. But no clues as to the whereabouts of the old woman. No clear sign it was even her behind the murders."

"That's fine," Thumann said, puffing his pipe. The air was cold, and the lake was still; a few geese argued between themselves on the water's edge.

"I had more luck in Berlin," Shrake said. "The crime scene seemed laid out as a message for your Dr. Cuba friend. One body, that of Professor ten Brinken. Strung up, but this time forced to consume his own blood until he died."

"That's horrifying," Ximena gasped.

"She was carrying out her rage," Thumann said. "So, the crone was operating out of Berlin as well."

"That's why we didn't find a sign of her here," Ximena said.

"Ten Brinken's finger had been painted red," Shrake added. "A message for Dr. Cuba, we assume."

"Specifically, a warning," Thumann said with a nod. Then, Thumann paused. *We? Who is he talking about? Who was with him in Berlin?*

"Warning?" Shrake asked.

"The crone is killing off the homunculi, one by one," Thumann said, pulling his overcoat's collar up to chase the cold air from his neck. "She's warning Dr. Cuba that he is next."

"And what did you learn in Kirchdorf?" Shrake asked. "Did you find this Rabbi Broda?" Clearly, Ximena had brought him up to date on everything, as instructed.

"The Rabbi is dead. Killed by the Golem, the locals say. They insist the beast has gone mad and now operates without any control."

Shrake crossed his arms. "That's not good. The Rabbi might have been able to stop it."

"We have a breakthrough, however. I found the notebook that started all this mess," Thumann said. Both Ximena and Shrake looked at him in surprise, but Thumann held his hand up. "Before you ask, I have it hidden. I'm not quite sure what to do with it."

"You must not let anyone find it, Inspector," Ximena said. "With all this talk of building a master race, that notebook could well help someone do it."

"Indeed," Thumann said, nodding. "I may have to destroy it. I wasn't entirely sure it was real until I saw it with my own eyes."

"But you read it?" Shrake asked.

"I tried. I couldn't understand most of it, but I learned some important details about our homunculi adversaries. They are grown, as we thought, not born. The book provided the methods for creating them, in fact. They have unusual anatomical differences, too, the result of being grown from what are called 'birth-masses.' Their bones are not single, rigid forms, but instead complex structures of shell-like lattices. This explains how Dr. Cuba was able to alter his facial structure to change his appearance."

"Sweet Jesus," Shrake said. "Do they have any weaknesses?"

"A few. They don't sleep, apparently, so after a month or so, they have to regenerate. They take in a special mixture to regain their energy. They can also use this to heal injuries."

"Blood?" Ximena asked.

Thumann nodded again. "Blood and gasoline, if you can believe it. The preferred method is injection using complex devices that the notebook referred to as 'iron maidens.' But they can simply drink it, if they must."

"The scene in Berlin was fitted with equipment that seemed to fit that purpose. The bodies drained into a large metal chamber, which was also fed by a separate tank of gasoline," Shrake said.

"Her version of the iron maiden," Thumann said. "She would have learned how to build it from the Professor."

"And our black-coated homunculus must have done something similar on the *Eustis* to survive his sea journey," Ximena said.

Thumann scowled. "This makes them effectively immortal, so long as they have access to their cocktail. The devil said he was born in 1870."

"There's plenty of blood and gasoline in the world for them to use," Shrake said.

"I learned another important fact," Thumann said, stamping his feet a little. "Blast this cold, I need new socks. These homunculi also share the memories of their original creator, whom the notebook referred to as the 'progenitor.'"

"Share memories?" Shrake asked with a frown.

"They are born with all the memories of their creator," Thumann explained.

"That implies some psychic link between them," Ximena said.

Shrake resisted raising an eyebrow at Ximena's astute insight, though he thought it very clever.

"I suppose there is no way for us to tap into that psychic link?" Shrake asked.

"If Blavatsky were here, we could try," Thumann said, knowing Shrake likely recognized the old mystic's name. "And we don't have time to search for a psychic right now and experiment. But I may have found a way to stop this Golem, at least."

"How so?" Shrake asked.

"The Rabbi's notebook contained some handwritten notes added by Broda himself. These were related to how he modified the homunculus formula to animate the clay beast. A lot of it was mystical mumbo-jumbo, and I understood none of it. Tree of Life, alchemy, and all that. Even Tarot, I think. But it did indicate that he programmed the beast with two words. One word to animate it, and another word to shut it down."

"Aemaeth and maeth," Shrake said.

Thumann and Ximena both looked at him in surprise. "Those were the words, yes," Thumann acknowledged, begrudgingly. "How did you know that?"

"The ancient golem myth," Shrake said with a shrug. "It is said that the original golem was animated after its creator carved the word 'aemaeth' on the creature's forehead. It means 'God's truth,' but one could kill the beast by erasing the letter aleph and turning the word to 'maeth,' which means 'death.'"

Thumann huffed to himself at how well-read the son of a bitch was. Collecting himself, Thumann continued. "In this case, it was more like a hypnotic suggestion, whispered to the Golem rather than carved into it. If I am right, simply saying the word 'maeth' into the beast's ear should deprogram it. Immobilize it, perhaps even kill it outright."

"So, we need to find the Golem and then get close enough to whisper in its ear. That will not be easy," Shrake said.

Ximena disagreed. "There is a way," she said.

Thumann's eyebrows hiked up. "How, young miss?"

"Our problem is that we always come after one of the Golem's attacks happens. We need to be alerted as soon as he appears. To do that, we need a network of contacts throughout Stuttgart."

"The military police?" Shrake asked.

"No, another network," Ximena said confidently, sure her plan would work. "One with more eyes in the city than even the American Army."

"Dr. Cuba," Thumann surmised. "You mean we need Dr. Cuba."

The Homunculus received Thumann's invitation clearly

enough. It was a ham-fisted, blunt affair: Thumann gave a newspaper reporter a brief, exclusive interview, announcing he was back in Stuttgart and not only closing in on the vampire killings but that he was close to tying them to the Dr. Cuba organization. Thumann's information was surprisingly vapid, lacking any details, but the giant German had become a media focal point, so anything he said to the press would end up published. Thumann knew the Homunculus would recognize the article as an invitation for a second meeting.

And he did.

Just as he did not know his assignment to Stuttgart was no accident, Thumann could not have known his unusual adversary was already in the city, pursuing the meaning of the psychic messages now filling the telepathic signalways shared by the homunculi.

COME TO ME.

COME TO ME.

The Homunculus smiled, realizing the hag was likely summoning the Golem with as much finesse as Thumann had summoned him. None of this was necessary; there was an endgame to be met, and the Homunculus was eager to see this matter finished once and for all. If people wanted to use crude methods to do so, it was irrelevant.

As expected, Thumann was waiting in the restaurant of his hotel. The Homunculus stood outside, a towering black figure marked only by the pearl white skin of his face and the bright red hatband. He sent a bellboy to fetch Thumann and bring him out.

Thumann emerged but was not alone. With him, as usual, came his young assistant, but another man followed, as well. This fellow was muscular, well-dressed, and nearly, but not quite, the height of the Homunculus himself.

"Do I still call you Dr. Cuba?" Thumann asked. There would be no handshaking or back patting between them.

"That will do," the Homunculus said. "Although you'll have

to take the blame for reviving the name in the local press, Thumann."

"This is Dr. Cuba?" the muscular man said, shocked, his eyes darting over the Homunculus's intimidating form, looking for weaknesses and weapons. The man was clearly a professional; his posture gave him away.

"This man wants me dead," the Homunculus said, aiming a gloved finger at this new player on the board. "I hope he understands our temporary truce, Thumann."

"This is Shrake, from Scotland Yard," Thumann said, albeit clearly thrilled about having to do so.

"Shrake of the Five Shields?" the Homunculus asked, looking at the newcomer curiously. He could tell Thumann had no love for the man. There was a tension between them, which made him even more curious. "Interesting."

Shrake seemed taken aback, while Thumann and Ximena simply appeared confused. "What?" Thumann asked, looking between the two.

The Homunculus shook his head once. "Never mind. We all have our secrets." The Homunculus turned to Ximena. "And, yes, your mentor has his, too."

Thumann fumed. He did not want this devil revealing to Ximena the gun under his mattress. "Leave her out of this. We called you here for a reason."

"Yes, I'm curious as to what that is," the Homunculus said.

"We need your network," Ximena said, showing no fear of this menacing figure before her. "We need spotters in the city to alert us as soon as the Golem attacks. The military police are too slow. If your network is as good as you claim, you should have a thousand eyes on every corner."

The Homunculus regarded them for a long moment. Had they found a way to kill the Golem? If they had, he knew they would not admit it.

"My network is a faint shadow of what it was. I never

claimed it was much of anything. The press and…," he looked at Shrake, "…your team at Scotland Yard, well, they made the organization appear larger than it was. Now, with the death of my Brother-Son in the Americas, it is actually much smaller."

"You're lying," Shrake said. "We know you have acquired much of the original Dr. Cuba's equipment and organization. You are regrouping."

The Homunculus maintained his posture as fixed, not even granting Shrake a shrug. "That is your information. I have mine. The truth is, however, there are not enough 'spotters,' as you call them, in Stuttgart to help you."

"We have to reach the Golem!" Thumann insisted. "For now, the thing is killing Nazis. Eventually, it will run out and start killing innocents."

The Homunculus smiled. "There are always Nazis."

"Nevertheless, you can help us find it. Use your network. I know you can."

The Homunculus paused. In the brief silence, the sound of a few cars passing behind them rattled softly through the cold air. "You found the Rabbi's notebook," he said finally.

It was Thumann who remained immobile this time, not wanting to give anything away.

"So," the Homunculus said, his brain connecting information in wet silence, "the Rabbi is dead, then."

Thumann cursed internally. The devil was piecing everything together without Thumann even speaking.

The Homunculus allowed a thin smile. "You found the Rabbi's last camp, along with his notebook. And you read it, so now you know that homunculi share memories of the progenitor."

Thumann maintained silence, though the Homunculus was clearly piecing even more together.

"And you think we can also communicate telepathically, then," the Homunculus continued. "That's why you think I can help. You want me to call the Golem here, right now. Serve the beast up to you."

Thumann pulled out his pipe; it was another attempt to ensure the Homunculus knew he was not intimidated by his deductive skills. "It would certainly speed things up," he said.

"And you have figured out that the hag is killing the homunculi one by one, as well. So you'd like to simultaneously use me as bait to draw out the hag, so you can take shots at her."

"The thought had crossed my mind," Thumann said.

"Well done, Thumann. But she is not only killing the homunculi, she's also killing their creators," the black-clad devil said.

"We found the Professor dead in Berlin," Shrake admitted.

The Homunculus remained stoic. "A shame. He would have been useful. But as you see, she is wiping out the entire species before it can get an evolutionary foothold."

"Then you are next," Thumann said pointedly. "You are a homunculus and a creator of them. If she's keeping lists, you're on both of them."

"You're quite the man, Thumann," the Homunculus said after a moment. "It will be a shame when we have to fight each other." Shrake twitched. "Don't worry, Inspector Shrake. You'll get your chance, too."

"So, can you do this thing?" Thumann asked.

"I cannot. To be entirely honest, I've only recently discovered the psychic connection between homunculi. I cannot seem to issue commands to them."

"But," Ximena said, finally adding herself to the conversation, "you know where they are. You can sense it."

The Homunculus turned, eyeing Ximena with appreciation. "Thumann is training you well. You are smart. I've asked Thumann himself to come work for me, and he's refused. Perhaps you can make a better decision."

Shrake stepped up suddenly, putting himself slightly

between Ximena and the Homunculus. The Homunculus just smiled.

"Inspector Shrake, that is very chivalrous of you, but I daresay this woman doesn't need your protection. Nor yours, either, Thumann," the Homunculus said, addressing both men. "She will outlive you both."

"I wonder if I should just kill you now, and we can worry about these other two creatures later," Shrake said menacingly.

The Homunculus was not, however, menaced. "You won't be able to kill even one of us, never mind three. And you probably should have killed me years ago, when I was hampering the efforts of your little gang of self-appointed white knights. But then, you didn't even know I was doing it, did you?"

Shrake fell silent. He was already stunned that this creature knew of the Five Shields' existence; he did not want to ask anything and risk exposing even more in front of Thumann and Ximena.

"Am I right?" Ximena insisted. "Can you sense them?"

"Yes, but it's faint. The Golem is on the move, as is the hag. It's why I was here in Stuttgart."

"Are they together?" Thumann asked.

"No. The hag is summoning the Golem in the telepathic airwaves, I think. That implies she doesn't have him, and that, for now, I'm *not* her next target. But they are not currently close. Once the two are together, the telepathic signal I receive should become stronger, as if they merge into a single broadcast, if you will, and double their transmission strength. I will be able to sense them easily, then."

"So, we will wait," Thumann said.

"Yes, but it shouldn't be long. I warn you, though: the hag seems to have much better control and mastery over the telepathic links. This is some side effect of the Professor's work, I suppose. If we make a move against her, she will likely sense me coming. We will not have any advantage of surprise."

Ximena sat quietly. She, Thumann, and Shrake had taken a position across the street, in a café, to bide their time over coffee. The black-coated Homunculus remained standing, outside in the cold, as if he were now simply an antenna mounted on the sidewalk, awaiting a radio message. His ability to remain fixed in place, without so much as a waver or muscular twitch, was unsettling.

Something was off, and Ximena sensed it. With Shrake present, however, she did not wish to raise it with Thumann. Shrake was part of the problem.

There were more questions being raised than answers. She wondered what Homunculus meant when he mentioned Shrake and this group, the "Five Shields"? Why did Shrake react with surprise to the comment? Shrake was hiding something.

As for the homunculi, the pieces were coming together, but they still did not fit completely. If this "hag" homunculus was killing both her kind and their creators, what was her motive? If she was the beautiful woman created and then abused by the Professor, why did she appear as an old, hideous crone now? What had happened to her since her abuse by the Professor?

And what of this telepathic frequency shared by the homunculi? Was the black-clad homunculus telling the truth about his limited abilities? Or were the three homunculi secretly plotting among themselves to entrap Thumann and his team? If so, it was working.

Ximena instinctively slid her hand under the café table to the bag that hung off her shoulder and down at her hip. She felt her pistol still inside; a relief. Ximena had trained well on its use at both Scotland Yard and Interpol, and was becoming a good shot, but the gun was hopelessly small and underpowered. Still, it was better than nothing. Thumann's Celtic-knot brass knuckles would not be much help against these inhuman creatures.

She whispered to her ghosts, asking them to remind her of

the permissions they had given her. *It is better to live in the service of good than die in the service of evil.*

Thumann and Shrake were not talking, she noticed. This meant Thumann was thinking, and he, like her, was not willing to share his thoughts in front of the Yank from the Yard. No doubt, her smelly bear of a mentor was also mulling the "Five Shields" comment. Or perhaps Thumann knew what the Five Shields were and had not yet told Ximena. Either way, Shrake was not to be trusted. Given his prior treatment of her, Ximena felt comfortable with this decision.

Ximena was also greatly concerned for her giant German. Thumann was vacillating between bouts of silent introspection — no, she would call it what it was: *depression* — and near-manic confidence in his progress in the investigation so far. He was tortured by his memories of Hilda, Ximena knew, even though he had not spoken her name out loud once since arriving in Berlin. Ximena struggled to fully understand what he must be feeling, but she imagined it was horrible.

There was little she could do about it. She wanted to comfort him, but that was not her role. She was moving past being the daughter-like apprentice of the older German and needed to assert her own professional independence. All she could do was remain supportive of Thumann's decisions relative to the investigation and continue to do the best work she possibly could.

With this in mind, Ximena tried to solve the case as they sat there in the café. As ludicrous as the idea was, doing so would have relieved Thumann of at least one burden, and they could all get out of Berlin quicker. Perhaps if Thumann were back in Paris, back on the fourth floor of ICPO HQ, he could distance himself from his ghosts once more.

But the truth was that Ximena could not solve this case over a cup of coffee. There were still details missing, facts that the black-clad homunculus standing statue-like outside probably knew, but which he was not sharing. And she knew there was no way he would reveal them to her.

Shrake, however. He knew something, and she could confront him.

"Inspector," Ximena said, interrupting the tense silence that blanketed their café table. She would just ask him, and professional courtesy be damned, she thought. "What are the Five Shields?"

Shrake twitched slightly despite his training. This was something he clearly did not want to talk about. Thumann perked up, turning his head to watch Shrake's reaction. Ximena sensed that Thumann was glad she raised the question, sparing him from having to do so.

"Nothing," Shrake said, hoping to dismiss it.

It would not be that easy. "A valid question," Thumann added. "This homunculus outside seems to know you, but not from the press clippings of your Scotland Yard adventures."

"If you know something," Ximena added, "you are obligated to tell us." She was pressing hard, but given the dire situation they were in, she felt it was warranted.

Shrake put down his coffee cup with a sigh. "The Five Shields is an organization. I am a founding member, along with four others."

"What is its purpose?" Ximena asked.

"The five of us operate within various nations, using the resources available to us to help track and resolve political crises before they happen."

"And Scotland Yard is the resource you bring to the group," Ximena surmised.

Shrake nodded, but only slightly. "Well, yes, or more like Scotland Yard provides me with valuable intelligence. Between the five of us, we can collect the various bits of intelligence we gather and see patterns that individual nations or agencies might not see."

"How is that different from Interpol, then?" Thumann asked.

"Well, the Five Shields predates it. When it was formed, there was no Interpol, or whatever you call it," Shrake said. "Even still, I would guess that Interpol is still crippled by bureaucratic policies and pencil-pushers, making it only partly effective. No offense, Thumann."

"None taken. Interpol is already creaking under the weight of its remit policy," Thumann admitted. "But I'm not comfortable knowing there's some secret group of five self-appointed narcissists running around trying to control world events. Apart from their superhuman abilities, what makes the homunculi and Dr. Cuba organization different from your gang?"

"They are trying to destroy civilization. We're trying to save it," Shrake said pointedly.

"So, you do know something," Ximena said. "You knew about the homunculi and Dr. Cuba long before we did?"

"We knew the Dr. Cuba of the Americas was in league with the Doktor in Germany and the Fantôme in France, yes. But this business about them being grown in labs, that's new to us."

"Why didn't you stop Dr. Cuba back then?" Thumann asked.

"We don't solve crimes, Thumann, and we thought Dr. Cuba was just a criminal organization. You were the one who put the pieces together, showing Dr. Cuba was striving for more than just robbing old ladies of their pearls, Thumann. The credit is yours."

Thumann remained unimpressed and steadfastly unflattered.

Shrake continued, undeterred. "I trust you know this is all highly secret —"

A movement at the café door had the three looking up in surprise. The Homunculus appeared.

"Now," he said. "We go, now."

Chapter 19: The Broken Tower

The Golem wanted to scream. He was being flooded with noise and information, and the artificial mass that pretended to be a brain inside his head was not built for such a torrent.

A new scent was upon him, a Nazi hiding in a small three-story home. The Rabbi's programming drove him towards it, even as the beast tried to stop himself. He was sick of the death and murder, but could only watch his giant clay body perform its singular task without any ability to take control. He wanted to sleep, he wanted to die, but his body pushed forward, stumbling over crushed rubble and breaking through twisted trees, all to find the next victim.

Worse still was the opposing decree to destroy, murder, steal, and abuse all who opposed him. Not just the Nazis, but everyone. The pain caused by this clash of commands was growing more intense by the day, and now a third voice fought for control.

COME TO ME.

This, the Golem sensed, was a command he could not fulfill. First, he did not know where to go, and second, his programming drove his body in other directions.

The bastard beast knew, or at least as much as he could know anything, he was a slave to the demands of others. Creators, men, ... gods? He could not be sure of anything, but the curse of being trapped inside this giant clay prison was burning his soul. Destroying the little mind he was born with, turning it into an endlessly burning fire inside his huge clay head.

The Golem pressed forward, seeking the house, a part of his half-formed mind hoping that if he just killed one more Nazi, followed one more command, he might find peace at last. He might be free to die.

The beast felt the scent grow strong, the Rabbi's demand more powerful. The Nazi was there, in that three-story house with the wooden fence and yellow flowers outside. There were lights on inside; a few on the ground floor, where the Nazi would be found, and another set of lights on the top floor, an attic turned into a flat. The neighborhood had been bombed at some point, but was being rebuilt, albeit slowly.

The Golem did not care. He would destroy the house. He would kill the Nazi and, perhaps, find a final peace.

The beast's giant clay fist smashed through the front wall of the house, sending shards of wood and brick inward, as if a grenade had gone off. Inside, the old woman screamed in terror. The monster swung another fist and destroyed more of the wall, leaving a hole large enough for its huge, eight-foot-tall body to enter.

As it closed in on the old Nazi woman, Petra screamed as she ran down the staircase.

"Frau Jannings! Run!"

Jannings had not heeded Petra's warning. The old woman must have suspected the Golem was real, but, like so many, never imagined it might come for her. Now, the great gray beast stood over her, his fists ready to crush her small body into dust, giving no thought as to whether Jannings believed in it or not.

Jannings could not run in time. Not only was she simply too old to flee, but the Golem had her cornered in her own parlor; escape was impossible. The same parlor where, just days before, she had plotted to help three Nazis get out of Germany and on a ship to Argentina; Nazis who had been responsible for the slaughter of at least thirty Jews between them.

Petra ran but could not reach Jannings in time. Nor would it have mattered; there was simply no way to escape. The Golem's arms raised, his voice creaking and groaning with its metallic, stone-on-stone scream, and then its fists came down. Jannings was turned into a pile of flesh and crushed bone in a mere five seconds.

The scent of the Nazi disappeared in an instant. The Golem stood straight, his head scraping the ceiling of the parlor, and fell still. Petra looked on, wondering what it was doing, as blood dripped from the beast's huge stone hands.

The Golem was waiting. The scent was gone ... but would that be enough? Could he have finally finished his tasks? Would he be set free?

And then, a new scent. A new directive.

The Golem screamed. Petra covered her ears; the roar was unlike anything she had ever heard. It was horror and despair and fury all at once. Terrifying and heartbreaking.

The Golem was not set free. He would have to continue. There would be no death for him that day.

In a fury, the thing turned and set its eyes on Petra. She stood at the bottom of the stairs now, just outside the parlor, frozen. The Golem stepped forward, the top of his stony head scraping the parlor ceiling as he walked toward her.

Petra remained immobile, watching it curiously.

The beast reached forward and grabbed Petra, her lovely pink dress suddenly caught up in his huge, hardened clay fingers, her body nearly bending in half from the force. The Golem picked her up with that single hand and smashed his way out of the house, carrying her with him.

Petra screamed.

Ximena pulled out her pistol, immediately knowing it would not be of any use. The Golem strode out of the smashed house, carrying Petra in one hand like a limp doll. A .22 caliber bullet was not going to stop this stone creature. To her left, Thumann and Shrake were poised for a fight, but no doubt making the same calculations as Ximena had; Thumann's brass knuckles and Shrake's .45 Colt were equally useless.

To her right, however, the Homunculus stood, straight and tall, stoic as always. Ximena admitted silently that their only chance to stop the Golem rested with this dangerous devil.

But something was off. Ximena tried to think, but with the giant creature striding towards them, her brain fell into a thick fog. Her body was screaming at her to run, and in her panic, she could not piece the facts together.

Thumann grabbed her, shaking her from her paralysis, and darted them both to the side, away from the approaching Golem. He was right, Thumann knew they were outmatched, and this fight would not be for them. They only needed to get close enough to say the word into the beast's ear, but that would not happen yet. Shrake, meanwhile, opened fire; his huge, silver-plated pistol shouted bullets at the creature, making small chips in its body and neck; it did not even notice.

The Homunculus remained still, almost as if he did not even see the gray thing coming at him. Now at a pace away, the Golem swatted Shrake to the side with his free hand, sending the Golden Boy into the dirt, face down. Ximena could see Petra clearly now; her body *was* limp, and she was either dead or unconscious. As Thumann placed them both behind a parked car, Ximena lost sight of the Golem and his prize.

And then, the Homunculus finally moved. With one fluid movement, he dropped his black overcoat to the ground and leapt in the air, cartwheeling as he did so. The red-banded fedora flew in the opposite direction. The entire scene appeared as if in slow motion to Ximena, who peered from behind the car; the Homunculus, his body careening with precision over the moving Golem, rotated once again and came to land on the beast's shoulders. The Homunculus wrapped his legs around the beast's neck, either to anchor himself or to try to strangle it, and began shattering blows down on the creature's stone-armored head with his fists. Chips flew, but despite the jackhammer-like strength of the Homunculus, the Golem appeared unfazed.

"It's not reacting to the Homunculus," Thumann said. "It's almost ignoring him."

"None of this makes sense," Ximena said, nearly out of

breath. "Something is wrong."

The Homunculus continued striking down on the Golem, trying to slow it down, or perhaps trying to break through the hardened shell casing of the creature's head and access whatever it used for a brain. The effort, as forceful and dramatic as it was, seemed to be having little effect. The beast continued to walk forward, crushing stone and brick under his feet, heading — somewhere — with the limp Petra in his hand.

Finally, the Golem appeared irritated by the pearl-skinned creature on his shoulders. With a single swat of his free hand, he sent the Homunculus backwards into the street. The Homunculus took a moment to shrug off the blow and stood once more.

Abandoning her stealth, Ximena stood now, too. She knew what was wrong now; she had it figured out. The facts had all assembled themselves. She raised her tiny, impotent pistol and began running towards the beast.

"Ximena!" he shouted, not realizing what was happening until it was too late. "Don't do it!"

The Homunculus was once again behind the Golem, and this time he attempted to grab the creature's burlap garment to slow it down at least. At the same time, Ximena charged forward, firing her pistol. The bullets had no effect but came dangerously close to Petra.

"Ximena, stop firing! You'll hit the girl!"

The Homunculus, using all this strength, managed to stop the creature. The burlap nearly tore in his hands, but he was able to grab the Golem by the waist and, in a stunning display of raw power, lift the half-ton creature over his head. Ximena continued to fire. Unable to concentrate on both Petra and the Homunculus, Petra's limp body fell from the beast's grasp to the ground. Free of its burden, the Golem rotated its body, loosening the Homunculus's grip until the Golem, too, fell to the ground with a thunderous thud, landing on its feet. The beast stood straight and reached one arm back to shove Ximena backwards, away from him. She fell to the ground, her pistol sent skittering across the pavement, her jacket sleeve torn from the rough street.

"Ximena!" Thumann roared, running towards her.

The Golem, meanwhile, turned to face the Homunculus now. The creature roared his metal-and-stone bellow with absolute fury before his giant knotted fists struck. The Homunculus flew backward nearly twenty yards, smashing into the brick wall of one of the street's rebuilt homes. This time, the Homunculus did not get up immediately, allowing time for the Golem to turn again.

Thumann did not reach Ximena in time. Whether confused or simply unfussy, the Golem now reached down and grabbed her instead, leaving Petra lying in the street. The beast began running, Ximena in his hand, her body flailing like a rag doll.

"Ximena!" Thumann shouted, but only the sound of the creature's massive boots hitting the street with each stride echoed back to him.

Thumann charged after the Golem, spotting Shrake from the corner of his eye. Shrake was still trying to shake off the dizziness from getting thrown by the beast.

"Shrake, pull yourself together, man!" Thumann shouted. "We have to free Ximena!" It was enough; now Shrake, too, began charging in pursuit.

Thumann had lost track of the Homunculus, but in his blind need to save his protégé, he no longer much cared for whatever the black-clad villain might do. The Homunculus was strong, yes, but that strength had not benefited them yet. Thumann could not be sure if the Homunculus knew the beast's shutdown word, but he assumed he did not. No, Thumann himself would have to get close enough to say the word and end this nightmare.

The Golem was heading towards an old tower; the structure was likely once used by Germany's military to watch for Allied planes, to issue an air raid alert. Now the tower, at least eighty to a hundred feet tall, was abandoned; it had not yet been dismantled.

As Thumann wondered why it could be going there, Ximena struggled to free herself from captivity. She pressed with all her might against the beast's fingers in a vain attempt to extricate herself; she was simply not strong enough. Soon, the Golem entered the base of the tower and began to climb the stairs.

Shrake reached Thumann. "What is it doing?" he asked, running alongside the big German now.

"I don't know," Thumann said, out of breath but pushing forward. "Perhaps there's a Nazi hiding in the tower. I just don't know. We have to get close enough to it to say the word."

The Golem now scaled the stairs past the second floor and onto the third. It was headed upward, towards the roof. Ximena continued to struggle but was losing strength; her movements were becoming weaker. The Golem carried her but paid her no attention at the same time; she was just cargo. Seeing Thumann and Shrake below, about to enter the stairway, she shouted, "Inspector! Get Petra! Petra!"

Thumann continued up the stairs, losing more of his breath. He did not fully understand why Ximena was worried about Petra, and as far as Thumann could tell, Petra was already safe. For now, they had to save Ximena, and that was his sole focus.

Shrake, in far better shape than the big German, shot up the stairs faster, his silver Colt .45 ready for action in his hand. "I can't fire!" he shouted to Thumann. "I might hit Ximena!"

Soon enough, the great gray monster arrived at the roof of the tower. It overlooked the blackened streets and sky of Stuttgart, lit by a bright moon that made the clouds shine with silver. The Golem moved to the edge of the roof and stopped, Ximena still weakly struggling in its grasp.

Then, the Homunculus again appeared. He had not climbed the stairs, and instead had — out of view of Thumann and Shrake — scaled the tower wall. With ease, he raised himself up and over to stand on the roof just feet from the Golem and his captive.

Stop there, Golem, the Homunculus telepathed. *Don't move.*

The Golem did not move, but the Homunculus could not be entirely sure it was due to his mental command. In fact, the Homunculus thought the beast may have already stopped.

Drop the girl, he telepathed. *Put her down on the roof. Do not harm her.*

The Golem turned and stared at the Homunculus. Only now did Shrake arrive at the roof, Thumann still a few stories below and winded.

The Golem looked at the Homunculus, his face contorted in torment.

Put down the girl.

The Golem, slowly, relaxed his grip, letting Ximena fall gently to the roof's floor. Thumann now arrived at the roof and ran as fast as he could to Ximena's side. His legs ached, his heart pounded, and he was sure he was near a heart attack, but he ignored his pain and dragged Ximena away from the two creatures.

"I couldn't remember the word!" she said to Thumann between desperate breaths. "I couldn't remember it."

"We'll get another chance," Thumann grunted, bringing Ximena further away from the creatures.

To the others, it seemed as though the Golem and the Homunculus simply stood facing each other in silence. It was not at all clear what was happening.

Shrake raised his pistol, this time aiming it at the Homunculus. "You there. Let Thumann approach. If you do anything, I will shoot you in the head."

The Homunculus turned to look at Shrake, then turned back to face the Golem. It was not clear if he was acknowledging Shrake's command or refusing it. Thumann nevertheless stood and began walking towards the two. His legs were in agony, cramping from exertion, but he continued forward.

As the Homunculus returned. His gaze fell on the Golem,

and he realized it was not looking at him at all. Instead, the bastard beast was looking past him. The Homunculus turned.

There, approaching from the stairwell, was Petra. Her dress was torn and dirty, but she was alive. She walked towards them with a slow deliberateness.

"Shrake!" Thumann shouted. "Lower your gun! The girl! Be careful!"

Shrake, seeing Petra approach, did as Thumann asked. She was now close enough to the two homunculi to make it too dangerous to shoot.

"No!" Ximena rasped, her voice weak and coarse. "Petra! She's one of them!"

Within the beast's clay brainpan, more voices emerged. The Rabbi's voice was telling him to continue on, follow the next scent, continue to defend the Jewish people and destroy the next hidden Nazi villain. At the same time, the progenitor's memories told the beast to create chaos, prepare the world for something terrible, and above all, survive. But then, a new voice issued a quiet command.

Do not harm us, Golem. I can repair you.

The Homunculus stood, fixed, telepathing his message with a new level of clarity. *I can repair you.*

But louder than all the voices was one other.

COME TO ME.

The Golem did not move. He did not need to. He had already arrived. He had obeyed.

Petra, her torn dress still diaphanous and angelic, her blonde hair shimmering in the moonlight, now stood in front of the beast. Thumann and Shrake looked on in silence, not knowing what to do; in the noise and chaos, Thumann had only half-heard Ximena's warning, but there was little anyone could do with the information. The Homunculus also stood in silence, observing, as if wanting to see how this would unfold.

Slowly, Petra placed a hand on the beast's breast, over the

spot where its heart might have been, had it had one. She was trying to calm it, soothe it. The Golem's head tilted downward and looked at the lovely Petra. Suddenly, the torment that had appeared hand-carved into his face dissipated. The beast's brow softened, the lines of stress across his forehead and cheekbones disappeared. His eyes, once wide with rage, fell into relaxed slits. Even his arms appeared to drop slightly, losing their tension.

Slowly, the Golem reached his massive, burlap-covered arms upward and grasped the frail Petra. Gently, almost lovingly, he lifted her into his arms. No longer was the clay beast a thing of fury and vengeance; now it appeared protective, caring.

And then, with the smallest of movements, Petra placed her mouth near the Golem's ear and whispered.

"Maeth."

The Golem's eyes were the first to transform. Where they had shown a spark of life, now they fell gray, appearing nothing more than those of a museum statue. Then, there was a subtle alteration in his posture, nearly imperceptible, but indicating that whatever processes drove the creature's ability to move had been stripped from him. The face froze; one of peace, even joy, but now immobile. A statue.

Still a silent observer, the Homunculus could feel the Golem's signal leave the telepathic space; it was already dead.

In the next moment, the frozen thing fell backward under its own half-ton weight, toppling over the side of the roof, its frozen arms carrying the waif with it.

"Petra!" Thumann shouted.

Eyes wide with horror, Thumann and Shrake rushed to the edge of the roof; Ximena, unable to walk, stayed behind, lying on the ground. The two men watched as the heavy shape crashed downward, striking the tower's wall once before hitting the ground with a tremendous, thunderous impact. The thing, now nothing more than hardened clay, shattered into a mass of shards, random bits, and a cloud of gray dust. So much dust, it made seeing anything impossible.

Now the Homunculus joined Thumann and Shrake, peering over the edge at the clay explosion. Ximena, crawling, reached the edge, too, watching in stunned awe.

When the cloud of dust finally cleared, they saw light gray streaks of dust splaying outward from the impact point, where bits and debris of the dead Golem had flown in all directions, a small crater now in the center. And in that crater, Petra's light pink dress, covered in dust.

"Sweet Jesus," Shrake said.

The Homunculus did not react. He knew exactly how this ended. He watched.

The dress shifted, not from the wind. From Petra herself. As Thumann and the others watched, Petra rose up, her body mangled and her limbs misshapen from the fall. But only for a moment.

Her body changed. Her arms snapped back into place, her legs repositioned into a normal posture, her neck straightened. Then, looking up at her audience on the tower roof above, she smiled. The smile, too, changed. No ... her entire face. The bones of her face were shifting, moving; had they been closer, Thumann and the others would have heard small creaks and cracks. First, the face filled up slightly, appearing to be a slightly older girl with rounded cheeks. But it continued to morph, now becoming sunken, hollow. The bones turned inward, leaving skin to hang more loosely, forming wrinkles. The creature's spine curved, creating a slight hump; the cheekbones emerged, sinking her eyes inward, giving her a skull-like appearance.

With a short movement of her hand, the creature stripped away its hair, leaving a bald beast behind.

"I was trying to tell you," Ximena said breathlessly. "Petra was the hag."

The hag's high-pitched cackle reached upward past the tower to the glistening moon itself as she scurried, spider-like, out of the crater and into the adjacent woods.

"Only one more!" she screamed before disappearing entirely. "One more!"

Chapter 20: The Yard's Yank

At the foot of the tower, Thumann and the others gathered to examine the remains of the shattered Golem. Both Thumann and the Homunculus were curious if there would be anything other than dust and broken clay found in the small crater left by the creature's fall.

In the impression, there *was* something unusual, something that appeared quite different from the rest of the gray, dusty debris that otherwise covered the area. A solid shape, a blob of gray but with a slightly pink color.

"The birth-mass," the Homunculus explained. "Or, what's left of it."

Thumann knelt near it. The shape was clearly dead and could be mistaken for a long-dead animal or mossy growth. There was nothing about it that suggested it had been capable of animating a giant clay beast molded by the hands of a desperate Rabbi.

Thumann took out his box of pipe matches and set the thing on fire.

"That seems extreme," the Homunculus said, but did nothing to stop Thumann.

"Just in case you can reanimate this thing," Thumann grunted gruffly. "I don't know what you devils are capable of."

"One more advantage for us, then," the Homunculus taunted.

Thumann stood and turned to Ximena. "You knew. How?"

Ximena swallowed, planning her words. "The Golem arrived at Petra's house. And, previously, we were led to believe she had also encountered him," she said, pointing at the Homunculus. "For one person to have accidentally encountered both homunculi in just a few days seems far too coincidental to be an accident. I don't like coincidences, either."

Thumann's face grew stern. He was angry that he had not put it together.

"And you said he told you he had never robbed Petra," Ximena said, once again indicating the Homunculus. "So, she lied to us about the robbery. It was a trap to get us to go to Berlin. Petra wanted us to summon him so she could follow him and kidnap the Professor."

Thumann scowled some more. "You're right," he said. Turning to the Homunculus, he repeated, "She is right."

The Homunculus remained stoic as usual, refusing to nod. They could figure it out on their own, he surmised.

"It never made sense that the Professor said he created a beautiful woman when we believed the old hag was the homunculus," Ximena continued. "But it made sense that she could change her appearance. She was Petra, Alraune, and the hag ... all of them. She summoned the Golem to destroy him."

The Homunculus turned to Ximena now. "And how did she know the word?" he asked, knowing the answer. He wanted to hear her say it.

"The hag killed the Rabbi. She had already been to Kirchdorf and read the Rabbi's notes. The Golem never killed his master. It was her all along."

Shrake watched with great attentiveness and respect as Ximena laid out the plot. She was even more intelligent than he'd suspected,

Thumann was conflicted. He was frustrated that his protégé had to figure so much of this case on her own. Yet he was also happy that Ximena had graduated to become her own investigator and might no longer require a mentor at all.

"I'm her final target," the Homunculus said.

Shrake looked at the Homunculus curiously. "Will you let her?" he asked.

"Let her what?" the Homunculus responded.

"Kill you," Shrake answered. "Will you let her kill you?"

"Of course not, Inspector Shrake," the Homunculus said,

folding his arms. "I have much work yet to do as Dr. Cuba. You of all people should know that."

"I suspected as much," Shrake said. Then, quickly, his hand emerged from his coat pocket, and he pointed the silver-plated Colt .45 at the Homunculus's head. "I'm not going to allow that."

The Homunculus did not flinch. "Inspector Shrake. This is a bit crude, even by the standards of the Five Shields," he said.

Thumann held up a hand. "Hold on, Shrake. We still need him to help us destroy the hag."

"He won't help us," Shrake said, pointing the gun directly at the Homunculus's forehead. "Not in the long run. He wants mankind to be led by a race of technocratic, authoritarian homunculi. His goal may be to kill this Alraune homunculus now, to purge his bloodline of defectives, but he still just like the Nazis. We can't risk it if he creates a purer set of these creatures."

The Homunculus did not move. His silence acknowledged that everything Shrake had just said was true.

"We have an arrangement," Thumann said.

"Technically," the Homunculus answered, "our arrangement is complete. I only needed you to find the Rabbi. You did that, you have the notebook. Of all people, I trust you not to publish it, Thumann. You don't want any more of my kind running around half-made and out of control any more than I do."

"So perhaps Shrake should pull the trigger, then?" Thumann asked with a raised eyebrow. "Without an iron maiden to revive you, you won't survive a shot to the head. We can end this Dr. Cuba nonsense right here and now."

"But I promised you a gift, Thumann," the Homunculus said.

"And I told you I was not interested in bribes. There is nothing you could give me that would lead me to risk the social order of the entire world, if you are left to expand your organization."

"Don't be too sure, Thumann," the Homunculus said. "Remember what the first Dr. Cuba's people told you. Do you remember?"

Thumann froze. He did remember. The message came through Ximena, after her rescue of Gentleman in Lima, Peru: "*They said they can take your Hilda.*"

Thumann ran those words through his head countless times, and countless times he chose to toss them aside. They made no sense. Hilda was dead; how could they take her from him? The Nazi concentration camp had done that already.

But ...

"You're putting it together, aren't you, Thumann?" the Homunculus asked. "You know what the gift is."

Thumann's mind raced. They could only take his Hilda if she were still alive.

This devil knew where Hilda was. He was offering her back.

Thumann's hand darted upwards, grabbing Shrake's pistol. He shoved it downward. "No!" Thumann shouted.

Shrake reacted with shock. "What the hell?"

The Homunculus placed a smile on his lips. This was not a reaction his body made for its own purposes, but rather to signal to Thumann and the others that he understood exactly what was racing through the German's mind. "You see now, Thumann," he said. "We both still have use for each other. You can help me defeat this Alraune, and I can deliver what you want most."

Thumann's face grew red with rage, but he tried to calm himself. If he could be reunited with Hilda, all his pain would be lifted. He could be happy again. If only ...

The Homunculus turned to Shrake. "You, on the other hand, are a problem for me," he said. "The Five Shields will become a nuisance of significant strength if not stopped."

"Then," Shrake faced him, a smug look on his face, "you may want to —"

Before he could finish his sentence, the Homunculus's hand had darted out, nearly faster than the human eye could see, and grabbed Shrake's neck. There was a crack like a twig being snapped in half as his neck broke. Within two seconds, the Golden Boy's body fell limp with paralysis. Within another five seconds, Shrake was dead.

Thumann and Ximena had barely any time to process what had happened. Only when Shrake's body fell to the ground did they realize what they had just witnessed.

"Inspector Shrake!" Ximena screamed, dropping to her knees to check his body.

Without thought, Thumann cocked back a mighty fist and threw it forward. It was stopped, midair, by the Homunculus's far more powerful hand. Thumann felt the muscles in his arm shudder from the return force, as if he had struck an invisible force field.

"He was not on your side, Thumann," the Homunculus said, Thumann's hand still clenched in his powerful grip. "The Five Shields obey no laws. They sit above them. If you oppose Dr. Cuba, then you would have to oppose Shrake and his friends. You just don't know it yet."

"Beast!" Thumann shouted, trying to extricate his hand from the black-clad devil's hold.

"I'll leave you now. When we've finished with Alraune, I will come back to give you your gift. It is a promise. Then, you can try to kill me, if you still have a need to."

The Homunculus released Thumann's fist and turned. Before Thumann could cock back his hand to attempt another blow, the tall black-coated creature was out of arm's length. Within another few seconds, he was trotting down the street at inhuman speed.

Dr. Cuba had escaped once more.

At a local military hospital, a medic bandaged Ximena's

knee and shoulder. She was only lightly bruised, and the injuries were, thankfully, superficial. The relative quiet of the hospital, as compared to their last few hours, allowed Ximena and Thumann some time to not only process what had just happened but also to plan their next steps.

"Inspector," Ximena asked, "what is this gift the Homunculus intends to give you?"

"It may be nothing," Thumann said, pushing the image of his beloved Hilda out of his head. "Or it may be everything. For now, it's not worth discussing."

"I know this trip has been difficult on you, Inspector," she said, looking into his eyes for a reaction. "We've solved one of the crimes already. We could return to Paris. Let someone else take this over."

Thumann shook his head, as Ximena knew he would. "This is our fight. We have to stop the remaining devils here before this gets worse."

Ximena nodded. "I know. I'm just concerned for you."

Thumann placed a meaty hand on Ximena's shoulder. "Thank you, and I know I have been ... distracted. You are right, coming to Germany brings up many memories. You've done a fine job filling in for me here. It seems no matter how stressful or dangerous our situation becomes, you always remain able to process the facts. This is a crucial element of becoming a criminal inspector. I daresay the days of merely being a translator are long behind you."

Ximena blushed, but she knew there were still many roadblocks ahead of her. "Shrake seemed to think I did not belong here, in this position," she said.

"Why do you say that?" Thumann asked with a frown.

"He told me outright. He said that as a woman, I didn't deserve this job. His frankness was ... hurtful, I suppose. The others at Scotland Yard and ICPO share this view, I know. But no one had ever stated it so plainly to me."

Thumann waved a dismissive hand. He knew Shrake would

never think such things of Ximena. "No, dear girl. He was testing you."

"What?"

"Shrake must have been testing you. I don't know why, but it must have been some sort of probe. You see, he was one of your most forceful supporters at the Yard. Without him, you would have never been approved for the Fourth Floor."

Ximena looked at him in confusion. "How is that? He told me directly —"

Thumann cut her off. "He was probably pushing you. Seeing how you'd react, I suspect. In truth, my request to bring you to Interpol was initially rejected. The brass at ICPO saw no need to have me bring an assistant. It was Shrake who wrote a recommendation to Brühl, insisting that you come with me. Shrake laid out all your capabilities and instincts for this profession. No one was listening to me, but they listened to Golden Boy."

Ximena looked away, trying to process what she was hearing. She wondered what Shrake could have been testing her for. She felt even worse, now, knowing he was dead and that she could no longer thank him.

She would find neither solace nor answers at this moment. A nurse appeared, tapping Thumann's shoulder lightly. "Sir," she said, "there is a man in the hall who wants to speak with you."

Thumann patted Ximena's arm. "Let them finish up with you here, I'll go see what this is about."

Thumann walked out of the room and into the hallway. A tall man of Japanese descent stood waiting. He was smartly dressed, with neat, slicked hair and an expensive, tailored suit. He extended a hand to Thumann.

"Inspector Thumann, I am Goro. I am an associate of Inspector Shrake."

Thumann shook the man's hand; a firm grip. "Goro?" Thumann asked. "I've not heard Shrake mention you, I'm afraid."

"He wouldn't have," Goro admitted. "I'm here to collect Shrake's body and return it."

"You're not with Scotland Yard," Thumann said curiously.

"No," Goro answered. "I am not."

The certainty with which the man answered had Thumann sure the man was one of the Five Shields.

"I think the Yard will want to see the body first," Thumann said, wondering just who these Five Shields were. "He died while working an official case."

"Well, no. Scotland Yard had no idea he was here," Goro said.

"I received a telegram from Brühl at Interpol saying otherwise," Thumann countered.

"The telegram was fake. I can't go into more detail, but let it suffice that Scotland Yard was not involved."

Thumann grew frustrated. "Enough games, then," he said. "Who are the Five Shields?"

Goro raised an eyebrow. If he was trying to appear unaffected by the question, he mostly succeeded. Mostly. "Shrake told you, then?"

"Not Shrake. The villain we came here to defeat."

Goro nodded. "I see. That's ... problematic. All the more reason I need to bring Shrake home. I cannot say more. For now, however, the hospital won't release the body to me without your permission. You are the known head of this criminal investigation, so they are deferring to you."

Thumann paused. There was nothing secret this man would uncover by examining Shrake's body. A broken neck, nothing more conspiratorial than that. "Fine, but I need something from you first," Thumann said.

"What is that?" Goro asked.

"A means of contacting your group. I have a feeling I will need to do so at some point."

Goro paused, considering Thumann. His organization had been, up to now, successful in keeping its existence a secret. He wondered just how far the information had leaked already and whether allowing Thumann some level of access would make it worse.

"Fine," Goro said, reaching into his breast pocket. He pulled out a small notepad and pencil and scribbled something. Tearing off the page, he handed it to Thumann. "Publish these words, in this sequence, in the Swiss newspaper Neue Zürcher Zeitung. We will contact you forty-eight hours afterward."

Thumann took the paper and glanced at it. There were five words, seemingly random. It was a code, so Thumann understood it was not intended to make sense. "Very well. Shrake's body is down the hall, fourth door on the left. I will sign the release."

"Good luck, Inspector Thumann. I hope you succeed." Goro turned and headed down the hall to collect Shrake's body.

Chapter 21: The Chameleon Witch

Once again in Berlin, the Homunculus rejuvenated himself in his iron maiden. The laboratory and facility around him were still heavily damaged, but he had ordered the site to be demolished in one week. With so many of the facility's operatives dead, so much of the equipment wrecked, it made little sense to try to rebuild it. Worse, Alraune knew the location and could return at any time. The Homunculus was taking a risk by using the maiden, leaving himself at least partially helpless inside it, but trusted that his improved ability to sense other homunculi would warn him if she was near.

Within the maiden, the Homunculus once again stopped his heart, killed himself, and let the silence magnify his reception. He reached out, trying to sense where, exactly, Alraune was at that moment.

But there was nothing.

The Homunculus could feel the gap in the signal where the Golem's tortured mind had once been. The signal was cleaner, with less noise and a bit less distortion. But alongside this was another gap; the Homunculus could not sense anything from Alraune, either.

If she were alive, which he knew she was, she should be leaving some trace inside the signal. Where was she?

The Homunculus did not send a telepathic signal of his own; he remained in a passive listening state instead. There was the possibility that Alraune not only had mastered her ability to send messages and commands clearly through the telepathic ether but also had learned how to obfuscate her presence entirely.

Thankfully, the Homunculus had calculated for this possibility. This was why he told Thumann he still needed him to help find Alraune. If his telepathic powers were of the same strength as Alraune—which he hoped was true as he had been improving—and assuming she had no jamming capability, he would not need Thumann at all. He would merely sense her location, go there, and kill her.

But the Homunculus suspected it would not be that easy, and he was being proved right.

And, so, he remained in the maiden for a full eight hours, not so much to rejuvenate — his body had not received much damage in the fight with the Golem — but more to spend time surfing the telepathic wavelengths.

His thoughts were interrupted by something.

There it was, hidden and faint. Her presence. She was there, after all. If she had learned to hide herself in the waves, he was breaking through.

Alraune's telepathic fingerprint was like the scent used by the Golem to identify his victims. With the faintest whisper of her presence in the signal, the Homunculus could isolate it, ignore the surrounding noise, and focus more deeply.

She was in the bookshop. What was she doing there?

The Homunculus tried to focus further, to see a view of what she saw. He tried to step behind her eyes. This was a mistake.

Get out, Brother! he heard, clearly and nearly deafening. Alraune had sensed him.

The Homunculus did not cut off his telepathic probe immediately, lest Alraune think he was panicking. Instead, he faded it out, as if he had only momentarily gained access to her mind and then lost it. He wanted her to think his signal faded. He would attempt to reach her again later, when her guard was down.

Finally, he emerged from the maiden, fully rejuvenated. New strength coursed through his veins. He dressed and trod through the demolished laboratory to the hallway, and from there towards the other lab where Professor ten Brinken had been working. There, the Professor's birth-mass was struggling. The Homunculus knew what he needed to do to ensure its survival. It would require him to re-enter a maiden once more, but this time bringing the mass with him. He was not entirely sure his plan would work, but the experiment was nearly wholly without risk, at least to him, and the birth-mass was otherwise expendable.

But first, the Homunculus had to correct the birth-mass's intended gender.

Another female would not do. Creating women was the Professor's obsession, not his.

Ximena approached the old bookshop with caution. Once again, she reassured herself by patting the leather bag at her side, finding her pistol waiting for her. And, once again, she was relatively sure it would be ineffective.

When she got back to Paris, she would ask her ghosts if she could find herself a bigger gun.

The street was dark, as it was already nearing 11 p.m. A few working gaslights did as much as they could to throw some light down on the pavement, but these were outnumbered by the broken lamps that surrendered to the dark. Another single light, above the door of the bookshop, flickered slightly. It was not quite an invitation as much as a warning.

Ximena pressed on, however. This was Thumann's plan, and she would help implement it. It was a good plan, but, to be realistic, it was their only plan.

She opened the door, which scratched noisily across the wooden floor, crying out with a desperate, rasping plea. It only opened halfway, and Ximena angled her body to slip through the rest of the way.

As she entered, her eyes adjusted. A few more dim gaslamps flickered inside, in a somewhat resigned effort to show off the shop's offering of books, but without much enthusiasm for the job. A lit fireplace behind the counter provided additional light and welcome heat.

In the pale light, Ximena could make out that the books were nearly all German-language titles, with a few English and French scattered about. Most were on the subjects of history, with quite a few literary works, or at least as far as Ximena could tell; she still could not read German particularly well. It was quite a different selection than that of Madame Blavatsky's occult library, for sure. Which made it all the more unusual that this would have been the shop that sold the copies of Dr. Cuba's notebook.

If the female homunculus had abandoned her warehouse hideout elsewhere in Berlin, Thumann assumed she might return to the bookshop.

"Hello?" Ximena said, calling out in a firm but quiet voice. "Is there someone here?"

There was no answer, but the door had been unlocked, so Ximena was sure someone must be in the back.

And so, she waited. Ximena intentionally made enough noise, rustling through books and allowing her feet to scrape along the floor, to announce her presence to anyone in a back room. Eventually, someone did emerge.

"Well, this is unexpected," Alraune said. "Inspector Thumann sent you?"

Ximena did not recognize the woman in front of her. Perhaps twenty-five years old, with auburn hair and a round face. She was neither Petra nor the hag. Ximena was not sure what she was expecting. She kept her hand near the opening of her leather bag. "Yes, he sent me. I ... I don't recognize you, I'm afraid."

"I am Alraune," the woman said. Her voice was polite but stern, not the creaking cackle of the hag nor the saccharine pitch of Petra. Something in between. "This is my born state. How I was designed, by Professor ten Brinken, to appear."

Ximena felt a tiny bit of terror run through her spine, but summoned all her strength to prevent this from being obvious to the creature in front of her. "I see. Dr. Cuba could change his appearance by, I believe, manually manipulating his face. You adjust it by sheer will?"

Alraune nodded. "As much will as it takes for you to walk or lift your arm. There are muscles involved. I control my facial muscles; they shift the bones. I am, frankly, not sure why my so-called 'brothers' have to do this with their hands. It's all very messy for them. Are you here to kill me?" Alraune tacked the question onto the end of her explanation as if she intended Ximena to miss it entirely. Ximena did not.

"No," Ximena said. "I doubt I could if I tried," she admitted.

"You're smarter than your colleagues, then. They think I am weak. But then, that's something I am sure you experience, as well."

Ximena did not react, choosing not to reveal too much about herself. "Why do you take the form of the hag? It seems ... well, unnecessary. Almost ..."

"Melodramatic?" Alraune said, finishing Ximena's thought.

"I wouldn't have used that word," Ximena said.

"To be honest, the shape of the old woman makes it easier to perform certain physical actions. But most of all, it helps me hide. No man would ever expect an old woman to do what I have done. If there is a dramatic side effect, that's a bonus. Would you prefer me to change now, and hiss and claw at you?"

Ximena shook her head. "I would prefer it if you didn't. I only come to bring a message. Well, more of a request."

"In due course," Alraune said with a wave of her hand. "But first, you have to answer a few of mine."

"Well, yes, that's fine," Ximena said, though she wondered what the woman was up to. "I may not be of much help, but I can try to answer you."

"How did you find this shop?" Alraune asked. "The Homunculus—or the one who uses the name Dr. Cuba now, at least — he was here. Your Thumann was not."

Ximena pulled out the notebook and put it on the counter, face down. On the back cover was a small sticker with the name and address of the bookshop typed on it. It was a gamble to expose the notebook this way, but Thumann thought it might act as a calling card to let Alraune understand that Ximena truly was his agent in this matter.

"Oh," Alraune said. "I see."

"You did not know the notebooks were labeled?" Ximena asked.

"No. I took over this shop after the books were sold. To find the records and to find out who bought the second copy. That was how I found the Rabbi." Her hand reached out towards the notebook. Ximena did not flinch. "I had not, however, found his copy of the notebook. Your Thumann must have found it, but now you would risk losing it? To me?" she asked.

"Inspector Thumann does not want anyone to have the book. He thought you might be the only other being alive that would agree with him on that," Ximena explained. "It is a sign of his trust in you."

Alraune took the book, opened it, and spent only a few moments glancing at its pages. She was checking to see if it was, in fact, the same as the book her own Professor had obtained. Slowly, she closed it and then threw it into the fire behind her. She turned back to Ximena to gauge her reaction.

Ximena, again, did not flinch. "Inspector Thumann did not make any copies," she said, as if to reassure Alraune.

"Your inspector is a strange beast, then," Alraune admitted.

"Do you know who made these copies, though? How did the book get here?" Ximena asked.

"I cannot be sure. An organized crime group, unrelated to our dear friend Dr. Cuba. French, I believe. It is said they were responsible. Does he treat you well?" Again, a question tacked onto the end of a statement.

"Who?" Ximena asked.

"Your Inspector Thumann. Does he treat you well?"

Ximena was taken aback slightly by the personal question. "Yes," Ximena said, wondering why she would care. "Yes, he does."

Alraune nodded, though her expression took on a faraway

look. "To be a woman in this age, and in your profession, must be difficult. Do they harass you? The men in the police organization. Do they let you be who you want to be?"

"Within limits," Ximena said hesitantly, then decided to tell the truth. "Yes, they do, but there are limits placed upon me."

"Such as?" Alraune asked, her gaze now boring into Ximena's.

"Well," Ximena said, trying to find a rudimentary example. "All my reports must be signed by a male officer. Thumann or someone else at Interpol. Nothing I write can be escalated any higher than Thumann without a man's approval."

"I see."

"There's great pressure upon me that the men don't have. I can't have even a minor error, or it would be jumped upon as evidence of my natural weakness, while the men around me can bumble and fail without consequence."

"Do they rape you?" Alraune asked casually.

Ximena was jarred, and it showed. "No. They don't rape me," she said in surprise.

"I see."

Ximena watched the creature's face and realized this was her reality. She had only known physical abuse and torture since being birthed by the Professor. As much as Ximena struggled, it was still nothing compared to this creature's experiences. The woman could not even imagine a day without rape or horror.

"I'm ... I'm so sorry for what you have been through," Ximena said with genuine emotion. "My troubles must seem insignificant to you."

"There are no insignificant troubles for we women," Alraune said. "There are only differing degrees of reaction to them. You have your methods, and I have mine."

"I have to ask you my question," Ximena said, hoping Alraune would now be open-minded. "It's important, and your answer may help you as much as it can help us."

"Ask."

Thumann paced as he waited for word from Ximena. His anxiety was not entirely due to the danger Ximena was walking into — Thumann was confident the Alraune creature would not harm his assistant if Ximena played her part correctly — but also over what was coming next.

He would have to destroy both homunculi, but Thumann and Ximena were armed only with brass knuckles and an underpowered .22 caliber pistol. The playing field could not be more tilted against them. There was no army coming to save them, no air support, no hired muscle. Just an old man and a young woman against two of the strongest, strangest creatures ever to have walked the earth.

Thumann, however, had come upon a theory. It was something that might have come to him sooner, had he not been stuck in his memories of his past life with Hilda. He slapped his leg in frustration, wondering if he might have been able to end this entire mess much sooner.

No, he thought. The truth was that his plan, however late it came to him, might still not work. He and Ximena would be in grave danger if it failed, but they would only be the first two to fall. If the homunculi were able to kill them, they would not stop. The black-clad homunculus in particular, who had been building a new criminal empire under the name of his predecessor, Dr. Cuba.

But if this worked ...

Thumann shook his head. There was no time to worry and second-guess himself. All he could do now was execute the plan. Wait for Ximena to return, and then do their part in it.

Chapter 22: The Radar Trap

The Homunculus strolled into the squat, boxy, single-story building. This was some sort of military installation, now abandoned and yet to be either destroyed or repurposed by the Allies. It seemed an unusual place for Thumann to want to meet, but the inspector's coded message, published in the Berlin newspaper, appeared to suggest some urgency on Thumann's part.

Thumann called to the black-coated figure as he entered. "Over here," he said. The Homunculus saw his temporary ally sitting in a small chair near the center of the room. Around him were tables and filing cabinets and various sorts of electronic equipment, all broken, scattered, or otherwise beyond repair. It now appeared this was some sort of German communications post, probably to support the giant Freya radar dish sitting outside the building on a now-crumbling concrete pad.

"Your message seemed desperate," the Homunculus said, bringing himself to stand in front of Thumann. "Do you have something for me, or are you asking me to deliver something to you?"

"Both," Thumann said, motioning that the Homunculus should also sit. The black-clad devil had no reason to sit but did so, if only to show some level of respect for his German adversary.

"Why here?" the Homunculus asked, pointing his hand to the building's broken ceiling and crumbling interior.

"I cannot be sure those Five Shields lunatics are not following me. This seemed a safe space," Thumann said. "I don't know what they are up to."

"You are right to treat them with suspicion, Thumann. They may appear to be on the side of 'mankind,' but they have their own very specific agenda."

"I met one of them at the hospital to pick up Shrake's body. I could sense he had multiple motives," Thumann said, exuding the aura of someone relatively unmoved by Shrake's death.

"Did you bring me here to get your revenge?" the Homunculus asked.

"As I said, I have something for you. But, first, I need to know something."

"You want to know about the gift," the Homunculus surmised.

Thumann nodded. "I have tried to ignore your offer. And tried to push ahead. I cannot. And I am sure you knew that."

"I did," the Homunculus said.

"Hilda," Thumann said, finally saying her name out loud. "You know where she is?"

The Homunculus shifted, crossing his legs and leaning back slightly. "Very good, Thumann. Hilda is, in fact, my gift. To answer you, it's not so much that I know where she is, but rather I know how you can rejoin her."

Thumann scowled. "Don't waste my time, devil. If this is one of those clever tricks where you kill me and say I am free to rejoin Hilda in the afterworld, I have no patience for it. Don't insult me."

"Afterlife? No, no, no, Thumann. In this life, in this reality. You in that flesh," he said, pointing to Thumann's frame, "and she in hers. Or, at least, by appearances."

Thumann froze at his words, his mind trying to deduce what "by appearances" could possibly mean.

The Homunculus knew he had released a scrap of information that Thumann needed time to process; he remained silent.

It took only moments for Thumann to understand what the Homunculus inferred, and only moments after that to grow angry. "You don't have Hilda."

"I do not," the Homunculus said.

"You have something of hers. Her body. Her corpse. Something."

"I do," the Homunculus again confirmed.

Thumann's spine froze. "You can't revive her. Even you can't bring back the dead. No. No, you intend to *recreate* her. As a homunculus. And gifting her back to me in that state."

The Homunculus remained stoic, immobile. He was letting Thumann comprehend the full weight of the offer.

Thumann swallowed, hoping his giant beard would hide the movement. He breathed in a bit and exhaled. This was to ensure the black-coated devil in front of him could not sense the full fury that Thumann was now feeling.

He had no interest in a soulless copy of his Hilda. But he knew this devil could never understand that.

"You have answered my question," Thumann said.

"Now, what do you have for me?" the Homunculus asked.

"Alraune. I know where you can find her. We can end all of this," Thumann said.

"She's at the bookshop. I already know this," the Homunculus said.

"She is not. She is most certainly not at the bookshop," Thumann said. "She is here."

The Homunculus allowed himself to smile, for Thumann's sake. "Thumann, she is not here. She is not even close. Have you forgotten that I can sense her, and that her signal is stronger when we are nearby? I sense nothing. She is not even close by."

Thumann stood, shaking his head once at the Homunculus, as if to say how wrong he was. "As you entered, my dear Ximena ordered the radar mast outside to be powered on. Normally, it rotates, of course, but we brute-forced jammed it so the beam is pointed directly at us. Right now, we are being bombarded with powerful radio waves. We had the Americans tune the transmission to a frequency of 150 megahertz, with a pulse repetition of 1,000 hertz. We have it running at full power, well beyond the normal watts used in wartime service. I daresay, we are running enough power through the damned thing, I will probably end up with a sunburn and the machine may well blow up."

The Homunculus stood, just as expressionless as ever.

"This," Thumann continued, "should have the effect of blocking your telepathic ability. In fact, I think I can say, without any hesitation, it worked."

"And why is that?" the Homunculus asked.

"Because she's right behind you."

Alraune, in her auburn-haired form, leaped from the shadows behind the Homunculus, a long iron pipe in her hand. With incredible strength, she shoved the pipe forward, impaling the Homunculus straight through the front of his chest, sending a spray of blood and meat onto the ground in front of him. Even the stoic Homunculus was unable to contain his shock, and for the first time, Thumann saw the black-clad devil — now spurting blood — look worried.

The Homunculus turned, the spike in his back rotating with him and nearly hitting Thumann. With lightning speed and without showing any concern for being stabbed through the chest, he sent an arm forward to grab Alraune. But she was faster; she dipped below the incoming hand and sent her own hand upward, into the pipe, forcing it upwards so that it began to turn the single puncture hole into a bloody, gushing slit.

The Homunculus had more luck with his second attempt. His other hand made contact with his female counterpart, grabbing her by the hair. As he attempted to pull her upwards, the hair separated from her bald skull, and the great black-clad devil was left holding only a wig.

Alraune used this distraction to her advantage as well. She punched upward, with her hand's fingers extended out, and thrust her hand into the Homunculus's sternum. With a single, violent move, she tore out shreds of the devil's chest, a mixture of skin, blood, and bone hitting the floor beneath him with a splat.

The Homunculus reeled from the pain and loss of blood.

The air smelled of a mixture of copper and gasoline, and Thumann wondered if the beast knew his end was now upon him. It was Thumann who struck the next blow, sending one of his mighty, oak-knot fists at the Homunculus, and making a pounding, thudding connection to the side of his head. Blood pooled in the devil's eyes, which no longer showed their usual confidence, but instead seemed to be searching around for some way to save himself. He fell backwards, legs struggling to find footing, and eventually landed on his back.

Thumann stepped closer, standing over the Homunculus.

"Your gift is refused," he said. "I have no need for an artificial Hilda so long as I have the memories of the real one." He swung down again, straight at the Homunculus's skull.

But this time, the beast caught Thumann's hand in mid-thrust. It once again felt to Thumann as if he had punched an invisible brick wall, and he felt two of his knuckles snap. He grimaced.

"It will take more than this," the Homunculus said, gurgling through the blood in his mouth, and with a voice that nevertheless sounded like a dying animal.

The Homunculus stood, the metal pipe still sticking through him, and with one hand, he raised Thumann off his feet and dangled him. With astonishing power, he threw the giant German at Alraune, and the two crashed down against a set of tables and filing cabinets, filled with heavy electronic radio equipment. Thumann could hear the sound of air being pushed out of Alraune's lungs from the impact.

Thumann shook his head, trying to shake off the sudden vertigo, but the female homunculus was already on her feet again, leaping at the black-clad, bleeding devil. She landed not on him, but in front, taking a crouching position, and grabbed the Homunculus's legs. Now it was she who threw him into a wall of electronics. Without power to the room, there were no sparks or fire, but shards of metal, vacuum tubes and dust filled the air. More blood poured from the angered Homunculus.

Getting to his feet, Thumann tried to steady himself before joining Alraune to stand over the Homunculus.

The Homunculus sputtered, no longer able to speak. The smell of blood and gasoline reached Thumann's nose once more as the Homunculus tried to pull on the metal spike stuck through him.

Thumann relaxed. It was nearly over now. He removed his pipe and tobacco pouch and calmly stuffed a pinch of latakia into the pipe.

"Devil, you have been a plague on the world. I think your time as Dr. Cuba is ended," Thumann said. He lit the pipe with a single match and puffed. Thick wisps of Latakia smoke filled the air. "But I really cannot be sure you won't hop into one of your damned machines and regenerate."

Thumann, still puffing his pipe, knelt in front of the Homunculus. "So, you will have to forgive me if I just take one more extra precaution."

Thumann removed the lit pipe from his mouth and plunged the apple-shaped bowl into the Homunculus's open chest. There, the lit tobacco met gasoline and burst into flames.

Thumann stood up as the fire within the Homunculus's body quickly spread. The room now filled with a new smell, not of burning flesh, but something else entirely: the acrid stink of a burned cellular mass, not human tissue. The Homunculus tried to scream, but no sound came out.

Within a few minutes, the body was charred beyond any recognition. It was now simply a smoldering mass of ash and bone, with a large iron pipe lying on top.

Ximena emerged and joined Thumann.

"You can shut down the transmitter," Thumann said.

"No need," Ximena said. "It blew up."

Thumann laughed. He turned to Alraune.

The woman was bloodied and disheveled, her bald head

exposed and scarred. Thumann and Ximena could not be sure how many of those scars she had gotten from her violent acts as the hag, or how many had been put upon her by the Professor. Now, in the light, Thumann could see some resemblance to Petra, after all; the eyes and teeth, things Alraune could not change the shape of. Thumann was suddenly sad.

Alraune straightened her spine, not wanting to resemble at all the hideous hag she had so often appeared as.

"I cannot apologize for what I have done, Inspector Thumann," she said. "An apology would require that I could have made different choices, and that I might not do the same things again. As you well know, I cannot change. I am fixed, after all. My creator made me a beast, and that is my permanent nature. What I do next is all I can do now."

Ximena stepped forward, tears in her eyes.

"You knew it was me," Alraune said, her gaze going to Ximena. "When the Golem was carrying me as Petra, you were shooting at me, not at the Golem."

Ximena nodded, ashamed. "I did know, but I thought you were controlling the Golem. With your telepathy."

Alraune smiled. "I was. I was forcing him to climb the tower. You did well."

Slowly, Ximena held up her trembling hands; in them was her pistol. Alraune took it.

"I hope your people find peace," she said, looking at Ximena. "I hope your women find peace."

Alraune raised the gun to her temple and fired. The bullet, at point-blank range, was effective. She dropped to the ground and, within just a few seconds, was dead.

Thumann had understood that he never needed to fight both homunculi; he needed only to defeat the black-clad devil. Alraune had always intended to destroy herself once the Homunculus was dead, and she had carried through with her destiny, with the help of Ximena, who now stood with tears in her eyes.

Outside, amidst the exploded wreckage of the German Freya radar mast, a bent, metal shape glimmered in the sunlight. It was jammed into the mast's wheel mechanism, locking the rotating base into position, aimed directly at the small, boxy building below.

Thumann had managed to kill the Homunculus with his Celtic-knot brass knuckles after all.

Chapter 22: The Lover's Ghost

Thumann sat in his comfortable leather chair, allowing it to catch his full weight. Once again in his Fourth Floor office in Paris, he leaned back and then reached forward. His hand searched his desk drawer, but he had neither alfajores nor macarons.

Turning himself around, Thumann checked the cabinet behind him, hoping at least that his Scotch had not run out. With a slight grin, he produced an unopened bottle of White Horse. Thumann opened the bottle and poured himself a full glass. He swigged.

Thumann was at peace. Like the Golem, the business in Stuttgart had freed him of the noises in his head. Clarity was returning to him. The Homunculus's offer had the opposite effect it intended. The "gift" of a lab-grown version of his Hilda as some sort of inducement was so blasphemous, so obscene, it shook something in Thumann permanently. His Hilda was gone. There was no bringing her back. No amount of sobbing, praying, slamming doors, or clomping feet would do it. Time ran in one direction only, and even the bizarre science of the homunculi could not alter that universal law.

But Thumann still had his memories of Hilda. And, to a great extent, her oppressors had lost. Germany surrendered, the Nazis were being rounded up and would be held accountable under international tribunals. This would have to be enough.

And, suddenly, after returning from Stuttgart, it was.

Ximena entered the office, hung her coat on the rack, and then threw herself into her chair. She held a bakery box. "Good morning, Inspector. You seem chipper this morning," she said.

"It is eight o'clock, and I have a fresh bottle of Scotch. The villains are all dead, Dr. Cuba's organization is effectively dismantled, and we stopped a rain of murders. This is a good day, I would say." He *was* chipper.

Ximena opened the box and pulled out an alfajor. A *genuine* alfajor, soft and crumbly, covered in powdered sugar. Without saying anything to Thumann, she ate it, sending sugar all over her sweater. Thumann stared in surprise, his mouth practically watering.

Ximena feigned ignorance. "What is it?" she said, taking another bite and allowing the sugar to fall everywhere. She was taunting him.

"Where did you get those?" Thumann demanded.

"Oh, these?" Ximena said, holding up another alfajor. "I made them."

"You made them?" Thumann asked.

"Yes, my friend sent me my mother's old recipe. Not surprisingly, Paris had all the ingredients available. The *manjar blanco* was the hardest part, but I figured it out." She took a bite of the second alfajor, and Thumann strained to see inside the box. He estimated there to be at least a dozen more.

When she took yet another bite without asking if he'd like one, Thumann grunted, like an annoyed four-year-old.

Ximena teased him further. "Did you want one, Inspector?" she asked, her cheeks covered in powdered sugar.

"I could order you," Thumann said sternly. This was his humor.

"I want to be clear with you, Inspector," Ximena said, beginning to pass the box towards her mentor, but then holding it in the air, just short of his reach. "I made these for myself. I am letting you have some of them. I did not bake for you."

Thumann's mustache twitched in amusement. "Of course not, dear miss. Of course not."

Ximena smiled and relented, handing the box to Thumann. "You can have six," she said. "The rest are mine."

Thumann nodded gratefully, gobbling the first alfajor. "My God," he said, closing his eyes briefly in bliss, "the Spanish were fools. They invaded the continent for gold when they could have returned with these instead. Absolute fools."

Both of them were now covered in sugar. Thumann looked up and noticed something. "You are *not* chipper," he said. "You're hiding something behind this alfajor business."

Ximena's face changed. "I will be fine," she said.

"You were instrumental in the defeat of that devil. Much of our success was due to your insight, your ability to think clearly in the middle of chaos. I lost sight of everything, and you brought us to victory while I obsessed about ghosts. You should be happy."

Ximena swallowed and cleaned the sugar from her face with a napkin. "The final report to Dr. Brühl, closing the case ... who signed it?"

"I did, of course," Thumann answered. "It's all official."

Ximena remained silent. Then she popped another alfajor into her mouth. "Well, let's enjoy these. But don't get used to it, Inspector. I am not your bakery chef."

Thumann took another swig of Scotch and another bite of alfajor. "No, you are not my bakery chef," he said. "You are nothing less than my co-inspector. And a damned good one."

Deep below the sea's surface, the strange mass lay dormant. It was nearly shapeless, a green-and-yellow blob that conformed to the ocean floor where it rested. The thing was impossibly dense, and yet gelatinous. It appeared very much dead.

Elsewhere, very far away, men with faces masked with lead manipulated the elements and lit a fire that could be seen in the heavens. Beneath the sea, the light of that fire was not visible. The tiny particles spewed by that fire, however, settled into the ocean.

Then, imperceptibly, the mass came alive. If any man had been able to withstand the pressures of the depths and see the thing, he would not have noticed much. A slight shimmer of the yellow highlights within the greenish mass, perhaps; perhaps not even that. Instead, the changes were microscopic.

No, atomic.

The mass lifted itself from the seabed and began to float, drifting away from its resting place, away from the place its creators had placed it.

The villainy continues in

The Blasphemies of Dr. Cuba

www.drcuba.world

Author's Notes

This second novel of the DR. CUBA series was written immediately after completing the draft of the first. Fueled by a mix of coffee, scotch, and professional discontent – my profession of quality management has turned into a cesspool of corruption and grift – this book slithered out of me much like one of the Homunculus' birth-masses. With the characters more or less developed, a sequel is always a bit easier. I had the plot already sketched out, so it was just a matter of writing the words.

This one was a lot of fun. For Book II, I targeted a different series of old German films and other cinematic influences. Obviously, Paul Wegener's *Der Golem* films played a big part in this, but so did Henrik Galeen's *Alraune.* Once again, both films played with the idea of a manmade creature, lacking a soul, rebelling against its creator.

(Fun aside: Wegener not only directed *Der Golem*, but played the title role in his film series; he also played Professor ten Brinken in *Alraune.* Galeen, meanwhile, had also written the screenplay for F.W. Murnau's famous take on Dracula, *Nosferatu,* as well as for *Alraune.*)

The Golem has always been a favorite myth of mine, and Wegener's take on the character is iconic: the lumbering, burlap-wrapped beast with the strange Dutchboy haircut. In the 1990s, I self-published a comic book adaptation of Wegener's film, but (if I recall) it only reached about two issues before it was dropped. The story altered Galeen's screenplay quite a bit, and much of my take for that comic series appears here in this novel.

Alraune took a lot more work. I was familiar with the story, but for years had hunted down a copy of the 1928 film. Now, it's readily available on YouTube and long since out of copyright. For Book II, I searched for an English copy of Hanns Heinz Ewers' 1911 original novel, which helped give me more perspective on the character. In the end, though, the Alraune of my book does not particularly represent the character in either the original novel or film. I urge readers to seek them out, though. The film stars Brigitte Helm in the title role, coming after her compelling performance in Fritz Lang's famous *Metropolis*.

Writing Book II while Book I was with the initial proofreader was also beneficial. The relationship between Thumann and Ximena developed, and the latter suddenly grew into the main character of the series. Initially, Ximena was just supposed to be a translator, to help move the plot and explain how a German was fumbling around South America without much of a problem. While she grew into her own character in Book I, she was still somewhat of a side character in the first draft. After completing the first draft of Book II, I added significantly to Ximena's background and character, and improved the relationship between her and Thumann. Without giving too much away, I can say that Book III very much becomes Ximena's story.

This is not to say that Thumann has been sidelined. Book III will explore how the German Brain is handling his acceptance of Hilda's death and regaining his confidence in his profession. We see a refreshed, relaxed Thumann, less haunted and more focused. He might even make a new friend or two, even as he deals with a traitor in his inner circle.

Obviously, this book toys with the introduction of the Five Shields, who – if I'm being honest – may or may not have a greater role in the future books. They are there is I need them, but to date they keep getting cut from the drafts. They were inspired, to some degree, by the five supporting characters from *Doc Savage* pulp novels written by Lester Dent (as Kenneth Robeson). But each time I have tried to trot them out, the scenes come off a bit too much like Doc Savage, and it all becomes too jarring. Nearly a third of Book III has been scrapped due to this problem, and the manuscript is better for it.

What will we see in Book III? An unusual, and likely unexpected, return of Dr. Cuba alongside a new set of cinematic influences. The book may only jump a year forward from Book II, but the influences include some British science fiction films, which many may have long forgotten.

Random notes:

- Each book includes a chapter named after a Cornell & Diehl pipe tobacco; for Book II, it's "The Haunted Bookshop," a great blend of Burley and perique.
- Yes, *The Haunted Bookshop* is also a 1919 novel by Christopher Morley. It's on my reading list.
- Ilha da Queimada Grande is a real place, and it is really infested with pit vipers.
- "Big Gray Golem" was my Twitch handle. I played GTA V roleplay as Richard Nixon. I suspect you never thought you'd read those words in that sequence before. If you ask nicely and grant me prio, I might join your server.
- The chapter title for "The Red Herring" does exactly what it says on the tin.
- How Petra wound up in the river of leeches is entirely up to you. I have my theories, but they are irrelevant since she's dead now.

About the Author

CHRISTOPHER PARIS is an aerospace consultant, author, satirist, and cartoonist. He previously wrote the comic book *Reverend Ablack: Adventures of the Antichrist* and led the comic book self-publishing Small Press Syndicate in the 1990s. His business management books include *Surviving ISO 9001* and *Surviving AS9100.* He created and starred in the satirical political podcast *The Mark Spittle Show* and writes and illustrates *The Auditor* comic strip for his company Oxebridge Quality Resources. His aerospace clients have included SpaceX, Starlink, Piper Aircraft, JetZero, and NASA.

Born in New York, he lived in Florida until moving to Lima, Peru, in 2011.

Visit the Oxebridge website at www.oxebridge.com.

www.ingramcontent.com/pod-product-compliance
Lightning Source LLC
LaVergne TN
LVHW100523110826
845146LV00002B/759

9798999381217